I0583883

THE WITCHES OF
PORT TOWNSEND
BOOK 4

WHICH WITCH
Is willing?

TIFFINIE HELMER • **CYNTHIA ST. AUBIN**
CINDY STARK • **KERRIGAN BYRNE**

USA TODAY BESTSELLING AUTHORS

All rights reserved

This book is licensed for your personal enjoyment only. The book contained herein constitutes a copyrighted work and may not be reproduced, transmitted, down-loaded, or stored in or introduced into an information storage and retrieval system in any form or by any means, whether electronic or mechanical, now known or hereinafter invented, without the express written permission of the copyright owner, except in the case of brief quotation embodied in critical articles and reviews. Thank you for respecting the hard work of these authors.

This book is a work of fiction. The names, characters, places, and incidents are products of the writer's imagination or have been used fictitiously and are not to be construed as real. Any resemblance to persons, living or dead, actual events, locales or organizations is entirely coincidental.

Moira © 2020 Cynthia St. Aubin

Claire © 2020 Cindy Stark

Aerin © 2020 Kerrigan Byrne

Tierra © 2020 Tiffinie Helmer

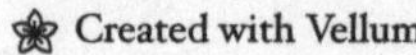 Created with Vellum

❧ I ❧
TIERRA

By Tiffinie Helmer

"I have a bad feeling about this." Tierra de Moray felt Killian Bane, aka Death, the fourth Horseman of the Apocalypse step up behind her and laid a possessive hand on her arm. They were all upstairs staring out at the scene below as her sister Claire verbally tried to pull the wool over Lucifer's eyes by using Satan's cyanide spell against her.

But it could easily go so wrong.

"Agreed. This is taking too fucking long," Dru Geddes growled. War's words mirrored the thoughts swirling in Tierra's mind like a hive of angry hornets.

Why had she gone along with this crazy-ass plan to let her sister face-off alone against Satan, the ultimate deceiver? There must have been something else they could have tried. Too many things were bound to go wrong, and had, since they'd opened the first Seal and brought about the beginning of the end.

The sun bled claret in a bruised sky. Bruised is how they all felt. Some of them had been bruised, broken, killed, and, in her case, resurrected.

She bit her lip and held her breath as Lucifer and Claire clinked the poison-laced glasses, each taking a toxic sip of the blood-colored wine.

Don't swallow, Claire, Tierra prayed.

She laid a hand over her swollen belly where her child grew. What kind of world would he or she be born into? Hell on earth? A new order with Lucifer ruling?

A fluttering kick hit her palm and love bloomed in her chest for this innocent life she'd somehow created with Death, the fourth Horseman of the Apocalypse.

Suddenly Lucifer vaulted to her feet, spewing wine and screaming at Claire.

Damn it, Tierra knew this would backfire in the worst way. Everything inside her tensed and she wondered if her bones might shatter like glass. She made a move to rush to her sister's aid, only to be held back by Killian's unbreakable grip.

"*Claire!*" Dru yelled, running for the balcony and leaping over the edge, diving two stories to the ground below.

Tierra stared in horror at the chaotic scene as Lucy tackled Claire, hissing and hacking, clawing at her throat. Then Lucifer jumped to her feet, pointed at Claire, but seemed unable to speak as her face started to melt. She ran from the grounds, and Tierra forgot about her as Claire struggled to her feet, stumbling toward the safety of the castle. She ground to a halt, her body lighting up like the hottest flame, and vomited up a fireball. The roaring mass of flames grew rapidly and spread to the castle.

"Everyone get out!" Nick Kingswood—Conquest— yelled just as Killian scooped up Tierra and ran for the open balcony doors, his massive onyx wings already extended as he leapt over the stone balustrade with her clutched in his arms.

"No, my sisters are still in there!" Tierra screamed. An explosion of flames, followed quickly by another deafening denotation drowned out her words.

The castle imploded on itself, sealing her sisters inside.

"**S**on of a fucking corpse fucker!" Lucifer busted into the deserted Palace Hotel. She was going to disembowel every last one of those feckin' gobshite sisters. How dare they try and trick her?

Her of all beings.

She was the embodiment of perfection, filled with wisdom and flawless in beauty. She'd walked through the midst of the stones of fire, had been named the Mother of Lies. The ruler of demons, the destroyer of mankind, the queen of temptation, and, her favorite, the punisher.

And yet, by all that was evil and blasphemous, she hurt. *Actually* hurt. She burned everywhere, from the inside and out.

They had tried to kill her with her *own* cyanide spell, and they might have succeeded if she'd ingested more than just the one sip of laced wine. She stumbled over to the large, full-length, glided mirror hanging in the Victorian foyer to assess the damage. The side of her face felt scorched and blistered. Cold air swept over her teeth from the area that should be covered by the skin of her cheek.

She gasped at her demonic reflection.

Her beautiful, perfect, angelic face echoed back at

her disfigured, the left side eaten away by the cyanide poison. She looked like a freaking zombie. The muscles and tendons lay filleted open, exposing her gums and teeth through what had been her cheek.

She whimpered. Her fingers shook as she raised them to touch the thin threads of derma and tissue that remained. The skin from her razor-edged cheekbones was gone, and the gaping hole continued down the side of her jaw, to the second hollow cavity in her throat.

So that's where the wheezing sound had come from—air being sucked in through the open pit of her tracheae.

Feeling down her sternum, her hand stopped at the wetness soaking her red, silk Armani blouse. She tore it off and found the source—another cavernous hole the size of a gladiator's head where her stomach had been.

"Come on, regenerate," she snarled through clenched teeth.

She'd never remained injured this long as her powers instantly started to repair any wound she received. She couldn't be killed, but she couldn't live looking like this.

Maybe it would just take a little longer this time to heal since the cyanide spell had been one of her own creations?

Her present state was scarier than when she donned her horns, cloven hoofs, and stingray whip of a tail.

She needed to find a body to wear until she completely regenerated, and then she would kill those fucking bitch-witches, starting with that turncoat Claire.

"Go back, damn it!" Tierra pounded on Killian's chest.

He landed them high on top of the cliff of Fort Townsend State Park, far enough away from Manresa Castle but giving them a clear view of the dust rising, turning red and black with the crimson sun over the carcass that used to be the Horsemen's hangout.

"I'm not taking you back there," Killian said, his voice as hard as his chest and just as unmovable. "You don't need to see what the destruction would have done to them."

"They could still be alive—"

"No way they could have lived through that."

"Don't say that. There are stories all the time about people surviving earthquakes, buried alive and found days later," she pleaded.

"Tierra—"

"Don't you dare Tierra me! Your brothers are down there, too. Don't you care about them?"

"Yes," he growled, the muscles in his jaw working. He was hurting too, worrying about them, she realized. "But they are immortal. They will survive."

"We have to go back. *Now*. If you don't fly me the fuck down there, I'm walking."

He grabbed her arm to stop her march down the hill. "Tierra, I don't want you to see me take their souls."

Tears sprang up and flooded her eyes. She had to swallow the lump of crippling emotion in order to speak.

"Do you feel their spirits?" she whispered.

He stood still, tense, dreading the task ahead of him more than she realized. He cared about them all, not just her. Her sisters had weaved their spell around him, too, at some point.

He suddenly frowned, his heavy brows angling over narrowed eyes. "No, I don't feel them."

"Could that mean—" She was afraid to hope. "They aren't dead yet."

He grabbed her, pulling her close against him. "Hang on." He shot straight up into the air and soared toward the remains of Manresa Castle.

As soon as Killian touched down, Tierra heard her name hollered in a broken sob.

Claire ran toward her, her steps staggering. "I thought you were—"

Tierra reached Claire just as she collapsed and they wrapped their arms tightly around each other. "I thought I killed you." Claire sobbed.

"I'm okay. How did you escape?"

"Dru tackled me as the castle exploded, shielding me with his body."

Tierra glanced around. "Where is he?"

"Clawing through the rubble looking for..." She couldn't finish, and Tierra was grateful that she didn't say bodies.

A thought entered her mind. She had the power over earth, didn't she? She could sift through the debris faster than any of them. "Can you call Dru back? I need to search the rubble. I can find them."

Claire closed her eyes and telepathically sent Dru a message over their special connection.

Tierra knew that Claire didn't mind having Dru in her head anymore, but no way did she want that kind of connection with Killian. The control issues he had were enough, deciding everything for her, not giving her a choice. Gotten her pregnant, though in reality that was just as much a surprise to him as her. But bonding her without her permission, and then squirreling her away for weeks on end to another world. While it had been beautiful there, and they had some incredible orgasmic moments, he still should have at least asked her first. At the very least, let her contact her sisters so they didn't worry when she disappeared, and given her time to pack a bag so that she'd had something to wear.

She'd been naked when she'd saved his sorry ass from Hell, and then spent weeks in another world, with not a stitch on. Sure, he hadn't minded, and while she liked seeing him in the buff, it had been too Adam and Eve for her. It hadn't helped that he'd taken her to the loveliest, lushest garden she'd ever laid eyes on to boot.

They really needed to have a talk about his bossy ways. As soon as they could catch a break from the damned Apocalypse, he'd be getting a piece of her mind.

Dru scampered over the broken bits of concrete, rushing to Claire's side, pulling her into his chest. He shared a worried look with Death, giving him an almost undetectable shake of his head.

Tierra ignored that and walked over to the edge of the rubble. Closing her eyes, she opened her other senses. Chunks of crushed concrete rolled out of her way as she searched for organic material hidden within.

In mere seconds, she located two beings. She couldn't tell if they were Moira and Aerin, just that they were alive.

Concentrating further, she raised her hands out in

front of her and made a large sweeping motion. Wood, plaster, brick and mortar moved as though she had swept a broom in a pile of dust. A few more swipes of her arms, and Nick's swearing could be heard.

"About bloody fucking time," Nick said, climbing out of the hole he'd been pinned in.

"How about you just say thank you?" Killian helped him down from the wall of rubble.

"Moira?" Nick asked.

"We don't know yet," Death softly delivered. "But I don't feel her or Aerin's soul."

"Thank the Goddess." Julian Roarke, Pestilence, the third horseman of the Apocalypse stood on the pile of destruction, carrying an ancient trunk. What could be in that trunk that was more special that he risked saving it, rather than make sure her sisters were ushered to safety?

"Where could they be?" Tierra asked. "There are no more organic signatures inside that mess." She gestured to what remained of Manresa Castle, the largest, grandest private residence built in Port Townsend back in 1892. It had withstood two hundred years of Pacific storms, two depressions that had taken the town down to a ghost of its former glittering Victorian seaport, only to be destroyed by one fire witch belching a fireball.

"Good thing we'd cleared the castle of the servants when we decided to use the place for a demonic meeting." Nick ripped off his tie. "Goddamn it, I loved this tie."

Claire sniffed back a sob. "This is all my fault. I thought I killed everyone, and I still might have killed Aerin and Moira."

"They aren't dead," Killian said.

"He would know," Dru said, rubbing Claire's shoulders trying to offer her comfort.

"What about Reaper? Would he have...?" Tierra trailed off.

"No. I would have known that too." Killian reassured her.

"I suggest we head back to the manor," Julian suggested. "They aren't here, and Maison de Moray will be their first obvious refuge. I'm certain they are as worried about you as you are them."

"Call up the horses," Nick said. "No way are we driving there." He pointed to where Tierra's beloved Prius lay crushed like a beer can under the rubble. "Shit, my Ferrari was parked in the garage."

"As well as my Hummer," Dru drawled.

"You wait for your horses," Killian said. "I'll take Tierra and meet you there."

Before Tierra could take in another breath, Killian had her airborne.

Tierra ran for the house as soon as Killian touched down in the front yard. She didn't pause when Killian bellowed out her name in warning.

Warning for what? The manor was warded up the ass. This was the safest place in the world for her and her sisters.

She came to a stumbling stop in the vaulted entryway, knowing the house was too big to run through all the rooms. She needed to do the same thing she did with the rubble of the castle. Open up her senses and search for organics.

Killian pounded up behind her, and she felt his need to reprimand her brimming off him in rippling waves. Without looking at him, she held up her hand for silence, and immediately dismissed him from her senses. A grinding growl over her actions vibrated from his chest and she knew he'd attempt to make her pay for that later. Like she'd allow that to happen. They needed to a serious "Come to Jesus" talk, and soon.

Taking a deep, centering breath, she searched for her sisters. She picked up their four familiars right off. Jinx, her ancient, immortal black cat perked up from where she slept on Tierra's bed as though feeling her probe. Jinx leaped off the bed and headed toward her direction.

Wow, this was freaking cool.

How come she hadn't figured out that she could do this before? But then she and her sisters had become more powerful each time they destroyed a Seal. They'd also been gifted with their wands and crowns from the Druids of old. Well, all but Aerin, that was.

Cheeto and Kai, Moira's pink, fire-breathing, teacup pig and Claire's sonic boom, tail-twitching red fox were outside digging up bulbs in her flower beds. Dang little varmints. She sent along a sharp "cease and desist" order over the magical channel, and both of them jumped, literally caught in earth's cookie jar, rich soil coating their furry snouts.

Dr. Lecter, Aerin's vampire bat was the last to be counted, sleeping high in the eaves of the attic. He just yawned at her, not seeming concerned that Aerin might be in trouble. Cheeto hadn't reacted with fear for Moira either, which filled Tierra with a groundswell of relief. They would know before anyone else if her sisters were in trouble.

She opened her senses further, going floor by floor of the manor. There were four stories of the mammoth Victorian to wade through, plus a basement. Eight bedrooms, solarium, multiple parlors, and bathrooms, not to mention, all the nooks and crannies.

Finding two humanoids on the second floor, Tierra raced for the stairs, though she was perplexed as to why Aerin and Moira would choose to be in Aunt Justine's bedroom of all places.

Aunt Justine was more tolerated than a celebrated member of the family. She'd had a major part in separating the identical sisters at birth, along with an order to kill three of them. She'd kept Tierra for some odd reason and raised her after their mother had died in childbirth. When Tierra had performed a spell to call home the missing parts—pieces—of herself, and her sisters traipsed into Port Townsend, Washington one by one, Justine had panicked. Knowing about the prophecy that four born of one would bring about the end of the world, she'd attempted to kill Moira.

Moira and Justine did mend their intransigent relationship when Nick Kingswood had held them prisoner for a time, and they'd been locked in a room together with nothing to do but come to terms. They more or less endured each other now, which was a welcome change over the attempted murder. Though, Justine still made living with her a challenge more often than not. But that was family, Tierra figured.

She reached the upper landing, with Killian hot on her heels, and swung open the door to Aunt Justine's bedroom. Only Aerin and Moira weren't there, and she wished more than anything she could unsee what she couldn't blink away.

Aunt Justine and *her* midwife, Lila Sullivan were playing the hokey-pokey in bed together, without any real pokeys. Both women were fifty plus, and in better shape than Tierra thought fifty allowed. But still. Her aunt fondled Lila's breast with one hand, the other thank the Goddess, was hidden under the sheet. Tierra didn't want to think about what the other hand was up to. Lila moaned with pleasure, her head tossing on the pillow, demanding more.

They were so caught up with each other, they hadn't heard Tierra and Killian barge in. Killian took charge of the situation as Tierra felt coated in bronze, her eyes wide, her body frozen in stupefaction. Killian lifted her off her feet and deposited her out in the hallway, shutting the door quietly on the mind-searing scene.

Amusement crinkled the crow-wings at the corners of his black eyes, his lips twisting with a smirk he fought, and failed, to keep hidden.

"Not one word," Tierra muttered, pointing a finger at him.

He made a motion of locking a key over his lips, which made him look ridiculous, mirth dancing in his eyes.

She slapped his arm with annoyance. "Stop it."

"Stop what?"

"You know what."

Jinx joined them and started up a figure eight dance around her legs. Tierra bent and picked her up and she climbed to Tierra's shoulder where she liked to perch. She hissed at Death.

Good girl, Tierra murmured at her, scratching her ears.

She traipsed down the hall, needing to get as far away as she could from what she'd just spied. The sight would probably haunt her the rest of her days.

Entering her bedroom farther down the hall, she embraced the earthy scents of lavender and roses, taking comfort in the chaos of color that greeted her.

She needed the black tourmaline that Julian had given her to help in rescuing Killian from Hell. She'd yet to return it to him, not in any hurry to relinquish the power the stone provided. Hopefully it would aid in finding Aerin and Moira. She couldn't feel them in the house. But how did she retrieve it with Death constantly dogging her steps?

Julian had made her promise not to let anyone know she possessed it. She figured Julian's *anyone* meant his brother horsemen too. Either way, she wasn't taking the chance.

"I need to be alone." She turned to face Killian. "You need to leave."

All amusement vanished from his expression, replaced by a look harder than diamonds. "Not happening."

"Please," she gritted out through a jaw clenched so

tight, her teeth ached. She hated asking anything of him, knowing he'd require a favor, or favors, in return.

"Until we know what happened to Lucifer, you will not leave my sight," he informed, his tone obstinate and rigid.

A sound of frustration escaped her. She needed a freaking break from him. He was too intense, too inflexible, and much too inviting. The more time she spent around him, the more she wanted him. They hadn't had sex since they'd returned from wherever he'd hijacked her to. She'd missed his touch, the way he lost himself inside her, stripping away his harder outer shell and letting her glimpse the softer side of Death.

Something must have shown in her expression, for he growled and stalked toward her.

"No." She held up her hand again, and Jinx backed up her verdict with another hiss. "That is not happening again."

"Yes, it is. You are mine."

Another thing they needed to talk about. He'd bonded her to him body and soul without her permission. While she loved his body—wasn't sure if the immortal had a soul—she would have freaking liked to have been asked. That was something she found that Death never did. He took. He damn well never asked.

"I need to find my sisters, and you are getting in my way."

"Get used to it."

Sanctuary, Jinx meowed.

Of course! Why hadn't she thought of that?

Men, they muddy the waters, Jinx returned.

"I need you to stay here, in my room, while I search...another part of the house."

"Tierra—"

"I'm not leaving the manor, so you can sure as hell stay here." She couldn't reveal the cloaked sanctuary to him. She didn't completely trust him. Didn't know if she trusted him even the tiniest bit.

Hooves pounded outside followed by whinnies that echoed over the landscape like a macabre thunder. Great, there went her grass, being torn up under their razor-sharp, chopping hooves. Again.

The door crashed open and Claire rushed upstairs, hollering her name.

Tierra hurried to the top of the stairs. "I'm here."

"Have you found them?" Claire asked, her eyes amber flames of worry and fear.

She shared a poignant look with Claire, praying she picked up her message and didn't mentally share it with Dru who stood on the riser below her. Claire blinked and then gave a slight nod.

"Where are they?" Julian asked, from the base of the stairs, his blanched skin even paler, looking more like a cadaver than actually alive. He clutched a large trunk in his hand, the one he'd refused to leave the bowels of castle without.

Nick started up the stairs, determination in his every step.

"You guys need to stay downstairs," Tierra said. "The room they are in is heavily warded. If it feels any kind of threat, I'm certain it won't allow me to enter."

"You have a room in the manor warded?" Julian asked, narrowing his eyes with interest. "Why?"

"None of your business, why. Just listen to me and stay." They looked at her like a pack of hungry wolves.

"We aren't men who can be ordered to stay like dogs," Killian said beside her.

"We promised each other no more secrets," Julian added.

Well, shit.

"Let Claire and I pass, we'll collect Aerin and Moira, and then the four of us will discuss it." This was not a decision she could make without the collective input of her sisters. One nod from Claire, sealed it. "We promise not to leave the manor," she added, though that hadn't seemed to sway Killian when she'd said it to him.

A door opened behind her, and Tierra cringed knowing who stood there. Just what they didn't need. Plus, she'd almost forgotten about what was going on behind door number one with Four Horsemen of the Apocalypse invading their home.

"Just what in all that is holy, is going on out here?" Aunt Justine asked, belting a floral robe around her waist.

Tierra slid a look over her shoulder, grateful Lila hadn't followed and that Justine had shut the door behind her.

"You're making enough noise to raise the dead," Justine said, her tone sharp and disapproving, then her eyes widened and she stepped back, seeing Death and the other three Horsemen. "What are *they* doing in *my* home?"

"*Our* home," Claire said. "And it's best if you return to your room and lock the door."

"I will not be a prisoner in my house."

"We can always lock you up somewhere else if you don't do what you're told, old woman," Nick threatened, having no affection for his onetime prisoner.

"Aunt Justine," Tierra implored, "Please, return to your room. I'll explain all this later."

"Yes, you will." She harrumphed and slammed her door shut, the lock clicking into place.

"I need a drink," Nick said. "It'll help rinse the taste of battle-axe from my mouth."

"Liquor is in the pantry, make yourself at home in the *kitchen*," Tierra stressed, grabbing Claire's hand. "We'll be right back."

Killian grabbed her arm, refusing to let her pass. "I don't like this."

"Get used to disappointment. I won't budge on this

and if you try to make me, I guarantee you will hate the result." She didn't back down from his thunderous look, but held his stare with one just as stormy.

"Bane, get your ass down here, and let the women retrieve their sisters," Dru said. "Knowing when to retreat, sometimes wins the battle." War should know.

Killian said something under his breath, warning Tierra that she would pay for this later.

Insolent man.

Jinx, still perched on Tierra's shoulder hissed her agreement.

Once Dru and Killian joined Nick and Julian in the large foyer, Tierra and Claire vaulted up the stairs to the fourth floor.

"I can't believe you stared Death in the face and *he* backed down," Claire said.

"The man is medieval in his thinking. He's going to get an education in the modern, magical woman as soon as I have a few freaking minutes to deal with him."

"So, your time away together didn't smooth things over between you?"

"Not in the least. He squirreled me away from my sisters with no chance to explain and no choice in the matter. Yeah, he's got a few painful truths coming his way."

"Damn, but we need a girls' night to catch up on what is going on with each other's love lives."

"Yes, we do." Though she really didn't have a love life. Killian never spoke of love, just possession. She wouldn't mind some sisterly advice on that and she needed to discuss what she'd witnessed with Justine and Lila, too. Maybe they could help her lock away the image so she didn't have to remember it ever again.

They reached the attic and found it quiet as a grave.

"Are you sure they're in there?" Claire asked, worrying her bottom lip with her teeth.

"About eight-five percent sure."

"If they are, why haven't they left and come looking for us?"

"That I don't know." But they were about to find out. Tierra recited the spell that revealed the cloaked door to their mother's sanctuary. She turned the knob and entered with Claire right behind her.

"About fucking time you two got here," Aerin snapped.

❅ 5 ❅

M oira rushed toward Tierra and Claire, sandwiching them both in a crushing hug. "You ain't dead!"

Tierra hugged her back, burrowing her face in Moira's hair and breathing deeply, cherishing the smells of magnolias and rain that always reminded her of her water witch sister. Thinking that she coúld have lost her today about broke her heart. She glanced over to Aerin, and motioned her over.

Begrudgingly she stomped over and joined the hug. Now the smells of the south fused with high-priced complicated notes of the east. That was Aerin all right. Complicated.

They broke apart, and Tierra moved to shut the door.

"*No!*" Aerin and Moira yelled together.

But it was too late. The latch caught.

"Well, shit," Aerin said. "We are now stuck in here."

"How do you mean?" Claire asked.

"Near as we can tell, this room acts like a panic room. And believe me, there was plenty of panic going on. Turns out Aerin's a touch claustrophobic."

"I am not," Aerin declared.

"Are, too," Moira fired back. "That wasn't me

screaming and ruinin' my manicure tryin' to claw my way out."

They had obviously spent too much time locked alone together.

"What happened?" Claire asked. "I thought I killed you. How did you get out and how come you didn't send us a message that you were okay?"

"This room plum locked us away from the world. It's like we've been shut away into another dimension. We couldn't even access the door to the Standing Stones." Moira gestured toward the magical door that Tierra had formed from the wood of the outside wall. It opened to the Standing Stones high atop the hill at Siren's Cry, roughly ten *miles* from the manor.

"Nothing was getting in or out," Aerin supplied. "All we could do was wait until one of you thought to look for us here. Took you long enough."

"Sorry," Claire said. "We came as fast as we could."

"So...how are the Horsemen? I know that they are all immortal and everythin', but are they hurtin'?" Moira asked, her huge, healing heart on her sleeve. Well, not really on her sleeve as she never wore much clothing. But winter was headed their way, and Tierra was interested to know if Moira would finally cover up her amazing attributes. Currently, she wore skintight jeans with frayed hems, and holes in the knees, paired a blue tank that showed her bare midriff and set off her startling aquamarine eyes.

"How did you get out of the castle before it collapsed?" Claire asked.

"Aerin poofed us here," Moira said. "It was awesome, like somethin' out of Star Trek." She turned to Aerin. "Think you could take me to the bayou to check up on Uncle Sal?"

"*Me*, in the bayou? I'd rather be caught dead in a flea market. Besides, I'm not exactly sure *how* I transported us here." She tugged on her ebony, designer pantsuit, adjusting the lay of the center buttons. She'd probably picked up the outfit right off the runway in Paris or Milan, and it most likely cost more than Tierra's pancaked Prius.

"Take us through exactly what happened," Tierra prompted.

"Death had just flown off with you right after War dived off the balcony for Claire." Aerin's lips tightened at the memory. "Julian, that douchelord, was more concerned over some dusty trunk than my welfare. He left me there."

"Now don't be too hard on him," Moira said. "He told you to transport us out of there."

"I've never transported anyone before. What if I couldn't do it on demand?"

"You poofed Julian to your bedroom for sexy times," Claire pointed out.

"That was different."

"I'd say," Tierra mumbled.

"There was no pressure, no life and death if I fucked it up. And I've never had a passenger before."

"He had faith in you. And he was right," Moira said. "We're here. We're alive. I thought for sure we were going to be barbequed."

Tears filled Claire's eyes. "I'm so sorry. I thought for sure I'd killed everyone. I wouldn't have been able to live with myself if I'd lost even one of you."

"Now, sugar, dry up them waterworks, or we'll all be cryin' and this room will flood with all the emotion I'm trying to contain." She sniffed. "Do you know what that twatwaffle Nicholas Kingswood did? Let me tell you. That immortal whip and chain-wielding, kinktastic, snatch hound didn't even attempt to save me. Didn't give me a backward glance as he hightailed his ass over to try and finish off Lucy."

Tierra knew this could quickly turn into a Horseman vent if she didn't stop it now. She had her own gripes regarding Killian's controlling and over-possessiveness. While Claire was in the blush of love—poor thing—she was bound to get her heart broken. The Horsemen were immortal after all. How long did Claire really think her relationship with War could last? If they actually survived the end of days, what future would they have together when Claire aged? The same applied to her involvement with Killian. The length of time they had with the men was a small chapter or footnote compared to the span of their lives.

"Why did you choose to poof into the Sanctuary instead of the kitchen or somewhere else like the castle grounds so we knew you were alive?" Tierra asked.

"I haven't a fucking clue. The only thought I had was to find safety."

And what could be safer than their mother's sanctuary? "So why wouldn't it let you leave once the threat was gone?" Tierra asked.

"Like I said, it acted like a panic room, the kind you find in mega-rich people's homes," Aerin explained when Tierra looked at her blankly. "You need to get out more."

"Rich folks are about as common as hen's teeth in the bayou," Moira said. "Only reason I knew what she was yackin' on about was that I caught that movie with Jodie Foster a while back."

"We're all safe now and together, so the room should release us." Claire moved to the door and tried to open it. Sure enough, it didn't budge. "Any ideas on how we break out?"

"THEY'VE BEEN GONE TOO LONG," KILLIAN SAID, standing with his ankles crossed, leaning against the kitchen counter as his fellow brothers finished off the scotch they'd found in the pantry.

Julian was lost in his head, obviously going over what they needed to do as their second command center in Port Townsend had been destroyed in as many months. First, by flood produced by a vengeful Moira, and now fire from Claire.

Would their next place be blown away by a tornado created by Aerin, or would Tierra have the earth swallow it whole, or Goddess forbid, send it to Hell with them locked inside like she had him? He mentally shuddered at the memory.

"Dru, you want to send Claire a mental IM and tell her to hurry the fuck up? First item on my docket is to instruct Moira in the finer points of self-defense. She would have been killed without Aerin's little trick. I won't have her unprotected like that again." Nick slammed his empty glass down on the table like a judge's gavel.

"I can't seem to reach her," Dru admitted.

Killian stood up straight. "I'm going after them." Tierra had promised not to leave the house, and if she lied to him, she would pay. "Julian, take the basement, Nick and Dru, the second and third floors. I'll search the attic." Something was going on up there in that room. He'd been puzzled over it ever since he'd heard about Tierra's collapse up there when the babe had erected a force field around her to block out a Satan-possessed Aerin.

He made to quit the room and then paused and warned them, "Don't disturb Justine. Trust me on this." Then he vaulted up the stairs.

The attic was empty except for Jinx, who sat on guard along a barren wall, staring at him with its freaky, intelligent glass-green eyes. Boxes and trunks were stacked neatly along another wall, which had to be Tierra's doing. He appreciated an organized woman. The kitchen was the same. While her bedroom was a type of logical chaos. More so to do with the abundance of color, flowing scarves, and draped clothing rather from messy clutter.

He stood and listened, scanning the room for any hidden doors. Nothing. But then why was the cat there?

Taking a step toward it, Killian stopped when it hissed, baring its sharp fangs.

"You really think you're a match for me?" He swore the feline lifted its lip in a sneer. Could it understand him? It understood Tierra, but then her powers as an earth witch included the ability to talk to the beasts of the forest.

He faced down the cat. "What are you protecting?" *I can't believe I'm talking to a cat.*

A low, hair-raising snarl emanated from the diminutive creature.

Definitely protecting or guarding something, but Killian couldn't see anything hidden, feel any magic vibrations, or mirages in the air. He walked around the perimeter of the room, taking in the size of the lower floors and the silhouette of the manor from outside.

Something was off.

Another low growl rumbled from the cat.

Yeah, he was onto something.

A bat flew at him from the eaves, and he swatted at it, missing the quick flying rodent.

What were the witches concealing up here?

"Did you find them?" Dru asked, entering the attic followed by Nick and Julian. Julian still carried his damn trunk. The man hadn't let it out of his sight since he'd located it in the castle rubble. Killian understood how important it was to Julian, hell to all of them, but he needed to find a way to cloak the thing. With his suit covered in concrete dust, torn and ragged, he looked like a carpetbagger.

"I found something." Killian indicated Jinx, now standing on all fours, with her ruff up and tail twitching, giving them a low warning roar that sounded like a diesel engine on a mac truck. "There's a hidden room here. Take in the dimension of the attic space that you see and compare them to the floors below."

Julian nodded. "The room does seem to be missing a considerable amount of square footage."

"So, where's the damn door?" Nick asked, his mood more sour than usual.

"Obviously, they shrouded it from us," Dru said. "What I don't understand is how the spell is preventing me from mentally reaching Claire."

"This is a disturbing situation," Julian said.

He was right. If the women could disappear like this, hidden from the world—*from them*—what else could they do that the Horsemen weren't aware of?

"By my estimation, the room is behind this wall," Killian said.

"How'd you figure that out?" Nick asked.

"The cat hasn't moved since I entered the attic," Killian added. "It has to be there."

"You thinking what I'm thinking?" Dru asked Nick.

A wicked gleam entered Nick's dark amber eyes. "There has to be a chainsaw around here somewhere."

❋ 6 ❋

"Hey, do you hear that?" Claire pressed her ear to the door.

"It's General Lee!" Moira exclaimed. "Why those destruction lovin' Horsemen. How dare they think of sawing into our sanctuary?"

"We need to find a release on that door, or we will lose it." Tierra planted her hands on her hips. Killian had to be behind this. Moira was right, how dare they destroy her home just to get to them? They had the patience of a rutting billy goat.

"Join hands," Claire said, holding out both of hers.

"Oh, hell no," Moira said. "Every damn time we've done that, we've opened a Seal. There's only one left. You want to end the world just to save a freakin' door?"

"Claire's right." Aerin took a position opposite Claire and offered her hand to Moira. "The room needs to know we are one. We say no spell. Just join in a circle and stand in your compass corners."

Moira shared a worried look with Tierra. She had the same doubts as Moira. But if they didn't perform any magic while connected that *should* prevent the last Seal from opening. Right? Saying a small prayer to the Goddess, Tierra clasped Claire's and Aerin's hand, standing north. "It'll be okay, Moira."

"It sure as hell better be," she muttered and stood south, completing the circle.

The second they joined, the door whipped open wide with a bang. The Horsemen stood gaping at the entrance. Nick slowly depressed the power on General Lee, looking thwarted that he didn't get to chainsaw through the wall.

Aerin was the first to speak, addressing her ire at Julian. "I see that you saved your precious trunk."

Her injured feelings over not being as important to Julian as that trunk vibrated over the room.

Julian devoured Aerin with his eyes, pride and something deeper in his expression as he raked her in. "I never had any doubt that you would save your sister. Otherwise, I would have sacrificed everything to save you myself."

Aerin harrumphed. While his words did seem to placate her somewhat, Tierra knew Julian still had a way to go to get back into Aerin's good graces, and her bed.

"What is this room?" Killian asked, advancing over the threshold.

Tierra was surprised when the room didn't expel him. "Our mother's sanctuary."

"It wasn't my secret to tell you," Claire said to Dru, obviously answering his mental question.

"All right, you two," Moira said. "No secret messages back and forth. And while we are at it, hands off General Lee." She strode to Nick and they had a little tug of war before Nick finally released his hold on the chainsaw.

"Good to see you are unharmed," Nick growled, his tone promising that no one marked her but him.

"No thanks to you." She turned and walked away from him without a backward glance.

Julian wasn't the only one who needed to repair fences. He moved to follow Killian into the room.

"Stop right there," Tierra said. "Our sanctuary is a Horseman free zone."

"Where does that door lead to?" Killian asked, ignoring her directive.

"None of your business," Tierra replied through tight lips.

"That is where you are wrong, my gazelle. Everything about you is *my* business." His tone was as hard as his black eyes.

Tierra wanted to shove him back, physically, magically, but held her ground without revealing just how much he infuriated her.

"Julian, show them what's inside the trunk," Killian said.

The other three Horsemen objected at once, talking so fast that Tierra couldn't make sense of the argument.

"Y'all go suck on a sock." Moira lifted General Lee in front of her like a sword. "I've had enough of this bitchin' and bickerin' between us. We have bigger things to worry about than fragile male egos. It's time we had a real truce and work together to find a solution that will save the world from endin'."

"No one has seen inside this trunk throughout time except the four of us, and you want to open it up for these neophytes," Nick said to Killian.

"*Neophytes*?" Aerin took a step toward Nick. "Moira give me that chain saw."

"Cease!" Julian said in a low, commanding voice that raised goose bumps on Tierra's exposed skin. "Bane is right. We will share with you what is inside this trunk, *if* you share the secrets of your sanctuary. Between the two, we might actually find a solution."

Tierra shared a look with her sisters. They met her wary one, with suppressed anger and reluctant agreement. They really didn't have much of a choice since Julian was mostly right. What did they really have to lose, other than the world, and that would happen if they didn't try everything they could to stop it.

Tierra stepped forward. "Okay, but first you show us what's inside that trunk as you are already standing inside our sanctuary."

Julian looked to his brothers. Killian nodded for him to go ahead while Dru and Nick stood stoic. Julian set the large trunk down and released the complicated locks on the front. It seemed antediluvian, and the locking mechanism was like those antique desks with all the hidden cubbies. Finally, he lifted the lid.

Tierra and her sisters peered inside. Narrow stone risers led down to a bottom she couldn't see.

"Is that a...staircase?" Tierra asked.

"You left me for dead to save a fucking staircase?" Aerin said.

"It isn't the staircase that is important, it is where it leads," Julian informed her.

"Why, don't that beat all," Moira exclaimed. "It's one of them Mary Poppins magic carpet bags. Remember how she pulled all those crazy things out of her sack? Everythin' from coatracks to a tasseled floor lamp. Don't tell me y'all haven't seen it?"

Aerin and Claire shook their heads.

"We need a movie night," Moira said.

"It really is an iconic movie," Julian said.

"*You've* seen it?" Dru shared an eye roll with Nick.

"Not all of us are out every night attempting coitus with anything on two legs," Julian said.

"There was no *attempting* about it," Nick muttered.

"We're getting off the subject," Claire said. "Where do the stairs lead?"

"To Julian's vast library in his gothic Châteaux high in the French Alps," Killian informed them.

"France." Aerin leaned into the trunk. "How is that even possible?"

"With all that has recently happened in your short

span of your staggeringly limited life, you can't figure that one out for yourself?" Nick pointed out.

"Listen you uncultured fuck," Aerin said, "I know its magic, but what kind of magic?" Tierra was surprised she didn't ask where she could get one for herself.

"Ancient," Julian said, clearly not willing to add any more information.

"Can we go down them?" Tierra asked, her feet itching to rush down the steps.

"Damn skippy," Moira said. "I've always wanted to go to France. It's the Creole motherland, after all. And just think. If we travel by magic staircase, I wouldn't have to get groped by those ham-handed TSA Agents who always seem to be lookin' for explosives in the general area of my tits."

"I'm not going down there," Aerin said, backing up a few steps.

"Turns out she's a mite claustrophobic," Moira added.

Claire sidled closer to Dru. "I'd rather stay here, too. I'm not a fan of dark, dank places." Especially now that she'd been held captive in the old cement Army batteries at Fort Worden.

"I suggest we split up," Killian said. "Tierra and I will go with Julian and Moira."

"How about hell fucking no," Nick said. "If any*one* is going any*where* with Moira, it's me."

"I'll go where I damn well please. You've got no claim to me."

"The hell I don't."

"It's best you give me some space, or you'll find yourself twenty leagues under the sea, buddy."

"Enough," Dru barked, wrapping an arm around Claire's shoulders. "Moira isn't the only one who can use a break from bickering. Claire and I will stay along with Nick and Aerin and we'll go through the sanctuary while you four see what you can find in the Châteaux's extensive library."

"Do I need to pack a bag?" Tierra asked. What did one wear in France?

"No, the Châteaux is equipped with whatever you might need, and if it isn't, all you have to do is climb the stairs back here." Killian took her hand, and in her excitement, she squeezed it before she remembered she was still upset with him.

Killian stepped inside the trunk and helped Tierra down. "Don't let go of me. The stairs are steep and I won't have you tumble."

Julian followed them inside and held out gloved hand for Moira. "My lady."

"She is not your lady and you'd better keep your diseased hands off her," Nick growled.

Moira took Julian's hand and climbed in behind him. "Stuff it, Conquest, and play nice with my sisters unless you want your right hand to end up as callused as your manners."

The sound of Nick's swearing followed them as they descended the rough stone stairs.

"This is a colossal waste of time," Tierra said, arching her back to help relieve the biting ache.

"We might not have found anything new regardin' the Apocalypse, but get this shit. Mermaids are *real* and so are unicorns. Atlantis actually exists. That is my next vacation spot. Have y'all been there?" Moira asked Julian and Killian.

"Indeed," Julian said not looking up from the large leather book in front of him. He sat in a brocade chair adjacent to a long, scarred walnut table, tomes stacked in towers on either side of him. "It's overrated, and any chance of you vacationing there will be moot if you don't advance to the next book." He pointed at the huge pile they'd amassed after going through the catalog on his computer.

Julian was an odd mix of the past and future. He was timeless, really. It had shocked Tierra that Julian had entered all the information of over thousands of books, along with pertinent subject matters, and his comments into a computer. It sure made their search faster, though they'd come up empty so far.

Tierra awkwardly got to her feet and stretched, and rubbed her lower back. She was feeling the pregnancy weight after days spent bent over and rifling through dusty manuscripts.

"You need a break," Killian said, standing and stalking toward her.

"No, I don't. I'm just stiff from sitting so much."

Moira glanced up from her cross-legged perch in the leather high-back chair. "Cool your heels, Tierra. Julian and I will keep at it. We're bound to find something useful soon."

"Agreed," Julian said. "Some vittles and more coffee would be helpful after you've had a lie down."

"I don't need a *lie down*," Tierra said. Just because she was pregnant didn't mean she had a handicap.

"You need to take better care of yourself," Killian growled. "You're with child."

"Like I don't know that." Hard to forget with the beach ball where her flat stomach used to be and the constant kicking from the little tyke. He or she had a promising career as a soccer player.

"Not to mention crankier than a pig in a bacon factory," Moira muttered.

Yes, she was cranky. She was in France and hadn't seen any of it outside of the granite medieval fortress Julian called Le Châteaux Morte.

Suddenly her world tilted as Killian swung her up into his arms. "You will take a break even if I have to force you to."

"Put me down," she demanded.

"No." He quit the room with her secure in his hold.

She wanted to wail at him, struggle in his arms, but didn't relish the idea of tumbling to the floor. Plus, if she were to be honest, taking a nap sounded like heaven. She'd been pushing herself, hoping they would come across something, *anything*, that would help them stop the progression of the Apocalypse.

Killian carried her through the grand foyer off the library and up the sweeping staircase to her bedroom as though she weighed nothing. She tried to stifle the feeling of being cherished, but wasn't successful.

Once they reached the room she'd been given, with its tapestry-covered walls, massive four-poster canopy and velvet bed clothes, he gently laid her on the soft mattress. "Stay."

She wanted to disobey his order—had felt compelled to argue with his every edict since they had returned from the vibrant garden he'd abducted her to—but she was too tired and sore to go against what her body craved. A yawn, large enough to crack her jaw, settled it. She needed a nap.

Killian lifted her feet and disposed of her shoes and socks. The Châteaux had been constructed eons ago and didn't have central heating. Just the oversized fireplaces in every room tall enough to stand completely upright in and wide enough to house three or four people easily. She wondered vaguely where Julian procured the firewood to heat each room. She hadn't noticed him feeding the flames either, they just continued to burn unattended. More magic that she wasn't privy to, she figured.

Once Killian tossed her shoes aside, he crawled onto the bed and settled next to her.

She stiffened when he pulled her into the curve of his body and felt his erection, hard and thick at her backside.

"Hey, *that* isn't resting." She was not up to making love with him again. She'd done a fine job of keeping him at bay with her sharp tongue. Who knew she had such a vicious side? But then Killian did seem to bring out the worst in her.

"Sleep. I'll not bother you...for now." He tossed a fur blanket over them, and she couldn't help snuggling into the pelt. No fake fur for the Horsemen, though she didn't want to consider the animal who'd been sacrificed for such a divine blanket.

With the warmth of the blanket tucked around her and the heat of Killian at her back, she instantly dropped off the planet into a deep sleep.

KILLIAN SMOOTHED BACK THE BURGUNDY-BLACK OF Tierra's hair, watching her slumber. The frown constantly marring her forehead relaxed and she looked peaceful and younger than her twenty-six years.

His heart swelled with emotion for his woman. She might not be ready to admit it yet, but she was his. He'd taken her virginity, impregnated her, and then bonded her to him. Eventually, she'd realize that she was good and stuck. While she'd offered her virginity to him, she hadn't been on board with the others.

What would she do when she found out—

No reason to think about that now. He figured he had time still to reveal what else he'd done to her without her permission. For now, he'd enjoy just holding her in his arms, sharing this moment and this space in time with her.

He couldn't remember when he'd ever just held a woman. Not to mention, actually *slept* beside one.

Laying his hand over her swollen belly, he marveled at the answering flutter.

My child.

The wonder of existing as long as he had and never being able to procreate until he'd met this enchanting earth witch, continued to cloud his thoughts and tangle his emotions.

Somehow, he had to heal this rift between them, but the damned woman bewildered him.

After an hour of watching over her sleep, she stirred in his arms, pressing her backside against his rigid cock. He'd been so hard for so long that he'd started to worry his condition might remain permanent.

His arms tightened around her, and he couldn't help from grinding his throbbing erection against her sweet ass.

She gasped, and he wrapped his hand around her long mane of hair, forcing her head to look at him over her shoulder. Her eyes were wide open, the emerald fire hardening to jade. Before she could utter a word, he sealed his mouth over hers, his tongue breaching the tight seam of her lips, glorifying in the heat that welcomed him back.

Gods, how he wanted to be inside her, lose himself in her softness, ease this tension between them with a dozen or more orgasms.

He had her trapped in his embrace, his leg swung over hers, keeping her in place, as he ravished her mouth. She couldn't push him away with her back to his front and his hand holding her head immoveable as he plundered her depths, showing her with his lips, his tongue and teeth how much he needed her.

She whimpered, and in his muddled mind he couldn't differentiate if the sound matched his desire or if it was a plea for him to stop.

Goddess help him, he couldn't stop.

Desire and need roared inside for him to take, to mark, to master. She was *his*. No other woman had ever infuriated him or raised him to such heights of passion that he lost all concept of consensus.

He lifted her skirt and tore off her panties, his fingers diving deep and finding her wet. Oh, so fucking wet for him.

That was all he needed. He continued kissing her, not wanting her able to utter one word. Lately everything that had come out of her mouth set his blood to boil.

It was boiling now with a completely different emotion, one that consumed him. He found the bud at the top of her sex and stroked it, glorifying in the jerk and shudder of her body against his.

He freed his cock from his trousers, his fingers never stopping in their deliberate and desperate ministrations. She tensed in his arms, mewling sounds transferring from her mouth to his, the smothered vibrations adding more heat and hunger to the kiss.

He felt her orgasm build and entered her from behind as it peaked. Only then did he break the kiss to bite her neck, sending her soaring into the stratosphere on a strangled scream of ecstasy.

The carnal contractions of her pleasure, sent him rocketing off with her.

❧ 8 ❧

Tierra lay there stunned, pleasure still quaking her body while anger twisted inside her like ivy choking a tree.

How dare he? Not only had he insisted she rest, then he basically decided to treat her body like his own private playground. Once again, he'd given her no choice.

The man was dead.

Just as soon as she could control her limp limbs, she'd send him back to Hell and let that she-devil have him. They were perfect for each other.

"Stop," Killian said, the breath of his command caressing the back of her neck, followed by a gentle brush of his lips over where he'd bitten her.

She shivered. The back of her neck was incredibly sensitive, making her body a traitor to her thoughts. "You forced yourself on me."

"You wanted me," he growled. "Don't deny it."

He jerked inside her, causing her to gasp as banked sensations awakened. He was still hard even though she knew he'd found his release. Everyone currently in Châteaux Morte probably knew it too—as well as any neighboring villages—by the guttural roar that had escaped him.

"Let me go," she whispered, praying that he would before her body completely betrayed her again. Holy Mother of Earth, how could she be this mad at him and still crave him with a hunger that never seemed to be sated?

"*Never.*" His teeth bit down on the cord of her neck again and she couldn't contain the gasp or the arching of her body into his, taking him deeper inside her.

An answering sound more beast than man rumbled up his throat, and he cupped her breasts, molding them in his large hands. Her breasts ached all the time, and having him knead them, pressing them against her sternum, altered her anger into an altogether different type of fever.

A fever with fangs.

"Use me, Tierra. Take *me* this time. Have your revenge upon me." He released her, slipping free of her body. She instantly missed his heat and the promise of pleasure his body always called forth from hers. He lay on his back, his arms splayed wide, a challenging glint in his ebony eyes for her to do with him as she wished.

Did she dare do as he urged?

He'd always controlled their lovemaking, and she had doubts that he could turn the reins over to her. At some point, he'd take them back, of that she was sure. But the thought of dominating him, for even a little while, was a carrot she couldn't refuse.

Dear Goddess, save her, but she wanted him.

She sat up on the bed, her eyes drinking him in. He was still dressed even though his cock pointed skyward from the opening of his trousers. "Take off your clothes."

His eyes heated with triumph, but he didn't say anything, he just slid from the bed and slowly stripped.

She gulped at seeing the muscles roping over his flesh. His shoulders were broader than any linebacker, his torso more chiseled than a bodybuilder's, and his legs as powerful as Hercules'.

She had to swallow in order to speak. "Lay down in the middle of the mattress." She climbed off the other side, to give him room to do as she demanded.

His nostrils flared and his arms tensed as though to reach out for her and drag her back into his embrace. Something in her expression stopped him, and he climbed on the bed, his full back tattoo of a shrouded Grim Reaper holding a scythe standing on the banks of the River Styx seemed to wink at her, encouraging her to continue. His tattoo had the power to house his raven-black wings. It had been a while since she had been cradled within their feathered softness as he made love to her.

In fact, this was the first time they'd come together in an actual bed. Each time before, they coupled in the forest, the Standing Stones, and what she'd started referring to as the Garden of Eden.

When he'd had her earlier, they hadn't taken advantage of the soft mattress. The joining had been fast, furious, and over too quickly.

Killian settled on the middle, adjusting the pillow behind his head, his eyes never leaving her.

Reaching for the hem of her loose-fitting peasant blouse, she slowly lifted it up and over her head. Next, she released her bra, shaking her hair so that it flowed around her like a curtain, hiding her swollen breasts.

He sucked in a deep, labored breath. She had his full attention and the power of it went swiftly to her head. Wow, she could get used to this.

She slid the skirt from her hips and let it pool at her feet, leaving her bare to his heated gaze except for the scrying crystal that hung from an ancient chain, nestled in the valley of her breasts, the multiple stones of topaz, jasper, and tiger's eye bracelets, and many rings adorning her fingers.

He raked in her nakedness, looking at her with pride as he took in her swollen belly. "Gods, you are stunning. My very own Earth Goddess."

She flushed at his words. While it had taken her a while to wrap her brain around being pregnant with the fourth Horseman of the Apocalypse's baby, her body had taken to it with ease. Though now that she'd reached her last trimester, she felt ungainly with her new shape that seemed to increase in size daily. Sexy was the last thing she usually felt when looking at her reflection, but the way Killian regarded her with desire, made her feel not only beautiful, but invincible.

She climbed onto the mattress, and he reached for her. "No. If I am going to take you, use you, get my revenge upon your body, you will have to do as I say."

He growled a warning low in his throat.

"These are my conditions, or this isn't happening."

His expression clearly said that he could change her mind.

"Yes, you could probably change my mind, but you won't like my mood afterward. It's my way, or no way."

He dragged in another deep breath and then reluctantly nodded his agreement to her terms.

Anticipation of having her way with him bloomed in her chest, and she trembled as she straddled him, sitting low on his hips and cradling his erection under the sensitive nub of her sex.

Killian groaned, his hands jerking up to grab her hips. She captured them and placed his rough palms over her breasts. Rather than fighting her, he took to lavishing her breasts with attention, causing her to moan, her head falling back on her shoulders with the pleasure.

He thumbed her nipples into hard peaks, causing her inner folds to weep and contract. She wanted to take him inside her body right now, but didn't want this to end so soon. She actually had carte blanche to touch him, taste him, have her way with him and she wasn't going to waste it.

She stroked her hands over his chest to the ridges of muscle in his taut stomach. They tightened under her caress and he arched his hips, his cock sliding along her sex. She sat too deep for him to enter her, but the rubbing against her most sensitive place caused the most delicious of sensations to blossom. She gyrated her hips in a steady rhythm that had Killian twitching under her, guttural sounds escaping his throat.

She wasn't going to last long and accepted the orgasm that burst through her on a cry.

The climax was instant, and while it satisfied her for a minute—much like a bowl of Rocky Road ice cream took the edge off her hunger—it ebbed too quickly, making her crave more.

She collapsed onto his chest, his breathing ragged under her. Killian's hands grasped her hips, and she felt him tense under her, ready to flip her over onto her back and thrust inside her.

"Don't you dare move," she warned.

He answered her with a desperate grumble. "Tierra, you are killing me."

She giggled over the irony of her killing Death with sex. She rose and gazed down into his strained face. This was taking a toll on him. She glorified in her female power over this ancient and formidable immortal. "I'm not finished with you yet."

She arched up and kissed him. His arms snaked around her, one hand splaying over her back, the other buried in her hair. She might have been the one to kiss him, but he took control of it. Colors flowered behind her closed lids and she lost herself in the feel and taste of him. His hand stroked down her backside to the cleft of her bottom, while his other held her head prisoner for his mouth to plunder.

His fingers slid between her slick folds, breached

her as his cock rubbed against her clitoris. Spasms shook her body, and she allowed him to play her like a violin until she sang, coming apart in his arms.

Killian emitted a low chuckle, continuing to stroke her curves as if he was a blind man and needed to read her body like a book of braille, committing the feel of her to memory.

"You'll pay for that," she muttered. He'd taken control of that orgasm, but she was far from done with him.

"Gods, I hope so."

She smiled, glad he couldn't see it with her face nestled in the crook of his neck.

Oh, yes, she'd make him pay.

KILLIAN GLOATED OVER TIERRA'S LATEST CLIMAX. Control him, would she? Never. He was just indulging her, and in the process, indulging himself *with* her. It was bloody brilliant to suggest this. Though, he feared he'd have the worst case of blue balls he'd ever experienced if she didn't take him inside her soon.

Tierra licked and kissed down his torso, and by the sounds coming from her, she reveled in his staggered breathing, the tensing of his muscles, as she lavished attention lower. When she reached his groin, she skipped it.

He cursed, making her smile.

She kissed his inner thighs, the sides of his knees and found the spot where he was ticklish, his reaction feeding her obviously delight.

"Tierra, you're driving me insane," he said through clenched teeth. "Take me inside you."

"Say please."

The little minx wanted *him* to beg? He begged for no one. "Be careful what you ask for," he threatened.

Drunk on power, she taunted him further. "Give in, Killian, and I'll ease your...discomfort."

He answered her with a warning growl. "Fuck me...*now*."

She laughed, her hand lightly cupping his balls. His hands clenched into fists to keep from grabbing her, tossing her off of him and onto her knees, taking her like a rutting bull.

"One word, just one little word," she purred and wet her lips with her pink tongue.

His heart pounded in his chest until all he could hear was his own pulse racing through his veins. "God-damn you woman. *Please*." The plea choked him, coming out harsh and dangerous.

Shocked that he actually said please caused her to hesitate, her eyes wide green pools of surprise.

"So help me Goddess, if you don't fuck me right now, I won't be held responsible for what happens next," he threatened.

She crawled up his body, taking her damn sweet time. His fingers flexed, and she shook her head, her hair brushing his oversensitive skin. She'd turned him into a twitching bundle of exposed nerves with her teasing.

No one in all his long life had ever teased Death. It wasn't done, yet his Earth Goddess had taken him on like an equal. She needed to learn a few things...or he needed to.

That was a sobering thought.

She rose above him, taking his cock in hand, squeezing his shaft until his eyes rolled back into his head and he snarled like a beast caught in a trap. Did she have any idea how close to the edge she played?

Obviously not. Only the thought of repaying her in kind, kept him from taking control.

Then she slowly took him inside her. The bliss, the

heat, the tightness of joining with her set his world to rights.

At least for a moment.

Inch by inch, she sheathed him with her perfection. Never had he felt pleasure like this with any other woman. Only she could make him feel this alive, this desperate, and this at peace.

Once she had him seated deep inside her, she released an unsteady breath.

Did her taking him like this pain her? "Tierra?"

"Just give me a second, you are really deep in this position. And I feel incredibly full."

"Am I hurting you?"

She shook her head, her eyes falling closed. Biting her lower lip, she started a gradual, rocking rhythm.

He groaned, needing her actions faster, but then the view above him as she took her pleasure was so erotic he never wanted it to end.

After a few long minutes of her slowly swaying over him, he grabbed her hips to help increase her movements.

She slapped them back. "No. I'm in control. Now you have to take it as I see fit to divvy it out."

"Sweetheart, you're tearing me apart."

Her lips quirked into the smile of a siren. "Good."

Good? Holy fuck. Who was this woman? While he preferred the seductress to the hissing kitten, both created levels of frustration he didn't know how to deal with.

But there were ways he could satisfy them both. When he found and flicked his fingers over her hidden pearl, she didn't slap him away. Nor did she when he rose and took her nipple into his mouth.

She moaned and started to rise and fall on his cock in a manner that had stars winking in the margins of his vision. Heat infused him until sweat broke out on his forehead. He needed, craved his release, yet he never wanted this to end. He'd happily be tortured like this until he expired from the rapture.

"Come for me, my gazelle," he urged, his fingers increasing pressure, circling the bud until she wantonly called out his name.

"Yes! Gods, yes," he shouted as the contractions of her release milked his shaft. Grasping her hips, he thrust harder inside her, dragging out her climax and generating his own mind-blowing orgasm.

She collapsed boneless on top of him, her breathing ragged. He wrapped his arms around her, using his embrace as an anchor to earth until he could get his wits about him again.

The woman had the power to unravel him. Part of him feared her effect over him, the other rejoiced.

"You win again," she murmured.

"I'd say that you won that last one." He gave a husky sigh of satisfaction.

"You weren't supposed to take over."

"This is new for me, so I believe we need to try it again." And again.

She slapped him. "I'm serious."

"So am I. Tierra, you rock my world until I can't find stable footing." He brushed her hair aside and knew she needed to hear what was in his heart. "Look at me." He waited until she timidly met his gaze.

"You'd better beware, my sweet gazelle, for this I vow. There is no existence on earth worth living, or any realm, without you by my side. If anyone can survive the destined destruction, we can, as long as we are one."

"How is that possible when all that we have is a constant battle of wills?" she whispered.

"Nay, not a battle of wills. A battle of love."

She stiffened, sucking in a breath and holding it.

He'd have to actually say the words that he'd never spoken to another soul. "I love you, Tierra de Moray."

She shook her head as though his declaration had

produced feelings of panic. "No, you want me," she said. "If you truly loved me, you wouldn't treat me like a possession."

"You are my possession just as I am yours."

She stared at him stunned. "What do you mean?"

"We belong to each other. As much of a hold as I have over you, yours is more powerful. You have the power to bring this immortal to his knees...if you so desire." Admitting he loved her had been scary enough, but to reveal how much control she really had over him, felt like he'd cut open his chest and exposed his heart in the most vulnerable of ways.

His words pleased her, by the smile that tugged her lips until her skin blushed, turning him to putty in her hands.

"How about we take a shower and then you get on your knees for me," she suggested wickedly.

His heart leaped in his chest at the vision her words created.

Much later, after their orgasmic shower antics, he cradled his exhausted woman in his arms, replaying their afternoon of debauchery.

With a stuttering of his heart, he realized that while he'd expressed his love for her...she had not.

9

"That was quite the *lay*down you had. Get any rest?" Moira asked Tierra when she entered the Châteaux library with Killian shadowing her steps.

Tierra ignored Moira's knowing smirk and Julian's all too-seeing eyes. They were still hitting the books, though it did look like they had taken a break to eat. The trays of cheese and crackers with an assortment of olives had her stomach rumbling. She was starved, but then she'd burned a lot of calories upstairs.

She loaded a plate and inhaled the food. "Where are we?"

"Good question," Killian muttered.

He'd been awfully pensive when she'd woken, regarding her with a constant frown marring his forehead. He looked more like he wanted to take up his scythe and behead someone and that someone was most likely her.

Regardless of his feelings for her, she couldn't express what she wasn't sure she felt. He had to understand by now that she'd never desired a man like she did him. Case in point, she'd offered him her virginity within hours of meeting him. She'd held on to that thing until the ripe old age of twenty-six. Unheard of in this day and age.

Why couldn't he be satisfied with that for now?

She sure needed a powwow with her sisters. They'd help her see through her foggy feelings.

Killian grabbed a book and took a chair in the corner near the fireplace, shutting her out with more than just distance.

Moira glanced from him to Tierra with a questioning look. Tierra slowly shook her head. Now was not the time. Moira accepted her silent message with one of her own, "We need to talk."

She had that right.

Tierra opened the book she'd been trying to read before Killian carried her from the room. She wasn't as good with old English as Moira seemed to be. She had a way with languages and perused the dusty tomes faster than Tierra.

Moira closed her book and stood, going over to the bookcase. "Hey, where is volume thirteen of the Paladin Planetary Magic?" She fingered the line of the hand-tooled leather bindings, cracked and worn with age.

"It vanished during Malcolm de Moray's—" Julian leapt from his chair. "That's it."

"That sneaky bastard," Killian muttered from his corner. "You don't think he—"

"It's just like him to do something like this," Julian said. "Hurry, we need to return to the manor. The book has to be there."

"Explain," Tierra demanded.

"Malcolm de Moray is your ancestor," Julian said. "We barely avoided the Apocalypse back in 1066."

Tierra shared a look with Moira. "Uh, he's more than just our ancestor."

"Might as well tell 'em. They're bound to find out anyway."

"Tell us what?" Killian asked, his nostrils flaring with irritation at her keeping secrets from him.

"Malcolm de Moray is actually our grandfather." Her

words dropped like a flashbang grenade. The Horsemen froze, taking in her reveal.

"That would mean Stian the Wanderer is your father, and that your grandmother the demon Vail," Julian said slowly through tight lips. "I knew he'd stolen the book from me, but I could never prove it or locate it."

"Stian must have taken the book through the Standing Stones to give to your mother," Killian finished. "Why would he do that?"

"We need to find that book. The only reason I can see for him bringing volume thirteen of the Paladin Planetary Magic to this time and place is that he knew his offspring would fulfill the prophecy."

⚓

"ABOUT TIME YOU TWO GOT BACK HERE," AERIN greeted them as they entered the sanctuary. "We have a huge problem. A Biblical Horsemen sized problem." She gestured with her hands spaced far apart above her head.

"You've destroyed two of our homes. The only way to prevent that from happening again is to move into yours." Nick had a smug look on his face as he turned to Moira. "So has research time with Julian stultified you into a coma yet, or should I wait five minutes?" He took a step in her direction and tugged the hem of her t-shirt. "I happen to know a fail-safe cure for boredom."

"And I know a fail-safe cure for stupid," Moira said. "It pretty much involves thinking of whatever it is you'd do, and doing the opposite."

"I take it you found something?" Claire asked, taking up the roll of peacemaker. Love seemed to have banked her fire.

Moira caught them up to date.

"I always knew Stian the Wander was up to no

good," Dru said, rubbing Claire's shoulders. Seemed he couldn't keep his hands off her.

"If he did, indeed, bring the volume forward through time, it must be in the manor. I would bet money that your mother kept her most sacred books here in this room," Julian said, already scanning the many shelves of books.

"Take your time, Julian," Aerin snidely remarked. He hadn't spared her a comment or a look since he'd entered the sanctuary, his attention caught on finding the missing book. "I need a few minutes to confer with my sisters."

"Won't do any good, Aerin," Nick said. "We're moving in."

"Over my dead zombie horde, are you fucking moving in," Aerin muttered under her breath, motioning for her sisters to follow.

They didn't speak until they'd reached the kitchen by mutual agreement.

Tierra went directly to the refrigerator and pulled out leftover quiche. "Anyone else hungry?"

"I need liquid calories after having been stuck here three days with that douchenozzle Nick and these two sickly-sweet lovebirds," Aerin complained. "Can't walk into any room in this huge house without announcing yourself first. Damn inconvenient, yet surprisingly educational."

Claire's face lit with a fiery blush. "Sorry about that."

Aerin threw up her hand in a signal to stop. "We made a pact never to mention it."

Aerin's reaction was similar to Tierra's when she'd walked in on Aunt Justine and Lila. Which reminded her. "Where's Aunt Justine?"

"We have some good news to report," Claire said. "Aunt Justine is in love with Lila and has moved out of the manor and is shacking up with your midwife."

"Well, damn if that don't explain a lot." Moira set the bottle of whiskey on the table and added three glasses. "Looks like we have another pressin' problem. We're running low on liquid courage."

"Exactly why we can't allow the Horsemen to move in here. Nick Kingswood drinks like a fucking fish." Aerin drained her glass. He wasn't the only one, Tierra thought.

"Yeah, he does." Moira gave them a dreamy smile. "You should see what else that man can do with his mouth."

Aerin covered her ears. "Enough. Yuck, overshare, Moira."

Moira shrugged her shoulders. "I bet it wasn't as disturbing as Claire's share." A glint of humor shined in her deep blue eyes.

"This is what I'm talking about," Aerin pointed out. "We let the Horsemen move in here and no room will be safe. While Claire and Tierra seem to be fine fucking destiny, I'm pissed at Julian and I'd just as soon put his balls in a blender than look at him."

"Don't lump me in with Claire," Tierra said. "I agree with you. I don't want the Horsemen living in our house." The last three days in Killian's company had found her in his arms again. Since she couldn't resist him, the best thing to do was avoid him until she could figure out these conflicting feelings he stirred inside her.

"We did kinda destroy their home, er... homes," Moira said. "There're plenty of rooms in this manor to house them."

"Agreed," Claire said. "We just need to come up with some rules."

"Are you two out of your fucking minds?" Aerin asked.

"I need a breather from Killian," Tierra admitted.

"What happened?" Moira asked. "Neither one of

you looked too happy when you returned from your 'nap.' Though Julian and I knew you didn't sleep much. Turns out Tierra here's a screamer."

Tierra felt heat envelop her face.

"See, another reason for the Horsemen not to move in," Aerin said. "There are just some things you don't want to know about your sisters."

Claire waved off Aerin's objection. "Tierra, what happened between you and Killian?"

Tierra squirmed in her chair and set down her fork, her appetite disappearing. She glanced around the room to make sure no one was eavesdropping. "Actually, I really need to talk to you about this, but not here. Let's go outside into the gardens where we have a smaller chance of being overheard."

Without another word, they rose in unison from the table and grabbed coats, sneaking out the back door. They reached Tierra's winter garden by the edge of the cliff, which overlooked an inky-black ocean with a bleeding moon hanging low in the torrid sky. Night had fallen or come early with all the changes the earth was going through since they'd opened the sixth Seal. Would they eventually lose the sun altogether?

In complete contrast to what was happening with the planet, her winter flowers of colorful, happy-faced pansies, rich-purple violas, kaleidoscope-flowering kale, and bleeding-yellow witch hazel, to name a few, thrived, giving her hope.

"Okay, out with it," Moira prompted when Tierra brushed her hand over her flowers and they responded with a riot of bursting blooms. "Though that there is one nifty trick. Do ya think it would work on chicken wings?"

"Highly doubtful." Tierra straightened and met her sisters' worried stare. "Killian told me that he loved me."

"I knew it," Claire exclaimed and wrapped her arms around Tierra. "I'm so happy for you."

"Wait a skunk-lickin' minute," Moira said. "The vibes I was pickin' up from the two of y'all when you got back to the library were distinctly of the *fuck you* variety. And I ain't talkin' about your afternoon boinkfest."

"That's because I didn't return his declaration."

"Ouch," Claire said, placing a hand over her heart.

"Now give her a break. It ain't like she doesn't have a lot on her plate, what with her oven baking a baby and all."

"But poor Killian," Aerin said. "And I really can't believe I fucking said that."

"Are you sayin' that Julian has declared his love for you and you him?"

It was Aerin's turn to blush. "He did, we did, but that was BP. Before Possession," she clarified when they all stared at her with confusion. "Since we kicked that soul-squatting bitch out of me, he hasn't said it again."

"Well, Nick—what did you call him?" Moira asked Aerin.

"Douchenozzle."

"Yeah, well if that douchenozzle tries that love crap with me, he'll be suckin' seawater quicker than he can shake his dick."

"Another reason not to allow them to move into our manor," Aerin said.

"How do you feel about Killian?" Claire maneuvered the conversation back on point.

"I don't know. I'm so confused. I desire him, obviously." She stroked her extended belly. "But he infuriates me with all his demands and high-handed medieval ways."

"He ain't alone in that particular flaw," Moira muttered.

"Speak for yourself," Claire said. "Dru is a modern thinking man."

"I'll admit even Julian treats me like an equal, though a girl doesn't mind being rescued from a fucking, burning building. Just saying." Aerin gave Tierra a sympathetic glance.

Moira's eyes suddenly widened. "Holy shit on a stick, is that..."

"Lucifer," Claire finished for her on a horrified gasp.

10

Lucy had been squatting in these godforsaken woods forever, waiting for her opportunity to get the witches alone. Interesting what she'd overheard. Hiding in the shadows, eavesdropping on her prey was still one of the most effective ways to obtain information, and she excelled at it.

So, Bane was in love with the fertile earth witch and by all accounts the bitch didn't love him back.

She smirked. Now, that was a torture technique beyond what she could have come up with. No wonder Bane wouldn't make a deal with her to give up his first born when she had him copper-staked in Hell doing all manner of unspeakable things. The poor reaper was besotted with this tree-hugging, crystal-loving, hippie. She was the last woman on earth Lucy thought Bane would hook up with, let alone give his black heart to.

Lucy would make her suffer for that.

Bane was a favorite pet of hers, and if the earth witch no longer existed, he'd come crawling back to her all heartbroken and devastated. Just how she loved her men. It gave her the opportunity to build them up so she could shatter them again and again until they were no more than drones to do her bidding. The thought of

Killian Bane as her personal slave sent shivers of delight through her.

This had to happen.

But first, she needed these damn witches and their destructive magic to repair her hideous face and body. Some might call her vain, but over the years she'd found that her beauty had the power to topple kings and destroy governments, while her nightmarish image caused her headaches, what with all the incessant screaming and all.

Lucy tottered from the trees wearing a black veil that reached her shoulders in an attempt to hide her grotesquely disfigured face. She reached her hands out in a pleading gesture and did her best to hide the contempt she felt for the de Moray witches. "Please, I need you to fix me. I have nowhere else to turn." And didn't that grate. She wasn't above groveling to get what she wanted, and at least two of the witches had bleeding hearts and might fall for her sob story.

"I'll fix you...with a nuke," Aerin sneered.

Though it certainly wouldn't be Aerin.

A part of her missed possessing Aerin. It was...nice being part of a family, having sisters, not being alone all the time, but she sure didn't miss Aerin's insolence. How Julian put up with an attitude that was as pleasant as knuckles on a cheese grater, she'd never know? The world was certainly in the last of days, with the Horsemen falling all over themselves for such unsuitable mates.

Lucy didn't spare Aerin a glance, focusing her attempts on Moira, the healer of the bunch, and Tierra, the earth mother. Anyone willing to birth Death's baby had to have a heart the size of Alaska.

"I can't go on living this way. I'll do anything, if you will just reverse the spell." Lucy tore off the veil with a dramatic gesture, revealing her destroyed splendor. She knew how to best use shock and horror to her advantage.

"Jesus H. Christ on a crutch," Moira said. "Ain't no amount of concealer goin' to cover that hole in your face." She cocked her head to the side. "Can you actually eat or does everything fall out of the new pie hole when you chew?"

Lucy narrowed her eyes, and then realized that wasn't meek and miserable behavior. Quickly, she lowered her gaze to the ground and faked stifling a sob.

"How'd you get past our wards?" Tierra asked, her tone suspicious and full of unease.

As well as she should.

"Not only did the spell disfigure me, it stripped me of most of my powers, including my regeneration abilities. I can't even return home to Hades." Not exactly truthful, but it did bite that she wasn't powerful enough to be expelled by their significant wards. She gave another pathetic sniffle, this one not so fake. "Please, you can't leave me like this. Either finish me off or allow me to live what days I have left as the beautiful woman I used to be."

"So, if the spell did this to you, why isn't Claire disfigured?" Tierra asked. "She swallowed enough of that cyanide brew to blow up a castle."

"Uh...it might be that tablespoon of Cheeto's spittle that I added to the mix," Moira added with a shrug. "It seems to alter the nasty in one's attitude."

"You poisoned me with *swine* spit?" Lucy's voice rose and she swiftly tried to disguise it with a pitiful wail.

"That's a new twist on casting pearls before swine," Claire muttered.

"Why come to us for help?" Tierra said. "There has to be others out there willing to come to your aid. The Sisters of the Serpent, or at the very least, your horde of Satan worshipers."

"You think I haven't tried? Nothing works." She

dried up the waterworks and got down to business. The pity thing didn't seem to be working. Let's see if they could refuse what she had to offer. "I'll make you a deal, you reverse this pig spell, and I'll guarantee you don't birth the Antichrist."

Tierra laid a protective hand over her belly.

"I call bullshit," Aerin said with a sneer. "How can you offer that when you just said you have no powers? Besides, I highly doubt even at high octane that *you* could deliver on *that* promise."

"I still have my knowledge of magic and spells. I'll share what knowledge I have with you." She addressed Aerin with what she knew the lovesick, air witch wouldn't be able to refuse. "I can also rescind the curse I bestowed on Julian. He will no longer infect others with the brush of his hand."

Aerin sucked in a breath.

"Don't do it, Aerin," Claire said. "I've never heard of a deal with devil turning out to be a good thing. There's always a loophole."

"But..."

"No buts and no deals, bitch," Claire said.

"Is that your final answer?" Lucy asked through clenched teeth. *Feckin' heartless hags.*

"You bet your sulphuric ass," Moira answered for them.

"Then *deal* with this." A pitchfork materialized out of thin air, and Lucy threw it at Tierra's chest, her aim deadly accurate. The three prongs stabbed sure and deep before anyone could react.

Take that, you earth whore, and your little spawn, too.

Tierra pitched backward like a fallen tree.

❧ 11 ❧

Pain exploded in her chest. Tierra lay prone on the cold, hard ground looking up at a foreign sky devoid of stars with russet clouds smothering the blood-red moon.

She couldn't breathe, couldn't move. Twice now she'd been stabbed in the chest, once by Conquest when he shot her with his arrow, and now that she-demon had skewed her with her devil fork. A note of hysteria bubbled up from her. She must look like someone planted a pitchfork in her sternum just as astronauts had pierced the moon with a flag so many decades before.

Damn it, she couldn't die. Not now. She had her child to bring into the world, and she needed to live long enough to make sure that happened. Darkness clouded her vision and she knew at any moment she'd experience that eerily comforting, weightless, pain-free state as she had when she'd died before.

Voices screamed above her. Her sisters. And then Killian's ferocious roar.

She blinked in an attempt to clear her vision. Focus. Maybe they could save her again? But in order to do that, they'd have to open a Seal. There was only one left, and her life wasn't worth destroying the world.

"Tierra!" Killian dropped to his knees beside her, taking her face in his hands and forcing her to look at him. He felt for the pulse in her neck, and froze, then a satisfied smile graced his face. "Do as I say, and just stay calm."

Calm? She was dying. She'd never hold her child in her arms, would in fact take her baby's soul with her when she died. Tears leaked from the corners of her eyes and trailed into her hair. Would she be able to raise her child in the hereafter? Goddess, she prayed it would be so.

Moira knelt beside her, her trembling hands hovering over Tierra. A soft drizzle started to fall and lightning flashed from Aerin, their anguish effecting the weather.

"Control your emotions," Killian barked to them. "Get her sisters out of the way," he addressed the Horsemen. Nick dragged a screaming Moira from her perch beside Tierra.

Good Goddess, she needed more time. Needed to know if she felt about Killian the way he felt about her. He had to know that she cared for him before he had to take her soul, and that of their child. She hoped he delivered them to Heaven. She'd even take the Garden of Eden. Any place but Hell. With all the indiscretions she'd recently done—what with opening the Seals, bringing about the end of the world, and killing zombies—she might actually be sent to Hell. One visit there was enough to leave lasting scars, but an eternity? She couldn't bare thinking of it.

"I'm sorry," she choked out.

"You have nothing to be sorry for," Killian said, smoothing the hair back from her forehead and wiping away her tears. "Don't cry. This won't take long, unless you fight it."

What was there to fight? No way she'd survive this.

Actually, how was she still alive? She knew one

prong of the pitchfork had pierced her heart as it wasn't beating, and her lungs had to be impaled, since each breathe she struggled to drag in had a bubbling sound.

"I'm going to pull out the pitchfork," Killian said, his hand wrapping around the staff. "This is going to hurt, but everything will be better afterward."

Better? How? "Wait!" She needed to ease his heartache, and time to say goodbye to her sisters. She glanced at her sisters' stricken faces standing over her. Each of their Horsemen restraining them from rushing to her side.

"There will be plenty of time to talk, but it's imperative that this is removed, and quickly." With no more warning, Killian yanked the pitchfork from her chest. Her body arched with the action. Pain screamed through her like a branding iron set to flesh.

Was that her shrieking like a Banshee?

"Holy shit! You're killing her!" Aerin yelled.

Julian wrapped his arms around her middle as she tried to escape his hold. Killian tossed the pitchfork, embedding it in a tree with a twang.

"No, he is not," Julian said. "He's saving her. The protuberance won't dislodge itself, thereby inhibiting her ability to heal."

"Healin' herself? How in the ever-loving hell is she doin' that?" Moira asked. "And why didn't that tricky tadpole throw up a force field like it did the last time Beelzebub touched Tierra?"

"You haven't told them?" Julian asked Bane, while sharing a look with Dru.

"Told us what?" Claire demanded.

"Now's not the time," Dru said. "We should get her inside." On guard, he scanned the area as though Lucy might return at any moment.

Killian carefully lifted Tierra into his arms. "I've got you. Just relax."

What the hell was he talking about, and how was

she still here? With each second that ticked by, it became easier to breathe. A stinging tingle generated inside her. It wasn't unpleasant, really, but wasn't like anything she'd ever experienced before. Definitely otherworldly. What was happening to her?

Killian carried her into the manor, up the stairs to her bedroom, and gently laid her on the bed. Everyone else traipsed into her room behind them.

"I'll get some water," Moira said. "We need to clean the wounds. Claire, be ready to cauterize them shut if need be."

"There will be no need for such barbaric measures." Killian reached for the buttons on Tierra's blouse.

Tierra attempted to slap his hands away, but she felt too weak, and in need of nourishment. She was suddenly shaky and starving like she hadn't eaten in days.

"If you want to help, bring up a tray of food that is easy to digest and has high levels of refined carbohydrates," Killian instructed.

"You know she's a health nut and doesn't believe in putting that kind of poison into her body," Claire said.

"Well, she *has* made an exception for pork rinds and bacon as the tadpole likes them," Moira said.

"I want to know what the fuck is going on right now," Aerin demanded. "Why isn't she dead? Not that I want her to be." She turned to the three Horsemen. "Why are we just standing here? Shouldn't you be doing something like chasing after that hideous harpy? No way is she allowed to live after she pitchforked my sister."

Killian succeeded in getting Tierra's blouse unbuttoned. She clutched the fabric to her with a whimper she couldn't hold in. Her body was on fire, the tingling morphing into a furnace of sensations.

"You peeping Toms, get out," Moira said. "Tierra doesn't want you seeing her undressed."

"She doesn't have anything that we all haven't seen

before." Nick scoffed. "You're identical, remember?"

"Shut your mouth, and get your ass out." Moira gave him a shove to get him moving.

"Please, my love," Claire implored Dru. "She needs privacy."

"Should you require assistance, you'll find us in the attic," Julian said to Killian. He gave the room a slight bow and took his exit.

"Tierra is the one hurt. Why would you need Julian?" Aerin asked.

Killian ignored her and addressed Tierra. "Come on, let me see," Killian said softly. "Everything's going to be all right. Trust me, my gazelle."

She released her hold on the fabric, and he bared her to his gaze.

Killian held his hand out. "A wet rag."

Moira ran for the adjoining bathroom and returned with a warm washcloth.

"Someone get her some food." Killian's tone brooked no argument.

"I'll see what I can find." Claire left in search of carbs.

He wiped the cloth across her chest, and Tierra braced herself for the pain. But none came.

Killian smiled down at her with pride. "You are doing great. Just a little more time and you will be good as new."

"How?" Tierra choked out, confused.

"That's what I want to know," Moira said. "What the hell kind of discount voodoo is this? She doesn't even have puncture wounds anymore."

"Is the zygote doing this?" Aerin asked. "That thing is getting bloody powerful if it can bring her back from the brink."

"No," Killian said. "This is all Tierra's doing." His eyes radiated pride and delight. "Her transformation is complete. She's immortal."

T ransformation?
  Immortal?

What the hell was he talking about?

Tierra sat upright in bed, surprised and horrified when she only felt a twinge of soreness. She patted her chest and found...nothing but some dried blood. Next, she smoothed a hand over her belly, relieved at the answering kick that followed. Her child was safe and she was somehow alive.

"Lie back. Your body needs to rest." Killian pushed her down to the mattress.

"What she needs is a fucking explanation," Aerin demanded. She and Moira flanked the other side of the bed. "We all do."

Aerin hit that square on the nose.

Tierra's mind raced, her heart beating hard enough to escape her newly healed chest.

"She needs to eat first," Killian said. "The healing process depleted her energy stores."

Claire entered the room with a tray of assorted cookies, a bag of pork rinds, and a soft drink to help wash it all down.

Tierra's appetite bared its teeth and she fell on the tray like a rabid dog locked in a cage and starved for weeks. She plowed through the bag of pork rinds first, not caring about the mess of crumbs falling on her bed and getting stuck in her hair. Guzzling the soft drink, to help swallow the barely chewed fried pork skin, she filled her cheeks with cookies like a chipmunk preparing for the coming ice age.

"Holy shit," Claire said. "Keep your arms and hands back from her, or we're going to lose some limbs."

Once every morsel had been consumed, Tierra dragged in a deep breath and felt her heart rate return back to normal and the shaking in her cells settle. A feeling of calm blanketed her. She leaned back and looked at her horrified sisters. "What?"

"Well, you know those salivating zombies after brains?" Aerin asked, continuing when Tierra nodded. "That display of feeding beat the hell out theirs."

She wiped a hand over her mouth, collected some leftover food particles and licked them off her fingers. "I was *starved*. I've never felt hunger like that before." She regarded Killian with suspicion. Had he somehow turned her into an animal? "What have you done to me?"

"Yeah, past time to explain yourself, buddy," Moira said. "What's this immortal shit you've been spoutin'?"

"First of all, I hadn't counted on this, but secretly hoped it would happen." Killian smoothed back Tierra's wild hair from her face, gazing down at her with his heart in his eyes. It made her uncomfortable to see his adoration that he didn't bother to hide from her sisters.

"Well, shit," Aerin said. "He *really* is in love with you."

Moira nudged her to keep quiet, while Tierra's eyes widened with panic, feeling like a net had closed in around her.

"Leave us," Killian ordered.

"*No!*" Tierra and her sisters hollered together.

Tierra continued, "You explain yourself right now in

front of my sisters. This concerns them, too." She thought she heard Killian mutter, *in-laws*, under his breath.

"It has been said that when an immortal bonds with a human, and the immortal's love for the human is pure, the human will be transformed into an immortal, too." He gave her a satisfied smile. "Welcome to the rest of your life, my gazelle."

Tierra sat there stunned, staring up at Killian. Immortal? She was immortal. "You're saying that I can't die? That I won't age?"

"Correct." He smiled as though he'd bestowed the most treasured of gifts upon her.

"Will she have to drink blood and sleep in the ground during the day?" Moira regarded Tierra with wariness.

"Nothing like that," Killian reassured them. "Other than the ability to regenerate, she remains unchanged.

"Except I can't grow old and die." She'd be forced to live forever...with Killian. A marriage lasting fifty years was a remarkable achievement, but eternity? How did one love someone for an eternity? Wouldn't he get tired of her? She of him? What about her child? Would she have to watch him or her grow old and perish? Her hand covered her belly and a sob gathered in her throat. Not to mention, she'd have to suffer her sisters passing too, as well as everyone else that she loved.

Killian placed his hand over hers. "There is a high probability that our child will also be immortal. So, don't fret."

"*Don't fret?*" she shrieked. "I don't want to live *forever*. I want to grow *old*. I want to experience every season of my life. Be a grandmother, one of those old biddies who everyone is always afraid of what they are going to do or say."

"You can still do all that, you'll just look the age you

are now," Killian said as though her objections were pesky flies to be swatted away.

"Take it back," she demanded. "I don't want to be immortal."

"Well, I sure as fuck do," Aerin said. "How do I sign up for this?"

"You'll have to consult Julian," Killian said.

"You can bet your ass, we'll be having a conversation," Aerin murmured.

"Wait," Claire said, a frown creasing her brow. "Does that mean *I* might be immortal as Dru and I pledged our souls to each other? How do we make sure?"

"Other than takin' a pitchfork to the chest?" Moira asked, sarcastically. "Sure would have been easier on my ticker if you'd given us a heads up. Seein' Tierra skewered like a shish-kabob took years off my life."

The thought of living forever further exhausted her. "I don't want this. I want to die like a normal human being."

"Even if that meant you would have died tonight?" A stiff note entered Killian's voice. "It wouldn't have been only you who would have died, but our child, too." His eyes hardened to chips of coal.

She was grateful she'd survived and that her baby still thrived inside her, but she couldn't comprehend the idea of living forever. Hell, she freaking *recycled*, and now she was basically a nondegradable plastic bottle, everything she abhorred.

"I need a shower." Killian's eyes flared with desire at her words. "Alone," she added in a tone that didn't leave room for debate.

"Shit on a shingle, I need a drink," Moira said.

"It'll take more than one to erase the image of her pitchforked. Several, actually, to help swallow the knowledge that I might be immortal, too," Claire said.

"We also need a battle plan. Lucy is top on my hit

list. That bitch needs to be eradicated." Aerin followed Moira and Claire the door, leaving Tierra alone with Killian.

"Let me help you." Killian scooped her into his arms again and carried her into the bathroom. Carefully, he set her on her feet. "Hold onto the counter. You might be wobbly after your ordeal."

Ordeal was right, but which was worse, being stabbed by Satan or finding out she was now immortal?

Killian turned on the shower and adjusted the heat and then faced her. He started stripping off what remained of her torn and bloodied clothes.

"I'm taking a shower alone," she stressed.

"As you said," he murmured, his eyes raking in her nakedness as he unveiled her.

"I'm serious."

"I can hear that."

"That means you need to leave," she stated, making her position clear.

"That is where you are wrong." His eyes hardened. "I will not leave you in your weakened state." He covered her mouth with his finger when she went to object again. "Save your breath."

Blasted, stubborn man.

When she didn't try to speak, he traced her lips with his fingertip, his pupils dilating until his eyes were pure black. She knew he wanted to lean down and kiss her, silence her objections with the desire he could so easily coax from her with the barest of touches. Instead, he surprised her and returned to undressing her.

Her thoughts continued to swirl like fallen leaves before a winter gale with questions she should have demanded the answers to when he'd first spoken of them being bonded. "What else does this bonding thing do?"

He stiffened and looked away

"Oh, no you don't. If you want any kind of relationship with me, or me to love you, then that means you need to start telling the truth."

"As you wish." Though he looked as though he'd rather have his feathers plucked than have this conversation. "There is nowhere you can run that I can't find you," he admitted. "It's the same for you, which is how you were able to locate me in Hell when no one else could."

Okay, that could be handy when she got into a scrap —which seemed to be happening too often of late—but what if she wanted to be lost, hidden from him? Be freaking alone? "Can you eavesdrop on my thoughts like Dru does with Claire?" That was sobering. Her thoughts were her own. And they needed to remain that way. There were just some things *no one* needed to know.

"Maybe in time, if you open that door. It's been a millennium since a human has become immortal, therefore the benefits are uncertain." He released the tie on her skirt and it pooled at her feet. He dragged in a deep breath, taking her in. She only wore a strap of thin white silk covering her nether region. He hooked his fingers in the elastic and slowly knelt, drawing them down her thighs. He held her hips as she stepped out of them. Instead of rising, he gazed up at her, letting her see the passion and love reflected in his eyes and the reedy hold he had on his control.

Slowly, he leaned forward and laid his lips to her extended belly, his hands splaying wide over her abdomen, wonder in his gentle caress.

Her heartbeat kicked up a notch and her breath turned choppy. How could he do this to her with just one look, one touch? She had to take control of their conversation before he had her under him again and she lost all ability to think straight.

"What are the consequences?" she asked.

He flicked her a glance, letting her know he was

aware of her tactics. "What is keeping you from admitting your love for me?" he countered, rising to tower above her. He reached behind him and grabbed a handful of his black t-shirt and pulled it over his head, revealing his glorious chest and ripped abdomen.

"You are *not* taking a shower with me."

"That is where you are wrong." He unbuttoned his jeans and slid the zipper down.

"See, there you go, making decisions for me again." She let her temper flood through her welcoming how it cooled the heat in her blood and the yearning to touch him, grab him, take him.

"When it comes to keeping you safe, I will do whatever it takes. You shouldn't be alone. Not until you are back to full strength." He dragged his boxers off with his jeans and stood resplendently nude in front of her, his erection jutting hard and proud.

She had to swallow in order to speak, her mouth watering at the sight of how much he wanted her. "That isn't what I was talking about." Well, it was, but it was just the zenith of the mountain between them when it came to him making decisions for her.

"What *are* you talking about?" He clearly looked confused.

Men.

They were clueless creatures, no matter if they were of the immortal variety or not. But then had she really taken the time to talk with him like this, state her concerns?

Probably not.

She'd just figured he should know why she was upset, and that was on her. How did she put into words what she needed? Wanted?

"Never mind," she mumbled, instantly regretting her choice of words. *Sure, give him the classic female response.* Never mind was right up there with fine. "Wait. I do mind. From the beginning, you have never asked for my permission, or for any promises from me. You have always decided what you think is best for us. That is medieval thinking and I don't like it. I'm not a maiden of old. I've been born of this day and age and it's past time that you adapted."

His jaw clenched at her words.

"What if I want a divorce?" she continued. "Or whatever the equivalent is for breaking this bond you've forced on me."

He grabbed her shoulders and gave her a hard shake. "That will not happen. Ever. You are mine. I am yours. The sooner you come to terms with that the better for everyone."

"Is that a threat?"

"Take it however you want it. I will never let you go." He yanked her to him and kissed her. There was nothing soft or loving in the meeting of his mouth against hers, it was a branding, a searing pronouncement of possession. He released her as quickly as he grabbed her. "Open your eyes, woman. I know you love me. What more must I do so for you to see the forest through the trees?"

Her heart clenched at his words, his soul stripped bare for her to see, the pain swimming in his eyes at her attempts to push him away. "I need time. You just told me that I will live forever, forever with you. That's a lot to swallow." Especially with everything else on her plate.

He released her, his fingers brushing over the tops of her breasts. "Do you remember that night when you danced naked under the harvest moon for me?"

She gave a jerky nod, feeling the heat of her blush at the memory. She'd been drunk on him. They'd spent the whole day getting reacquainted with each other after she'd rescued him from Hell, and he'd squirreled her away to the Garden of Eden. It had only been them, no end of the world problems to worry about, an abundance of food to eat, the temperatures tropical with just the right amount of humidity that the air caressed her bare skin. She hadn't been able to get enough of him.

"Remember how you felt that night. How you loved me unconditionally with your body, your essence. The peace, the joy, the euphoria? That is our future, what we can have together for eternity. I knew I loved you before then, but I fell deeper under your spell that night. You delight and enchant me, my gazelle, forever and always. There is no one for me but you." This time when he kissed her it was filled with wonder and tenderness like she was the most treasured thing in the world.

She melted against him, her arms tangling around his neck. He crushed her body to his for a brief moment and then broke the kiss. "Your body has never lied to me. It isn't only desire that brings us together. We've always been fated. Everything I have done is for your protection."

"Bonding me to you was for my protection?" Come on, she wasn't born yesterday.

He paused. "In truth, it was more for my...protection."

"How so?"

He shifted on his feet and it took him a moment to respond. "I couldn't face losing you."

"Losing me or access to our child?"

He physically struggled with his answer. "To be honest, in the beginning, both." Laying a hand on her belly, he continued, "What we have created is a miracle, one I thought never to experience. But you...you consume me." He laid his other hand over her heart. "You are my world, my everything."

And just like that her temper dissipated and something bright and promising blossomed in her heart. Her throat clogged with emotion and her eyes filled with moisture. Oh, Goddess, she did love him. It had been fear keeping her from realizing how much.

"Why are you crying?" he asked, his voice barely a whisper, as he wiped at the tears that trailed down her cheeks.

"Because, I love you."

"And that makes you sad?"

"Quite the opposite." She gently placed her lips over his heart.

He crushed her to him, his arms like bands of iron, and his body shuddered against hers. Then he was kissing her, her mouth, her cheeks, mumbling words she couldn't make sense of, but understood deep in her soul.

Steam from the forgotten shower drifted around them, cocooning them in their own enchanted haven. Tenderly, he assisted her into the shower and then lovingly washed every inch of her, taking his time, worshiping her until her need for him left her trembling.

He turned off the water and reverently dried her off, running his fingers through her hair to untangle the knots. Then he lifted her into his arms and carried her to the bed, where he followed her down to the mattress and preceded to show her the depths of his devotion.

Their bodies came together, until their souls intertwined, sealing the promises they'd already spoken.

❧ 13 ❧

Tierra woke in Killian's arms to find him raised up on his elbow gazing down at her. "Morning, my gazelle," he purred. Well, as much as Death could purr. Not quite the sound Jinx made, but it had all the contentment and satisfaction of an adored pet teeming in the deep timbre. He traced a finger down her cheek and then anchored a strand of her hair behind her ear. "I do apologize for not allowing you much rest."

"I highly doubt you are that sorry." Her lips quirked into a smile. She could get used to this, waking in his arms, starting her day losing herself in his dark and dreamy eyes.

"There you are mistaken. I've realized after our discussion, that I have failed in asking you a crucial question." He opened his palm and revealed the most beautiful ring she'd ever seen. Formed of silver and gold, a tree of life laced with emerald leaves glimmered in his palm. "Will you consent to marry me?"

Tears filled her eyes and her heart expanded in her chest, threatening to burst free. "Wherever did you find that?"

"It found me. I've had it stowed away at Châteaux Morte since Malcolm de Moray gifted it to me centuries ago and asked that I give it to the woman who would own my heart. You are that woman and my heart is truly yours. I love you with all my soul. Tell me you will be mine."

He seemed nervous, regarding her with anxious eyes. A smile spread over her face. Looked as if her medieval man was learning. "Yes," she whispered and held out her hand for him to slip the exquisite ring on her finger. Once the ring was in place, he lifted it to his lips, the action so sweet and tender that tears flowed down her cheeks. He wiped them away and kissed her, sealing their union.

"Are you well?" His fingers trailed down her neck to her collarbone where he lightly traced the outline of her bones.

She understood that he was asking if she was willing and able for another round of lovemaking. Case in point, the large member enthusiastically pressing against her hip. Mating with a Horseman, who by all accounts had a vigorous sexual appetite, was something to thank the Goddess for. She'd never hunger for orgasms like so many married women she'd talked to over the years. Another reason she'd waited so long to finally have sex. But one look at Killian in Sirens and she'd offered up her maidenhead without a second thought. Part of her must have understood that this man was her man.

She'd never believed in fate or destiny, but maybe there was something to it. After all, how did she discount them coming together like they had?

"I will always be well enough." She slipped her hand under the sheets and wrapped her fingers around him. He groaned and his head fell back on his shoulders.

He might have her number, but she was very adept when it came to figures.

A long time later, Tierra found her sisters in the kitchen cooking breakfast. Killian had headed upstairs to check on Julian's progress. Pestilence hadn't left the

Sanctuary since they'd returned from Châteaux Morte. She doubted he'd even taken time to eat or sleep in his search through their mother's treasured things.

The world might look bleak, but hers was all sunshine and rainbows after clearing the air with Killian last night and then making love with him until the sun rose. She couldn't get enough of him. Maybe it was the pregnancy hormones? Most likely it was the love she'd been suppressing. Not anymore, the gates had busted wide open.

Jinx hadn't even hissed at Killian when she'd jumped on the bed to find him curled around Tierra. Though she hadn't quite accepted him, eyeing him with that all-to-knowing green-eyed stare. They'd find a way to get along. Jinx would relax her guard once she understood how much Killian cared for Tierra.

"For the love of the Goddess, Tierra, dial it back," Claire grumbled into her coffee cup.

"Dial what back?" she asked.

"The sexual pheromones," Aerin gripped. "Have you taken a look around?" She gestured to the solarium where the plants had doubled in size overnight, their enormous flowers scenting the room. It resembled spring instead of winter outside the windows. Even the grass had repealed its dormant winter slumber, turning verdurous and now needed a good mowing.

"It's not only the vegetation she's affectin'," Moira mumbled. "I'm about ready to offer up an ovary to ride a Horseman."

"Amen, sister." Aerin looked wishfully into her coffee. "But Julian is more interested in books, than me."

"I take it you're over the whole immortal thing," Claire said.

"Not over, exactly," Tierra admitted. "More like I'm coming to terms with it." She didn't think she'd ever be over it. For now, she was choosing not to think about it.

"Have anything to do with all that orgasmic

screamin' comin' from your room last night *and* this morning?" Moira asked.

Heat flared in her cheeks, but she was too happy to be embarrassed for long. "Maybe." She filled the kettle and set it on to heat.

"Oh, dear Goddess, you *are* in love with him!" Aerin exclaimed.

"Guilty," she admitted with a sappy smile. She held up her hand and showed them her ring. "He asked me to marry him. Actually *asked*."

Claire squealed, jumping up and embracing Tierra. "I'm so happy for you. For you both. We have to plan a wedding."

"I'd love a spring wedding." She sighed at the thought. She'd always wanted a spring wedding as the season represented new beginnings and rebirth. By then —if they'd survived the Apocalypse—she'd be a new mom and wouldn't have to waddle down the aisle. She tried to dial back her joy as not all of her sisters were content with their love life. Part of her felt bad about that, the other wished they could see through their obstacles like Claire and she had.

Obviously, this Apocalypse depended on all of them. Each elemental witch and each Horseman mating together to form something epic. Goddess she hoped so. Claire had bonded with War, and her with Death, but the other two were still up on the air.

"Seems redundant to have a wedding when you are already bonded," Aerin muttered, "and immortal."

"Bonded without her permission, remember?" Moira said. "I think a weddin' is just what we need. We'll make sure there is plenty of booze at the reception so that you can suffer through it in style, Aerin."

"I've located the book." Julian entered into the kitchen.

Tierra stared. Normally Julian wore impeccable suits, some accessorized with a cravat. But this morning, his suit jacket was absent, the cuffs of his white dress shirt were rolled to the elbows, and his long black hair shot with strands of sliver and usually tied back with a strap of leather, flowed wild about his face and shoulders. "My brothers are waiting for you to join us in the parlor."

Tierra turned off the heat under the kettle and followed her sisters as they traipsed after Julian. He took up a position beside the hearth. Killian reached for Tierra's hand and drew her to the loveseat where he sat next to her, his arm anchoring her to his side.

Claire sat beside a frowning Dru on the windowseat, but left enough space that they weren't touching. It didn't seem as though Claire had taken the news of her possibly living forever any better than Tierra had.

Aerin and Moira took the sofa, leaving Nick to perch uncomfortably on the edge of the Queen Anne chair, glowering at Moira with lust and irritation.

Julian got the meeting underway by holding up a leather volume. "While this book matches the others in the Paladin Planetary Magic it has obviously not aged like the others have, which means Stain the Wanderer must have brought it forward through the stones like we believed."

"We don't need a history lesson. Get to the good part," Nick grumbled, his eyes never leaving the long expanse of Moira's bare legs.

"We've been amiss in how we've regarded the Seals," Julian continued. "In reality, they are tumblers in a complicated lock, each cleansing the earth in preparation for the Goddess to be released from her prison. We were created to bring about the Apocalypse." Julian shared a look with each of his brothers. "Yet we have failed her with our compliance, our contentment of living in this world. We've fallen for the temptations of the Devil, seduced into believing what she'd told us. When our real purpose has always been as the harbingers to lead the crusade for the Goddess, and we've lost our way."

"May I see that?" Moira reached for the book and started reading the page Julian indicated. "The Goddess will be released from her prison on the event of the seventh Seal being opened by the four born of one."

"Wait," Claire said. "Is that book *actually* saying we need to *open* the last Seal?"

"I knew it," Aerin said, her eyes alight with the promise of power. "*We* are the new order."

"You make us sound like Nazis," Tierra commented. "Besides, it says the Goddess will be released."

"Let me get this straight," Claire said. "This *one* book says we need to open the last Seal while nothing else we've come across even *hints* of something like that. Where is the proof to back this up? How can we trust that this book is right?"

"Moira, show them the picture on the next page," Julian instructed.

She turned the page and gasped. "It's...us." She held up the volume and showed the intricate drawing of four identical women standing in a circle, wearing their elemental crowns and holding wands from the tree of life.

"That's me," Aerin said. "And I have my crown. I'm finally going to get that sucker."

"There's more. Read the top of the next page, Moira." Julian didn't take his eyes off of Aerin as Moira translated the indicated text.

"The four born of one will conceive two children, one good and one evil, keeping all things in balance so that the earth will be restored for the coming of the Goddess' time to rule."

Moira glanced up at Tierra, and she laid a protective hand over her belly.

Please Goddess, let my child be the good one.

Killian tightened his hold on her hand, giving her much needed reassurance.

"One good *and* one evil?" Tierra repeated hoarsely. "I've had an ultrasound. I'm not pregnant with twins. Just one little baby swimming around in here."

Which left the question, who else among her sisters was pregnant?

"Fuck, no!" Aerin rose so fast to her feet, she almost toppled over on her stilettos.

"Holy shit!" Claire followed Aerin. "You think one of us is *pregnant,* too?"

"Oh, hell no." Moira flipped the book shut and tossed it to the coffee table where it landed with a slap.

A gleeful sound escaped Tierra. She wasn't the only one knocked up. "Fill your bladders, sisters. Looks like you're all peeing on a stick today."

II

MOIRA

By Cynthia St. Aubin

$$ \maltese \ \text{I}4 \ \maltese $$

"I got me a bad feeling about this."

Moira de Moray reckoned she'd had enough bad feelings in her short but exceedingly strange life to recognize that distinctive cocktail of foreboding and dread when it flooded into her heart like swamp water. Each time, it had arrived on the heels of some person or other telling her something she would have preferred not to know, and usually meant it would be dragging a gut-full of suffering in its wake.

The examples were plentiful and varied.

The time Uncle Sal had shared his plans for converting an extra pontoon motor into a moonshine bottling device.

The time she'd agreed to trade Nicholas Kingswood some nay-nay in exchange for his help in offing herself to stave off the impending Apocalypse.

The time she'd guilt-allowed her pet teacup piglet, Cheeto, to eat a whole head of cabbage.

And right the hell now.

Now, she sat on the edge of the antique clawfoot tub, aiming a serious stink eye at the slim thermometer-shaped gadget perched precariously on the edge of the sink.

A pregnancy test.

The kind that promised results six days in advance of a period in absurdly cheerful script on the front of the package.

The plan was, they'd all take the tests at the same time, come out into the living room, and unveil the results on the count of three, rock, paper, scissors style.

And believe it not, synchronized piddling had been the easy part of the plan. The hard part had been laying hold of a pregnancy test in the first place. Like everyone else and their flea-ridden dog, the sisters de Moray had done their share of pantry stocking against the End of Days, but pregnancy tests weren't something they'd thought to buy in bulk.

Just a simple trip to Port Townsend's one grocery store had become more treacherous than catfish noodling in a gator pit.

And if you happened to survive the gauntlet of people trying to shoot your ass full of bullets over the last package of non-vegan hot dogs a la Drustan Geddes or back over you in a fit of black-brained Nicholas Kingswood-esque road rage if you happened to take the parking spot they'd been after, there were those whose lives Julian Roarke had touched.

Like, with his hands and stuff.

You couldn't swing a dead cat—and Goddess knew the Apocalypse had produced an alarming number of those—without hitting someone hideously afflicted with some sort of face-liquefying super-plague.

Moira was getting awfully sick of hosing globs of skin off Tierra's eco-mobile every time she left the damn house, even if some of that skin may or not belong to that demonic twat Lucifer. Imagining what had become of she-Satan's face the last time Moira had clapped eyes on her brought her first smile of the day.

She'd seen half-eaten pork chops with more sex appeal than Lucy had now.

Something warm and wet nudged Moira's calf, startling her out of her thoughts.

Cheeto sat at her feet, velvety pink skin fuzzy in the glow of the bathroom lamp. His small eyes squinted as he gave an impatient grunt.

She didn't have Tierra's talent for yakking with critters, but she was pretty certain she knew what he was saying.

Get on with it, biped. That stick ain't gonna pee on itself.

"All right, all right. I'm going." Moira stood on legs gone numb from sitting too long on the edge of the tub and hovered over the toilet, pausing when she saw Cheeto blinking up at her from the bathmat. "If I wanted some male in here eyeballing me while I squat on the pot, I'd have invited Nick in here."

Not that she'd had to invite him.

He'd invited himself.

In fact, she'd practically had to slam the door on that chiseled jaw he was so damned proud of.

Even now, she could hear the footfalls of his expensive loafers echoing up and down the hallway where he already paced like an expectant father.

Nicholas Kingswood. An expectant father.

Now that there was a colon-loosening thought.

But no more or less troubling than Bane, or Julian, or Dru as a potential baby daddy Moira supposed.

And truth was, as of this particular moment, any of the immortals in question might have been the one to supply the de Moray baby batter, so to speak.

When Julian had toted Paladin Planetary Magic and Tierra had insisted that it mean one of them was knocked up, they'd all been forced to admit—after copious denials and general panic—that they'd each, at one time or another, boned their respective Horsemen bareback.

Moira, when chained to Nicholas Kingswood's bed, thinking she was going to die anyway.

Aerin, when she'd finally relieved Julian of his millennia-long virginity.

And Claire, when she and Dru had bumped uglies in addition to souls.

And Tierra...well, no one needed a pregnancy test to know she was heavily knocked up.

"All right." Moira sat down and angle the stick toward what she approximated would be the splash zone. "Here goes nothing."

❧ 15 ❧

Moira was the last to arrive in the parlor, a room that looked cozy when it was just the four sisters, but positively claustrophobic with the addition of the Four Horsemen, who'd they'd been sharing quarters with since Claire had accidentally reduced Manresa Castle to a heap of smoldering ash.

As was their way, each Horseman had chosen a strategic position. Death, as close to the bulging-bellied Tierra as the furniture would allow. War, with his back to the corner and his broad chest facing the exits. Pestilence, near the bookshelves from which he seemed to draw strength. And Conquest, where the architecture would best magnify the sound of his voice.

A surge of ardor doused the flame of irritation Moira had been fanning against him.

Hearing him was one thing. Seeing him was another.

Tall against the corner where wall met wall and the ceiling vaulted overhead, his head tipped back against the plaster at an insolent angle, the lamps casting amber sparks into hair the color of the brick roux it had taken Moira pert near ten years to master. Arms crossed over his chest, his biceps strained the midnight blue fabric of his tailored dress shirt. Not for the first time, Moira marked that Nicholas Kingswood didn't so much wear a suit as force each seam and panel to worship the planes of his body. Not that Moira could blame them. Lord knew she'd done plenty of worshiping at the temple of Conquest in the days of their acquaintance.

She felt his awareness shift from his favorite focus—himself—to her. A subtle rearranging of the room's molecules around her as a center axis. His gaze lasering away everything in the room that wasn't her, his warm whiskey eyes tracing the coastline of her body with a cartographer's zeal. Shores he had mapped with his lips, fingers, and tongue. His face slid into that particular grin he got when she caught him looking at her naked. Not that he ever really tried to hide it. Nick Kingswood wasn't prone to much by the way of remorse as a general rule. It was something Moira both loved and hated about him depending on the day.

"Finally. What did you do? Fucking forge the plastic from scratch?" Aerin de Moray perched on the edge of the chaise longue, her long legs creating sharp, slim angles in their expensive slacks. She still dressed every inch the high-powered, ball-busting businesswoman she'd been before coming to Port Townsend, just as Moira still favored her ratty cut-offs and threadbare tank tops. In times like these, a body wanted to hold on to everything, any shred of comfort or familiarity it could find.

"You try relaxin' enough to pee when you've got this guy marchin' up and down the hallway outside the bathroom door." Moira jerked her chin toward Nick, who detached himself from the wall and took a step in her direction.

"I just wanted to be nearby in case you needed any help."

That voice.

That goddamn talk a nun out of her starched knickers and sell a glacier to an Eskimo sinfully smooth drawl.

Her usual ritual of feigning indifference in Nick Kingswood's presence would be a hell of a lot easier without that voice. Not that the sight of him helped any.

"And how exactly were you gonna help me?" Moira asked. "Hold the stick?"

Nick's eyelids lowered, his wicked mouth tugging up at one corner. A subtle suggestion that he'd have been willing to do that and more.

Much, much more.

"Enough already." Claire pushed herself up from the sofa, the pregnancy test poking up from the hip pocket of her curve-hugging black jeans. Her face was drawn and pale, her lips as bloodless as her cheeks. "Can we just get this over with?"

Moira glanced down at the pregnancy test clutched in her own sweaty hand. It had taken every ounce of her meager self-restraint not to peek at the little window on the walk from the bathroom to the living room, which had felt more like a walk from a jail cell to an electric chair. "Y'all ready?"

"Ready like for a vivisection." Aerin sighed and stood, picking up her test from where it rested face down on the end table and holding it out at arm's length between her thumb and forefinger.

"Oh my hell, this is so exciting!" Tierra, swathed in layers of loose-fitting skirts and scarves, clutched her hands against her baby-swollen boobs. "I'm going to be an aunt!"

Killian Bane dropped a possessive hand over her shoulder, his obsidian black eyes drawn to the globe of her belly as if it housed a magnet rather than a miniature immortal. "You'll be a mother first," he said. "Or have you forgotten about the babe, my gazelle?"

Dark-haired, built like several brick shithouses, and capable of a sphincter-tightening glare, Dru made a sound somewhere between a gag and a grunt. "It's a fucking baby, all right? B.A.B.Y. We've all been around long enough to pick up the nuances of modern English language. Well, all except for Julian. But he makes that shit work for him."

Darkness seemed to gather around the region above Bane's head. A pretty impressive trick, Moira had to admit. "It's my child and I'll call it what I like," he said.

"I know what I'm going to call it," Nick said. "Road kill. Because it's half Death and half gazelle."

Julian covered his lips with one gloved hand, the fine lines stretching from the corners of his pale blue eyes deepening to an almost imperceptible degree. To anyone else, it might have looked like mild shock or dismay. But in the time they'd pretended to be a budding couple, Moira had learned a thing or two about interpreting his infinitely subtle expressions. This right here was amusement.

Bane's fists tightened. From the way his jaw flexed, he might have been trying to chew a rock. "So help me—"

Moira stuck two fingers in her mouth and whistled the way she'd used to when she had to call Uncle Sal home for supper from three bayous over.

"Look, we can bust out the kitchen scale and weigh your sacks after this is all over, but for right now, we need to figure out which one of us is baking a bun and what the hell we're supposed to do about it. So y'all two quit ruffling his feathers and hush up."

An uneasy silence returned to the room.

"All right," Moira said, turning back to Aerin and Claire. "We flip on the count of three."

They counted together. Same voice, three slightly different accents.

Well, two slightly different accents and one alien-strange Southern drawl.

"One, two, three."

They flipped.

They looked.

Three, big fat NOT PREGNANTs across the board.

Moira exhaled all her breath in a huge whoosh as Aerin fist-pumped the sky.

"Ha! Suck a bag of dicks, Paladin's Planetary Magic!"

Claire folded forward at the waist, hands on her knees, loose hair falling around her face. Moira had never actually seen anyone gag with relief before, but she was pretty sure that's exactly what Claire was doing.

Moira pressed a hand between her sister's shoulder blades. "You okay, sugar?"

Claire nodded, slowly rolling up to standing again. "I'm just...relieved."

But relief wasn't at all what Moira was picking up. The emotional signature rolling off her sister in erratic waves wasn't nearly so simple. It bled into the space around her like weeds in a swamp. When Moira tugged on one, several others came with it.

Sadness. Anger. Fear. Regret.

"But how could this be?" Tierra rocked forward on the couch, finally making it to her feet with Bane's assistance. "The prophecy said—"

"Perhaps we were a little hasty in our original interpretation of the prophecy." Julian, far too polite to glance at Tierra directly, cut his eyes toward the well-preserved leather-bound book on the coffee table instead. The volume of Paladin's Planetary Magic that their father, Stian the Wanderer, had brought through to their mother through the standing stones. "If you recall, it said the four born of one will conceive two children. It didn't say when, precisely. Tierra is obviously the first. The question that remains is which of you will be the second."

Icy fingers squeezed Moira's chest as she swallowed around a lump in her throat roughly the size of a duck egg. "Are you sayin' that in order to fulfill the prophecy, one of us is going to have to get knocked up willingly?"

Julian looked at her, his eyes full of the extra measure of kindness they'd brought to her ever since they had worked together to free Aerin of Lucy's unholy dominion. "That, Miss Moira de Moray, is precisely what I'm saying."

❧ 16 ❧

"Nope." Aerin backed out of the circle, her palms up like she was trying to stop an oncoming train. "Nope, nope, nope. No babies. Not me. Not ever."

"So you're just arbitrarily deciding that it has to be me or Moira?" Some of Claire's fire had leapt back into her amber eyes, flecks of gold sparking deep within their depths. "How is that fair?"

"I think the more important question is why does it have to be any of us?" Aerin had begun to pace, the color in her cheeks hectic and her silvery eyes wild. "Why are we making reproductive decisions based on the ramblings of some centuries-old fuckwit who uses ridiculously arcane and obscure terminology? I mean, four born of one and one good the other evil. I'm sorry, but no. Just. Fucking. No."

"Regarding that part of the text, I have a thought." Julian's smooth, imminently sane diction lowered the room's temperature by a couple degrees. "The medieval mindset was far more primitive in its understanding of the forces governing the universe. I would suggest we take a more enlightened approach. Rather than thinking of it in terms of good and evil, I think we could substitute light and dark. Entities neither good, nor bad, who will restore balance to the world."

As he so often did, Julian paced the length of the room as he walked, that long body, elegant as an undertaker, making liquid work of the steps from one end to the other. His dark hair, threaded with silver at the temples, tied back into a queue so orderly its mere existence seemed to rebuke the chaos of the world around them.

"Call them entities, call them babies, call them crib lizards whose chief exports are misery and shit, but the point is, none of them are welcome here," Aerin said gesturing toward her middle. Little hairs had escaped the tether of her bun, the sweat on her forehead making them coil up around her face like springs popping out of a broken watch.

Moira had to school a rogue smile away from her face.

Together, they'd faced down zombies, ghosts, apocalyptic Horsemen, and even the devil herself, but they'd just now stumbled ass-over teakettle into the thing that scared Aerin more than all of them combined.

Babies.

"Look, I ain't especially crazy about the idea either," Moira admitted. "I mean, if I wanted myself a, needy, immature boob-leech prone to temper tantrums, I could have soul-bonded myself to Nick."

"I heard that," Nick said.

Moira had been counting on it.

"Well if you aren't crazy about the idea, then why are we even discussing it?" Aerin asked.

Moira walked over to the windowsill, which she'd cracked open only minutes ago to allow in a blast of autumn air to cool the stuffy parlor. She dragged her hand across the surface then held it up for her sisters to see. "Look here."

"So we're not much for the housekeeping lately with everything going on." Aerin shrugged. "I think we can be forgiven for that given the circumstances."

"It's ash." Claire stared out into the middle distance, her eyes going wide and glazed. "Wildfires are eating up the coastline. I can feel them." She hugged herself and shivered.

It was a feeling Moira understood all too well.

She'd known about the floods long before they'd made the news. She'd awoken to a feeling of dread the likes of which she'd never felt before. A sick tightening deep in her guts. A profound ache in her chest. Not because she felt the pain of all those who had been affected, but because she felt the deep yearnings of the element that it was her curse and blessing to bear.

The water wanted this.

The same way it wanted to break on the shore and spit curds of foam against the rocks. The same way it wanted to spin eddies and form currents. To babble over river rocks and glide over fish scales.

It wanted to wipe the planet's surface clean.

To rinse everything clean away and start over.

And it would.

Until they put the world back to rights.

"What about the hurricanes?" Moira asked, turning to Aerin. "Don't even try to tell me you can't feel them storms tear-assing all the way up the east coast."

"Well, yeah," Aerin admitted. "The wind may be just the tiniest bit homicidal lately. But who isn't, really?"

"And what about this?" Moira walked over to the coffee table, picked up the book, shoved it at Aerin, cracking it open on the page of the illustration where four women stood in a circle, elemental crowns on their heads, wands in hand. "Are you going to try and pretend that this ain't us? That it don't give you a case of the all-overs just lookin' at it?"

"Yeah, but see, these four women all have their crowns and wands, and I don't, so technically..."

Tierra gasped, her hand going to her belly reflexively

as it did so often these days. "What if that's what you have to do to get your wand? Get pregnant!"

"It would require an act of bravery on your part," Claire pointed out. "That seems to be kind of a pattern in how we got ours."

Aerin assumed the haughty posture she often did when something had tweaked her tail good and hard. "Even if I agreed to this ridiculous plan—which I'm not —and Julian and I successfully...conceived—which we won't—who even knows what the...fetus might get with Pestilence for a father?"

Julian's already pallid skin turned a shade closer to chalk, whether because of the idea of fathering an ill child, or just a child in general, Moira couldn't be sure.

"Now, I know there ain't no one accusing me of being the sharpest axe in the shed, but last time I checked, Julian didn't infect himself and you're immune. So, stands to reason that your offspring would be, too."

"Yeah, but you're forgetting one vitally important thing," Aerin said. "It's the Apocalypse. Who even knows if my tailor is even still alive? I mean, have you seen how fucking hideous most maternity clothes are?"

Tierra folded her arms beneath her ponderous bosom. Which was, for the present moment, at least, clad in an empire-waisted peasant blouse she'd bought from some place with a name like A Bun In the Oven or a Pea in the Pod.

"I mean like, on me," Aerin amended. "On you, though—"

"We're the same person!" The copious bracelets ringing Tierra's wrists jingled as she threw up her hands. "How could they look bad on you, but not on me?"

"That's not what I...that is, what I meant to say..." Aerin's eyes darted desperately around the room as she considered her sisters, neither tact nor apology being her particular areas of expertise. "But Moira though!" she finally blurted out.

"Moira though what?" Moira raised a brow at her sister, as excited about this turn in the conversation as she would be to tongue wrestle a rattlesnake.

"Think about it," Aerin insisted. "She's a water witch. And what's a womb but a biologically complex water balloon? Think of how nourishing she could make that shit."

And all of the sudden, Moira started to sweat in places sweat had no business being.

Because everyone was staring at her.

Three sisters. Four Horsemen.

Not to mention, Jinx, Dr. Lecter, Kai, and Cheeto—who had, it seemed, been secreting themselves nearby all so they could add to the drama of this moment.

But the creepiest shit of all?

The way they were all looking at her.

With the same expression she'd seen on the faces of local farmers considering the prize brood sow at the county fair. Mentally prodding the thickness of her hide, calculating the span of her hips, already imagining the heaps of healthy piglets that could surely shoot from her cooter.

"It's not a terrible idea," Claire ventured. "I mean, Aerin isn't wrong."

"And you've always been a natural nurturer," Tierra added.

"Maybe so," Moira admitted. "But y'all are forgetting one very important consideration."

"What's that?" Tierra asked.

"I'm only one half of this equation," Moira said. "Raise your hand if you're comfortable with the idea of Nick Kingswood's child being responsible for restoring balance to the Universe."

The silence following her question was so total, Moira would have sworn she could hear a cricket chirping. When Nick failed to provide the searing rejoinder to her flippant insult, she hazarded a glance in his direction. He glowered at her. Sullen, but wordless.

It was so out of character for him, so far from the man—or whatever he was, exactly—she knew, that for a moment, Moira was quiet herself. For the briefest of moments, she wished she could dip into his thoughts the way Claire did Dru's.

"It doesn't have to be Nick." Dru, who had remained largely silent during the proceedings thus far, cleared his throat and stepped forward. "Once you've identified the field of battle, it makes sense to pick the soldiers best suited to launch an attack against that specific terrain."

Nick's cold laugh sent chills crawling down Moira's spine. "If you're suggesting that it's going to be anyone other than me conducting the invasion, you are seriously fucking mistaken, my friend," Nick said in a voice that was anything but friendly.

"I can't believe I'm about to say this," Claire began, "but I have to agree with Conquest on this one. We ran into enough trouble when Moira and Julian were just pretending to be a couple. We start swapping partners, and the world is going to end sooner than later."

"All I'm saying is that when troops need to be lead into battle, you always choose the best commander for the job, and I'm not sure Nick is it." Dru's perma-scowl deepened and he flicked a glance in Nick's direction.

"And you are?" Nick gave Dru's shoulder a shove.

Moira quickly slid between them, not that she'd have been able to stop them if they really got after it.

"Okay, first off, I haven't agreed to anything and second, if y'all could stop talking about my body like the beach at Normandy, and your immortal super-spunk as troops and soldiers, I'd sure appreciate it on account of it's squickin' me the hell out."

"I'm not saying I am," Dru said, ignoring Moira's attempt playing referee. "I'm just saying you're not." He planted a hand on Nick's chest and gave him a shove twice as hard as the one he'd received, nearly knocking Nick into a bookcase.

"Hey!" Tierra shouted. "No fighting in my living room! There are too many breakables."

But Dru and Nick didn't seem to hear this either.

"You know what I think it is?" Nick leaned in closer, his voice dropping a register as he towered over Moira, bringing his heat to bear on the left side of her body. "I think you're so bored with being soul-bound that now you're looking for any excuse to dip your wick in a different sister."

"Excuse me?" Color flared into Claire's cheeks as she came to Dru's side.

"Or maybe you're just so bitter that the water witch won't bind herself to you that you haven't stopped to consider why," Dru fired back.

Shee-it. Moira had sort of been hoping that wouldn't come up.

She was too close to observe the changes in Nick's face, but knew them all the same. The darkening of his eyes. The flaring of his nostrils. The thunderheads gathering in his countenance. Since the moment they met, she'd discovered she had a particular talent for teasing his meager irritation into a full-on, orphan-kicking rage.

Instinct made her step back as she felt every muscle in Nick's body tensing. Coiling. Ready for a sudden, violent release.

And then, as the saying went, all hell broke loose.

Nick lunged at Dru. Bane lunged at Nick. Julian, who was too polite to lunge, slowly rose to his feet and tried to pry his three brothers apart with more dignity than the situation called for. Tierra, jacked on pregnancy hormones and possessed of a terminal case of nesting frenzy, tried to wade into the fray, while Aerin and Claire did their best to hold her back.

The sounds of all their wrangling voices morphed into a high frequency whine that filled in all the blank spaces in Moira's head. She shut her eyes against it, preferring the darkness to the endless, painful gray of the world around her.

She heard screaming, and realized too late that it was her own. The words she'd shouted had been muffled by her hands pressed against her ears, returning to her only when the room and everyone in it had once again fallen silent.

"I'll do it."

I f Nick lived another ten thousand years, he'd remember this moment.

Standing beneath the canopy of trees, leaves and ash falling all around. The dying sun bleeding into the bruised evening sky as distant fires made lava lanterns of the clouds.

Moira in his arms.

Her long legs—clad in jeans one wash away from dissolving into denim confetti—draped over his forearm. The thin, ratty t-shirt she wore failing to conceal the gentle bounce and sway of her unbound breasts. Her whole, warm, living weight pressed against him.

It was so beautiful.

She was so beautiful.

That is, until she opened her mouth.

"You put me down this second, you skunk-licking snake turd! Just 'cause I agreed to birth some Universe balancing baby don't mean you need to haul me around like a sack of taters."

Truly, he hadn't planned on princess-carrying her out to the garden. Chivalrous shit had always been Julian's forte. But getting what he wanted? Definitely Nick's wheelhouse. What he had wanted was to talk to Moira immediately and alone in the wake of her volunteering to play broodmare without so much as a discussion.

As usual, she had balked, refusing first a polite invitation then second, a not-so-polite suggestion to accompany him outside for a walk.

So he'd taken the walk for both of them.

One small problem solved, a sack-shriveling large one looming.

"I think you surrendered your right to make demands right about the time you obligated me to knock you up." He lowered her to the ground feet first, stepping back to avoid the wild swinging of her fist. It gave him something to do, dodging a blow. All the better to ignore the odd tightening the phrase 'knock you up' had woken in his chest.

"I didn't obligate you." Moira folded her arms across her breasts—disappointingly depriving him of one of his chosen default focal points—as she cocked her hip and her head at an angle that usually meant trouble was coming and fast. "I obligated myself. You just assumed you'd be the one doin' the knocking."

Nick took a step backward, his mind infuriatingly empty of all but one soul-shredding thought: was it actually possible this woman was incapable of understanding the honor he would be bestowing on her by even considering putting his baby in her belly?

Nick didn't like to pace. Or he did, but not in front of people. It was a weakness. An outward physical display of the inner conflict and gave away too much. Just this moment, he couldn't stop himself from storming the length of the earth witch's devastated flower bed, his irritation growing with every step.

"Do you have any idea how many women have asked, no, begged me to father their children over the centuries?" he asked, pausing for dramatic effect.

"Not directly," she said. "For some reason, I just

didn't figure there would be a big line of broads begging for your nut butter."

She shrugged.

Fucking. Shrugged.

"These are women who changed the course of the world's history, and out of any man on earth, they wanted to breed with me. Me."

"On account of they were a bunch of pinchy-faced old harpies with leather twats?"

"Because they wanted their potential children to be born with even half of my intellect. My drive. My physical prowess. My—"

"Staggerin' humility? Gentlemanly lack of neck hair?"

"Humility doesn't build dynasties. Humility doesn't start revolutions or unseat despots."

"Well neither would our child if I had anything to say about it."

Our child.

The words pierced him like the flaming arrow he'd once shot into Moira's chest.

Fatherhood.

Family.

A legacy.

All his long years, this had been denied him. He, who had watched entire dynasties be born, rise, and return to the dust. He who had shaped not only nations, but entire civilizations. He, who had brought about entire legacies, had no legacy of his own.

No heir to carry on his name, as well as his genetic material.

He could see entire empires he had caused to be, but never a child with his own face.

If you gaze long enough into the abyss, the abyss also gazes into you.

Everyone thought Nietzche had said that, but it was really Nick.

Just one of the kings, conquerors and philosophers he had influenced over the years.

He looked into the abyss, and met with his own cavernous want. He wanted to have a child with this woman. He wanted to see her belly round with his seed and know he'd caused this thing to be. He wanted to see her waddle. To rub her swollen feet.

Worse, he wanted her to want this as much as he did.

"You want to stop lookin' at me like I'm a smoked turkey leg you're fixin' to shove down your neck hole without chewin'?"

It was this sentence that did it.

The pure auditory displeasure of it. The offensively crude diction and imagery.

His donkey-like bray of laughter startled them both and sent her damnable pig scampering in the direction from the porch. The walking pork sack was neither a fan of loud noises nor Nick, and especially not loud noises from Nick.

Nevertheless, Nick found himself unable to stop.

It was the hardest he'd laughed in years. Centuries, maybe.

"You gonna tell me what's so funny, or do I have to set Cheeto here to broil?"

Nick shook his head, one hand pressed against his aching abdominals, the other knuckling a tear away from the corner of his eye. "Irony," he finally managed to gasp.

"Irony?" Moira's sapphire blue eyes narrowed at him. Not, he knew, because she lacked an understanding of the concept. Presuming there was any correlation between her backwater bumpkin dialect and her IQ was a dire mistake and one Nick had only made once.

"I could have had any woman in the world," he said. "Any woman. Cleopatra. Catherine the Great. Marie

Curie. Frida Kahlo. Joan of fucking Arc. All women who would have paid dearly for the pleasure of jumping on my dick." Nick reached up and loosened his tie, suddenly aware just how much the unaccustomed feeling of laughing had made his throat feel swollen and strange. "I mean, why do you think Elizabeth was the Virgin Queen? Because I fucking turned her down. That's why."

"I'm assumin' you have a point and are plannin' on arriving at it sometime before the actual Apocalypse?"

Nick exhaled a long breath, taking a step closer to her. "My point is, for millennia, I've been pursued by the world's most remarkable women. Queens. Literary geniuses. Famous artists. All these women, and the woman I want is you. You. You, who come from a part of the country where road kill is a food group and the swamp is deeper than the genetic pool. You don't see the humor in that?"

"Right now, the only funny thing I'm seeing is how you'd look with a tire iron shoved up your ass." Moira's delicate chin tipped up a notch as the solid country stubbornness that irritated and turned him on in equal measure stiffened her spine.

"Look, it does neither of us any good for you to pretend you don't know what I'm talking about. Before you'd left the bayou and you didn't know that the world beyond the borders of the swamp was full of people with complete sets of teeth, I could almost understand you being nostalgic about the suck-hole from whence you sprung. But now that you've been in actual civilization—"

"Actual civilization?" Her eyes, usually a placid sapphire, flashed like lightning on the open ocean. "And what would you call the people who raised me? Gator bait?"

"No. Well, yes, but that's not what I'm saying at all."

"And what exactly are you sayin', Nicholas

Kingswood?" The animated pork chop was back, its beady little watermelon seed eyes narrowing at him in concert with his mistress's.

Gods, he loved it when she used his full name.

"I'm saying that despite your repellent upbringing and your hideous grammar and your appalling choice in clothing, it's you I want. I could have had any woman in the world, but it's you. It's always been you."

There.

He'd done it.

He'd said it.

She was apparently as shocked to hear it as he had been to say it.

Staring at him, her plush lips tightened into a perfect 'O', a shape that stoked a heat deep in his belly thinking of the puzzle piece he might fit there.

Understanding something of pride, he took the first step, holding his arms out in open invitation for Moira to rush into them.

"Why, Nicholas Kingswood," she whispered, floating over to him with more grace and poise than he'd imagined her capable of.

The heat of her body found his skin through his shirt as she closed in, bringing with it her signature scent of rain and wild muscadines. A shivery rush slithered over him as her lips brushed his ear.

He prepared himself for the sweet words that unnamable and unacknowledged part of himself had been so longing to hear.

"Fuck. You," Moira said.

And drove her knee up into his crotch.

Nick sucked in air against that particular sick, gutchurning ache dragging nausea in its wake.

And gods, the pain.

As his knees failed him and he crumpled to the earth, he hissed their names, welding them together with the filthiest words he knew in languages long dead.

Who's fucking idea had this been? Which one of them specifically had come up with the idiotic concept of chaining an immortal to a human body? When he found out who, he was going to personally rip their spine out of their ass and beat them with it.

He was wrath. He was ruin. He was Conquest. And yet he could still be felled by a knee to the nads.

Nick tasted ash as he writhed on the ground, hands pressed to his crotch and knees drawn up to his chest.

Moira squatted down next to him. Close enough so he could hear her but not quite so close that he could reach her. "Lord, Cheeto. I ain't seen a face that purple since Pervis Coy tried that auto-erotic asphyxiation stuff with an alternator belt and some engine lube. And just look at his eyes. You ever seen eyes bulge out of a head like that?"

The pig squeaked, a sound redolent with approval and good humor.

Nick prepared a scathing rejoinder, but when he opened his mouth to deliver it, all that came out was a strange, high-pitched, "Guhhh."

"I'm sorry," Moira said. "Say again? I'm afraid I didn't quite understand."

Nick dragged in a shaky breath and tried again. This time, he managed a very clear and emphatic, "Hu-uuurrrf."

"Right," she said, turning to the pig. "I think what he's trying to say is that he's awfully sorry for insulting Stump Bayou."

"Duurrgh," Nick gurgled.

"And he also wants to apologize for indicating that there was something to be desired in the way I talk."

Cheeto oinked his agreement with her assessment.

"Mmmmeerbb." A white curd of spittle flew from Nick's lips in the pig's direction.

"Furthermore, he wouldn't mind one bit if I went out and found another immortal to father my baby on account of he realizes that he's a self-centered donkey taint with a soul uglier than a lard bucket full of armpits!"

This time, Nick didn't bother trying to reply.

Moira stood, spanking ash from her jeans. "Well, I'm sure glad that's settled. I'll just let you rest there a spell since you're looking so comfy." Moira's hips swayed side-to-side in that effortless figure eight that so hypnotized him. Or would, if he could feel anything but the sickening ache in his offended testicles. The angry thwap thwap twap of her sandals kicked up little clouds as she made her way across the lawn to the back porch.

The pig, who had stayed behind, turned the pink pucker of its ass to him and hoofed dust into his face before trotting off after his mistress.

As he lay there, Nick's own words returned to his mind like a mocking echo.

It is better to be feared than loved.

Never interrupt your enemy while he is making a mistake.

It is better to live one year as a lion than a hundred years as a sheep.

He was used to not getting credit for his finer thoughts. After all, it had been engineered that way. He dropped gems in the ears of those in power and went on his way unseen. Unmarked in history's dizzying sweep.

Millennia of quotable shit, all attributable to him.

How was it, then, that the first time he attempted to express his feelings, he ended up with a knee in his crotch and ash in his mouth?

"Do I correctly surmise that your efforts didn't proceed especially well?"

So mired had he been in his own misery that Nick hadn't even heard Julian come. But then, Julian Roarke had always been one slick motherfucker. Like the virulent lifeforms that were his birthright, you didn't see him until it was already too late and you were bleeding out the ass.

With one dexterous sweep, Julian cleared his long coattails from the backs of his thighs so he could lower himself without catching them.

Nick took his proffered hand, gloved in the finest, buttery leather and was once again surprised at the wiry strength in his brother's grip when Julian hauled him upright. Nick remained seated, still unsure of trying his legs.

Unfailingly polite, Julian did not stand, his knees bent and his weight on the heels of his hand-tooled leather boots so they could converse at a level as egalitarian as possible.

"May I ask what you said that vexed her so?"

Some of the seizing pain having passed, Nick tried a breath. "I just told her that out of all the women I had known in my millennia on the planet, she's the one I wanted."

Julian narrowed eyes the color of a scrap of sky. "Were those the exact words you employed?"

"Well, not the exact words," Nick admitted. "I might have mentioned how ironic it was that I would fall for a woman with her disadvantages."

Chagrin dug a delicate crease at the center of Julian's forehead as he sighed. "Have you?" he asked. "Fallen for her, that is."

Something turned in Nick's gut, thankfully several inches north of the still-throbbing heat.

At first he thought it might be indigestion from one of the earth witch's meatless lunches or perhaps his testicles descending back into place from his diaphragm.

But no.

As much as he disliked those particular sensations, they weren't unfamiliar to him. They didn't come with the strange spreading warmth he felt now. Like someone had tipped a jar of heated honey inside his chest.

"It's possible," he said to Julian. "That I might have a kind of attachment to her that exceeds a general feeling of not-hate."

"Nicholas," Julian said, pinning him with the icy edge of his unfettered regard. "Slice the excrement. We know each other of old."

"I fucking love her, Julian." Nick paused, something like wonder dipping him into a beat of silence. "Holy shit. I really do."

The corners of Julian's lips tipped up in a knowing smile. "Then you must tell her. Preferably in a way that doesn't involve insulting everything she holds dear."

"How the fuck am I supposed to do that?" Slowly, carefully, and with infinite deference to his aching scrotal region, Nick rolled over to all fours and pushed himself to his feet. "You saw how this turned out."

Julian followed suit, lithe in his black suit as he stood. "Are you familiar with Pride and Prejudice?"

"You mean that one book by that one mopey chick who wrote lots of books about lots of other mopey chicks?"

"I'll take that as a no," Julian said, procuring an antiquated volume from the pocket of his suit coat and handing it to Nick. Like the trunk he kept in his room, it seemed Julian's bottomless pockets could produce any much-needed tome upon demand.

Like Mary Poppins, if Mary Poppins caused explosive diarrhea and imminent death.

"It might be helpful for you to study the case of one Mr. Darcy as you seem to share a similar penchant for inserting your loafers in your mouth," Julian said.

"And what did this Darcy fucker do to fix it?"

"In Mr. Darcy's case, it was to arrange for payment of an annual income so the heroine's sister can be legally wed to the man she'd eloped with, thereby warming the heart of the heroine and securing her affections."

"Jules, you beautiful fucking brain!" Nick clapped his brother on the back, seized by a sudden onslaught of inspiration. "A grand gesture. Bitches love grand gestures!"

"Yes, well, perhaps you ought not state your intentions in just such a way." Julian dusted Nick's dirty handprint from his velvet smoking jacket, cordial as a cat.

"Freak not, brother," Nick said, already jogging toward the Maserati parked on the street in front of the De Moray manse. "I got this."

✼ 18 ✼

I got this.

I got this.

I don't got this.

"Fuck!" Enraged, Lucy threw down the arm she'd been attempting to pop back into the gaping shoulder socket of the body she was wearing. The gleaming white ball of bone protruding from the wet red stump glowed in the moonlight.

Time to change.

She picked up the long, black leather duster from the hedge, shrugging one arm into the coat and draping the other over her shoulder to hide the damage while she limped toward downtown.

With any luck, people would think she was just a kinky amputee.

Luck, she sneered inwardly.

Luck was a rank twat who she hadn't been on speaking terms with for quite a while.

Not since the devastating cyanide spell that drove her from her own crumbling carcass into more pleasing —and also intact—vessels.

Trouble was, they never stayed intact.

Her powers had been compromised right along with

her face, and even a simple possession spell turned into a total fuckola.

Take this most recent body, for instance.

The taut, lithe, little boho yoga teacher she'd spotted browsing among the crystals at Phoenix Rising.

She'd chosen her.

She stalked her.

She'd deftly helped herself to the body the minute the hippie had ever so compassionately turned her back on Lucy's veiled and putrefying face.

And less than hour later, boom.

A finger popped off.

Followed by three toes on the left foot. Still, to Lucy's knowledge, scattered under the table where she'd been sitting at Siren's pub. She didn't envy whichever member of the t-shirted waitstaff found them. Just as she didn't pity the snooty tea-shop proprietress who had driven her out the second she noticed the scattering of teeth that flew from Lucy's mouth as she tried to order a chai latte. A dizzying act of hypocrisy, Lucy thought, from someone who sported horsey, ill-fitting dentures.

Judgy bitch.

Still, the body had lasted long enough to serve its purpose.

Which was pretty much the only purpose Lucy had these days—eavesdrop on the sisters de Moray.

From the fight she'd witnessed while lurking just beyond the de Moray house's wards, things were getting juicy.

Remembering the sound Conquest made when the backwater swamp witch had hiked his junk up to his sternum made Lucy forget herself for a moment and she grinned.

An action she immediately realized to be a mistake when with a pop her jaw came unhinged and dangled from the top half of her skull.

"Hun of uh itch," she growled, attempting to snap her face back together with her remaining hand. Her jaw flopped back down the second she released it. "Huck it," she said, deciding to let it hang.

Just then, a car pulled up alongside her, the passenger side window sinking down with an automated buzz. The driver—a polite and pony-tailed man wearing wire-rimmed spectacles—ducked down to lean across the arm rest.

"Excuse me, miss. I noticed you were limping. Could you maybe use a ride somewhere?"

Lucy turned to him, forgetting herself until his eyes widened. "Dear God," he gasped. "What's the matter with you?"

She tried raising her eyebrows to make it seem like maybe her mouth was only gaping from perpetual surprise, but the effort stretched her eyelids just a hair too far.

One of her eyes fell out of its socket and dangled against her cheek with the nerve still attached, dangling like a disco ball.

From the back seat, a toddler with hair a similar shade of chocolate brown shrieked. The tires squealed as the driver stomped on the gas and sped off, leaving Lucy coughing in a cloud of oily exhaust.

"Hum ack!" she shouted, casting off a few fingers as she attempted to wave him down. "Other hucker!"

What the everlasting fuck was going on?

Staring at the gutter where two of her fingers had landed in a somewhat appropriate peace configuration, Lucy began to wonder.

It couldn't be happening already...could it?

She knew they had stumbled upon the prophecy from what she'd overheard Nick say to the water witch in the garden. Which meant they knew one of them would have to conceive a second child.

But none of them knew what Lucy knew.

What Lucy had known from the second the earth witch's womb-rat had kept her from entering their mother's sanctuary.

The earth witch carried the Tugadh Solas. The Bringer of Light.

And while it nudged her closer to her demise, the earth witch's spawn did not spell certain disaster for Lucy because, after all, it was her darkness that balanced the light.

No.

From the way she had understood it, she wouldn't be relieved of her powers completely until after the Ceann Dorcha, The Dark One, was conceived.

Surely they hadn't had time to do that already.

From what she could gather, the water witch had volunteered herself as the vessel but had come to no consensus with Conquest as to his filling it.

Moira de Moiray had left Nick writhing in the dirt, and not even a being with Conquest's stamina could recover from a shot to the junk so quickly. Nor could they have successfully conceived already, immortal swimmers or no.

But they would try.

Soon, they would try, and if Lucy didn't stop them, they might actually succeed.

One thing was for sure and certain. She'd never be able to stop them if she kept shedding parts like a broken Barbie. She needed a new body, and she needed it now.

When she saw the headlights reflected in the eyes of the deer lazily strolling up the middle of the street, she knew she had her answer.

Moira had always thought of this as her place.

Just a simple pier crawling into the water on long, stilted legs. Gray, sun bleached wood complaining of its age under every stiff wind.

But it held so many of her memories.

Here, she had almost tried to drown herself.

Here, she had first kissed Nicholas Kingswood.

Here, she had crawled out of the bay with crown and wand in hand.

Here, she sat and spent long hours contemplating the end of all things as the waves crashed below her feet.

They crashed like that now. Angry curds of foam flying up as the water gnawed at the barnacled ankles of the pier pilings.

It wasn't just the end of the world that stirred the water so.

It was her. Her proximity.

Because she hurt. Because what Nick said had hurt her. Because what Nick said *could* hurt her. He had that power over her now, and she'd be damned if that didn't just chap her ass good and proper.

Two days ago she had jacked him in the junk, and he'd been missing ever since.

No word.

No call.

Big fat nothing.

"Can you believe the nerve of that shit weasel?" It was a hypothetical question in that all the questions she asked to Cheeto were hypothetical. It wasn't like he could answer, though he looked like he'd dearly like to. His curly little nub of a tail wagged happily the way it did whenever she was insulting Nick.

"I mean, saying those things about where we come from. There ain't a nicer place to live in the whole entire world."

Here, Cheeto's tail stopped wagging all together as his small, dark eyes slid to the side.

"All right, okay. So there were mosquitos big enough to rape a turkey and some cousins did a lot more than kiss, but that don't mean they weren't good people."

Cheeto sat down on his plump hindquarters, his velvety ears rotating backward.

"And yes, I do remember how I rescued you from Jo Buck Jones, who was using you to clear his acreage like a flame thrower, but I still think most the people there were essentially good."

Cheeto grunted.

"Everyone but Charlie Ray. But mostly people have forgotten about what happened with him and the goat."

"My point is, there are a lot of good memories there." Moira drew Cheeto to her lap, stroking the spot behind his ears that made his body go slack and loose in her hands. "Like, remember how Uncle Sal used to wake up first thing in the morning, pee out the window and say—"

"Hey, baby. What time do y'all eat around here?"

For a moment, Moira thought she might have heard a ghost. Some scrap of her uncle the wind had carried all the way from Stump to torment her.

Then, she saw it.

A smallish yacht, sleek and powerful as it knifed through the waves toward her pier. A tall, dark-haired man stood at the prow, waving his arms in opposing circles like airplane propellers.

Moira scrambled to her feet, upending Cheeto, who squealed in alarm. She had to catch him by the tail to keep him from going in the drink. "Uncle Sal?" she shouted into the wind. "Is that really you?"

The man on the deck stripped off his trucker hat and saluted her with it.

"It's really me, Moira Jo!"

Moira Jo.

The name opened up a familiar ache in her chest.

She'd been Moira Jo once. A simple southern girl who waited tables at the HooDoo shack. A girl who'd driven an old Barracuda she'd nicknamed the Badger down back roads paved with ground oyster shells. A girl who'd fallen asleep to cricket orchestras and woken up to rooster choirs.

A girl who had laughed easy and often.

Where had that girl gone?

She waited for minutes that felt like eternities as the boat pulled up alongside the pier at a rate far faster than seemed safe.

She saw the alarm darkening Sal's eyes as he motioned her away from the dock. "Watch y'self, Moira Jo! We's comin' in hot!"

Moira reached down the scooped neck of her shirt and drew out her wand from its appointed place in the bra she now wore to hold it snug between her breasts.

Aiming the pearlescent and sapphire jeweled tip at the water directly ahead of the yacht's bow, she whispered a quick incantation. The yacht stopped abruptly as the water molecules fused together, a solid somewhere between concrete and ice.

Uncle Sal nearly toppled over the side at the sudden stop, catching himself on the railing with a sheepish smile. "Stay where you are," he shouted down to her. "I'll be there directly."

"How are you going to get down?" she asked, eyeing the gap between the boat and the dock.

"Just you wait and see!" With no small measure of mischief and glee smoothing the wrinkles on his sun-weathered face, Sal raced to the bridge on the yacht's main deck.

Moira watched in wonder as a gangplank emerged from the side of the boat and extended out and down toward the dock.

As soon as it was within distance, she leaped onto it, running, running and not stopping until she'd barreled into Uncle Sal's embrace.

His wiry arms folded her into his chest, his chin coming down to the top of her head as it had so often when she was a girl. He held her this way while she gave into a gale of tears, stroking her hair and making the same reassuring noises she remembered so well.

"Now Moira Jo, you quit that snubbin'. Tears ain't gonna fix what's gone wrong with the world."

Wiping her tear-stained face on the sleeve of her t-shirt, Moira stepped back, taking him in. Noting the things that hadn't changed: his smile, his scent—tobacco and leather and salt and the sun—and the things that had: his dwindling frame, the dimming shine of his coal black eyes and inky hair, shot through with more silver than she remembered.

"How did you get here?" she asked. "Where in the hell did you get that boat?"

"Well, I'll tell you, he said, steering her toward the center of the deck, where a ring of aluminum lawn chairs was set up around an oil drum from which flames leapt and danced.

That, not ten feet away, there was a ring of padded seats around what looked to be a propane powered faux fire pit, Sal hadn't seemed to noticed.

"This is quite a set-up," she said, pointing to the drum. "But is it safe? I mean, the deck is made of wood and all, and it looks like they already built a—"

"None of that fake fire for me, please and thank you." Sal's chest puffed as he rose to the fullest extent of his lanky height. "I'll take the real stuff and the danger that comes along with it." He indicated one of the lawn chairs for Moira to sit in and slouched down in the one opposite. From a battered red cooler wedged between the chairs, he plucked a long silver beer can and offered it to Moira.

Why the hell not, she figured. For old time's sake.

She popped the top and took a swig, tasting the roasty grain as Sal popped open two for himself. Were they back on the bayou, Sal would have doctored it with salt and lime until it tasted something like citrus sea water.

"So how'd you come by this boat?" she asked. "And what are you doing all the way in Port Townsend?"

Uncle Sal's Adam's apple bobbed as he drained the last of his beer and belched through his nose. He crushed the can and threw it in the drum before turning to Moira. "It's one hell of a story."

"I'm listening."

Uncle Sal was in his element now, a country raconteur of the first order. He sat forward in his seat, his face becoming animated as he prepared to relay the details in all the vivid color he could paint.

"So there I was, sittin' behind the counter of the bait shack, when in walks this big city feller in a fancy suit."

Moira's stomach death-rolled like a gator.

"What did he look like?" she asked.

"Kinda like he thought his shit would smell like potpourri and he'd never been told no in his entire life."

"Whisky colored eyes? Sandy brown hair?"

Uncle Sal looked genuinely piqued. "How'd you know?"

"Just a guess. Go on. Tell me the rest."

"Well, of course I asked him if he was lost, 'cause he sure as hell didn't look like he belonged there." Sal reached for another can and slurped, his protuberant Adam's apple bobbing up and down within his skinny neck.

"What did he say?" Moira asked.

Uncle Sal leaned in, the barrel fire playing orange in his black eyes. "It's a good thing you're settin' down, 'cause this is where it gets real strange."

Real strange had become a much harder target for stories to hit just lately.

"He told me he wanted to buy my bait shack for five million dollars!"

Moira's head felt simultaneous hot and light as all the blood drained away from her face. "Why the hell would he do that?"

Uncle Sal sat up straighter, a look of wounded pride on his brow.

"I guess he knew a valuable piece of real estate when he saw it."

The real estate in question was a shack the size of a postage stamp on rickety stilts slicked with decades of moss. On a good morning, the seagulls haunting the local garbage dump one bayou over would serenade you with their cries before 9:00 a.m. On a bad morning, the dump trucks would.

"I suppose so," Moira allowed. "You used the five million dollars to buy this boat?"

A crafty gleam lit Uncle Sal's eyes. Moira had seen this look before. Usually when he'd just gotten $10 for a $2 bucket of worms from some unsuspecting tourist. "That's the best part. I traded him my pontoon for this here boat straight across. You believe that?"

Frankly, she didn't.

Nicholas Kinsgwood parting with five million dollars in cash and a yacht for a bait shack and a pontoon that didn't so much have a motor as it did a souped-up can opener.

"Well, it sounds like one hell of a deal," Moira said.

"And you ain't even seen the half of it." Sal grasped Moira's hand in his leathery palm and tugged her to her feet. "C'mon. I'll give you the dime tour."

A dime might have been generous, upon further consideration.

"The pool looks a little muddy," Moira said, regarding the scummy brown surface.

"That ain't a pool, it's a noodlin' pond. The pool's over there." Sal pointed to a sunken seating area, which he'd covered with tarps and filled in with water.

"Ohhh," Moira said. "I see. You brought catfish with you all the way from Stump?"

"Well, yeah," Sal said, looking at her like she'd just asked him if grass is green. "And they ain't the only thing!"

As if on cue, the door to one of the lower cabins opened and out tumbled a sweaty elbowing tangle of cussing, sunburnt redneck flesh.

Moira's heart lurched within her ribcage. "Red! Mookey! Little Earl!"

She greeted them one by one, her nose stinging with both unshed tears and the spicy scent of grain alcohol, sweat, and Old Bay seasoning—which Red insisted worked as good as baking soda on a toothbrush.

Little Earl with half his face grinning, the other half having been paralyzed from the stroke that felled him from a bar stool in the late 70's.

Mookey, with his pot gut and t-shirt tan—shoulders whiter than a fish belly, forearms damn near the color of brick roux.

Red, lanky as a scarecrow, his whisky-bloomed nose

a livid illustration of the color whose name he bore into the world.

"Speakin' of leaving Stump when did you?" Moira asked once they'd made their re-introductions. "How did you know where to find me?"

"I don't rightly know," Sal admitted, scratching his head. "Last thing I remember, me and the boys was sitting on the deck, havin' us a celebratory 'shine. Next thing I know, we're here. I wandered out hopin' to figure out where I'd ended up, and I seen you."

Moira smiled, certain now that supernatural forces originating with a particular immortal asshole of her acquaintance had been at work here. "Show me somethin' else."

The highlights included: the engine room, which Mookey had converted into a makeshift 'shine still. The stateroom, which had become a skeet shooting gallery with Little Earl's careful help. And the movie theatre, which Red had turned into a dedicated goat den.

"Ain't that somethin'?" Red wondered aloud, looking fondly over the heard of nannies and billies slowly stripping the seats of their red velvet upholstery.

"It's somethin' all right," Moira said, pressing her hand to her empty stomach. Traipsing up and down the spacious decks had given her a powerful appetite.

"You hungry, darlin'? I got me some pickled chicken livers down in the kitchen. And the fixin's for sloppy joes. They always were your favorite."

Moira tried to conjure a time when the prospect of ground meat—typically of dubious origins—drowned in tomato sauce served over a starchy bun had filled her with delight.

Truth was, her palate had grown a little more finicky in the days since she'd left Stump Bayou. No longer did she pass the carcass of an animal on the side of the road and wonder how fresh it might be. And it had been ages since she'd ingested any kind of rodent.

"How about we get us something in town?" Moira suggested. "There's a few places that still let you pick up things to take home with you."

"Oh, no," Mookey insisted, lifting a trucker hat bearing the words Camel Towing...Wedged in Tight, We'll Pull it Right. He replaced it after wiping the sweat from his forehead with a stained red bandana. "I don't trust none of them fancy restaurants. Last time I ate at one of them places I wound up with hemorrhoids the size a radishes."

"You idiot," Little Earl said, delivering Mookey a sound clap upside the head. "I told you you c'aint get hemorrhoids from eatin' fancy food. They're the Lord's way of punishing you for doin' that butt stuff."

"That ain't it either," Red insisted. "You get 'em from that cheap toilet paper you's always buyin' at the A&P. Rather wipe my ass with a corn cob."

Moira winced, even as a feeling of inexplicable fondness filled her chest with a drift of warm sand. This kind of good-natured wrangling had once been the sound of days and nights. Her fondest memories. Her home.

Though she was tempted to share what Tierra had taught her of the miraculous effects of fiber and probiotic smoothies, Moira decided she might have more straining matters—so to speak—in mind.

"Does that mean y'all ain't coming?" she asked, turning her shoulders toward the door.

"Nah," Little Earl, self-appointed statesman of the group said, a meaty hand scratching the back of his thick neck. "We'll stay here. Give y'all a chance to get all caught up."

"Suit yourself," Sal said. "I don't want to hear no bellyachin' when I get back."

"How does fish and chips sound?" Moira asked as they crested the deck.

"All right," Sal agreed, eyes narrowed. "But only if

you let me pay. Turns out, I have me a windfall at present." He produced a wad of money from his overalls, throwing it up in the air like green confetti.

"All right," Moira agreed, threading her arm through his. "You pay. Just don't throw any more of that stuff around, okay? It'll last longer that way."

They had barely reached the gangplank when Sal stopped abruptly.

"Hey!" he said, pointing a bony finger toward the dock. "That's him."

Moira looked up, afraid she already knew what she would see.

She both was and wasn't disappointed.

There, standing on the dock with the sunset at his back, was Nicholas Kingswood.

❋ 20 ❋

How it was possible to feel both touched and horrified, Nick did not know.

Touched at the name.

Horrified at the manner of its application.

Big, dripping hand-painted letters on the side of his yacht. Or the yacht that had been his, before he traded it to Gomer Pyle in an act of contrition.

An act he wasn't yet certain had actually had the desired effect.

He watched Moira descend the plank on her uncle's arm, trying not to think how it might look if she were clad in billowing white, and he, in a tuxedo. More helpful to focus on the ghost of the terrible pain she'd wrought in his crotch.

"Hey," Nick said when he was certain they were within earshot.

"Hey yourself." Moira's face bore its usual smirk. A maddeningly inscrutable expression that suggested she knew some secret thing about you that you didn't want her to know, but which amused her greatly.

Not exactly the untrammeled amazement for his generosity or undying ardor Nick had been hoping for. But not out and out dislike either.

Progress.

"Wait a minute." The yokel thumbed the straps of his overalls, aiming a querulous look his niece. "You know this fella?"

"Sometimes," she said.

Nick was encouraged by her sly smile. A smile that remembered, and not altogether unpleasantly, the more intimate details of their acquaintance.

"I know why you're here," Sal said.

"You do?" Truly, Nick had to try to keep his face empty of surprise at the suggestion that a man like Salvadore Malveaux could know anything.

"Sure do. And just so you know, the answer is no."

"No?" Nick bit down hard on the surge of rage driving up from his belly. Only two people had ever dared tell him no over the course of his long life, and they were both standing in front of him.

"No, you can't have Moira Jo." The man draped a possessive arm around his niece and squeezed.

Nick brought his hand to his eye to stop the sudden twitching. "I don't think that's your decision to make."

"Of course it is. She belongs to me and now that we're together, I'm keepin' her."

Nick glanced at Moira, shocked that she'd endure such patriarchal posturing without complaint. "Don't you think she should have a say in this?"

"Why the hell would she get a say?" Sal asked. "I mean, she's purty, but it's not like she has a brain."

"You listen, and you listen good," Nick said, grabbing Sal by the front of his bib overalls and shoving him against the dock railing. "Moira Malveux de Moray is one of the smartest, most cunning, most wickedly clever women I've ever met, and believe me, I've met a lot. If you dare insult her intelligence in my presence again, so help me gods, I will strip the skin from your bones and wear it like a Brioni suit. Do you understand me?"

"Oh I understand you, all right." But far from the

fear and cowering Nick had expected, Sal broke out into a smile that took over his whole face.

"What?" Nick said, releasing him. "What are you grinning about?"

Sal's shoulders shook, rhythmically jerking toward his ears with a hyuk hyuk hyuk sound before he doubled over, slapping his denim-clad knee. "You were talking about Moira Jo the person. I was talking about Moira Jo the boat."

Nick glanced at Moira, and from the half-pleased, half-amused expression on her face, gathered that she had known what both men were referring to the entire time.

"Right." Nick smoothed his tie and cleared his throat. "Of course. I knew that. We made a deal and I have no intention of reneging on it."

"Good," Sal said. "We have an understandin'. Now point me in the direction of the nearest grub shack. I'm starved."

Siren's gastro pub wasn't the nearest, but it was the nearest they could come to a compromise on. With Sal insisting that he couldn't eat "none of them fancy vittles on account of it gave him the galloping squirts" and Nick insisting that he'd not set foot in an establishment where at least two kinds of top shelf scotch weren't on offer, the upscale gastro pub seemed to be the best option.

What followed was sixty-seven of the most painfully awkward minutes in Nicholas Kingswood's life. And considering he'd been present at the Lisa Marie and Michael Jackson kiss at the Grammys, that was saying something.

Moira said little, folding and refolding her napkin, focused on feeding French fries to the pig-formed familiar hunkered between her and her uncle's hips.

The aforementioned pig-familiar mostly glared at

Nick, aggressively chewing scraps in his general direction.

And Sal Malveux, determined to make small talk, asked Nick a series of utterly inane and irritating questions.

Examples of their pained exchange:

Sal (wiping tartar sauce from his chin with the back of his hand): So what is it you do, young fella?

Nick (while sipping his scotch): I'm in acquisitions.

Sal: Of companies and such?

Nick: Of kingdoms. Of countries. Of continents. And occasionally the will to live.

Moira (clearing her throat, staring daggers across the table): He's kiddin'.

Sal: So how did y'all two meet?

Nick: A cosmic collision of forces destined to bring about the end of the earth as we know it.

Sal: Wait a minute. You're talkin' about that Tinder thang, ain't you?

Nick: Sure.

Sal (around a mouthful of crispy battered fish): Shooee is this good! What's your favorite thing to eat, Nick?

Nick: Your niece's—

Moira: <kicking him good and hard under the table>

Nick: —fried chicken.

Sal: Boy howdy, don't I know it. We sure have missed Moira's cooking back home. If you like her fried chicken, you ought to try her biscuits. Lighter than an angel's poot. Why, it seems like only...

The epistle continued, but Nick was no longer listening.

The unexpected jolt of pain from Moira's judicious flip-flop had somehow found its way all the way from his shin to his cock, which made an impromptu and inconvenient tent of the linen napkin in his lap. He shifted in his seat, drawing a knowing grin from Moira.

For the first time, he realized what an appropriate choice of venue this was for their meeting.

Sirens.

For that's what she was to him. A water witch with the power to draw him toward the rocks that would be his ruin.

And how well she knew him.

Well enough to slide her foot up the inside of his calf. Between his knees. Up the inside of his thigh.

Bare toes pressed against him. Nails painted the absurd red only used for very expensive cars.

He remembered that color.

It was the color of their first meeting. Her whole, improbable self in the first class seat he had reserved. Her feet stretched against the back of the chair in front of her, her long legs still burnished tawny from the low country sun. Breasts and hair and lips and hips. A composite he had scarcely considered before deciding he would have it. That he could have it. The way he'd always had everything he'd even half wanted.

Looking at her now, he wondered at his own ignorance. The ignorance still shared by every male within groping distance of her now.

They saw her, but didn't see her. Her native wit. Her unfailing gentleness. Her resilience. The simple joy she took in living.

Immortal that he was, he had been on this planet past recall and past time. All those centuries, attempting to carry out what he thought was his purpose. And still he was not finished.

Not even three decades had Moira lived on this planet, and already she had changed its trajectory irrevocably for good or for ill.

In the end, whose had been the greater destiny?

Whose, the greater power and the greater purpose?

Nick wrapped the fingers of one hand around her slim ankle, the other pressing the delicate bones of her foot harder against him.

Her toes moved with the dexterity of the woman who'd spent a lifetime with nothing between her and the earth. The undulating articulation common to those who dug their toes into the mud, the grass. Who let the water lap at the tender skin between them. Who probably picked up dropped fishing lines and household objects. With that same, unnatural knowing, she explored him through his strained slacks.

He let his eyes fall closed for the space of a minute, the pleasure rising in him.

Just as abruptly as it started, the pleasure stopped.

Nick opened his eyes to a triumphant expression on Moira's face as Sal droned on about marination and buttermilk and getting a good scald from the lard.

Words floated by him like leaves on a stream.

Moira had done it on purpose.

Making him hard. Leaving him that way.

She was playing a game.

When he got her alone, Nick Kingswood planned on showing her exactly what it meant to play with Conquest.

They were being followed.

Moira might have been sure of it sooner, but with Uncle Sal a few paces ahead of her, Nicholas Kingswood beside her, and Cheeto trotting along behind, she'd felt...safe. Contented. Like for just this handful of minutes, all was right with the world.

But of course, it wasn't, and she cursed herself for a fool and a simpleton for forgetting it.

She glanced back over her shoulder for the third time in as many minutes, her mind shifting from Nick's explanation of how he'd managed to get the Moira Jo from Stumps to Port Townsend so quickly—a tricky operation involving a few favorable trade winds generated by Aerin.

Nick stopped mid-sentence, his body tensing as he flipped on to high alert. "What?" he asked. "What is it?"

"Did you hear that?" she whispered, the deserted street falling suddenly silent.

Another rustle. A crash.

Sal came up beside them, lifting the baggy pants leg of his overall to retrieve the wickedly curved fish-gutting knife that had been his lifelong companion.

Nick put himself between Moira and the potential

danger, already reaching behind him to summon the flaming arrow that was his birthright.

They gave a collective exhale when a small, spotted fawn staggered from the alley, blinking broad brown eyes at them.

"Aww. Would you look at that? Poor little thing's lost his momma." She took a step toward it, but was quickly yanked back by Uncle Sal.

"Stay here, Moira Jo. That thing don't look right."

"I can't believe I'm about to say this." Nick shifted uncomfortably on the sidewalk. "But I think your uncle might be right. Julian's been rather busy of late. There's no end to the hideous diseases it might be carrying."

"Y'all don't be silly. I'm sure the poor thing's probably just hungry." Moira took a few tentative steps toward the small, spindle-legged creature, her carton of leftovers in one hand, the other stretched out in invitation.

When she was only a couple feet away, she popped open the carton, withdrawing a couple French fries and holding them out as enticement.

Cheeto snorted behind her, less a warning than a witness of his discontent at Moira sharing what would usually be his dedicated snack.

The fawn's shining black nose twitched in the direction of the fries, the little nostrils flaring before it eagerly snaffled them up.

Moira set the open carton down in front of the small, eager body, encouraged when it lowered its head and set to scarfing.

"See?" Moira said, looking back at the improbable group of the males spanning the sidewalk—a pig, an immortal, and a hillbilly. "It's just hungry." She reached stroked the deer's small head, beginning at the sleek indentation between its eyes and sliding her fingers up his small, silky ear.

Which came off in her hand.

Moira stared at the tawny scrap in her palm for an undetermined length of time before it occurred to her to gasp and drop it.

"Oh, dear God. Oh, sweet baby Jesus," she jabbered, panic reeling her back to the days when those had been her chief expletives. "Look what I did!"

"Moira Jo!" Sal hollered. "You come away from that thing. It ain't natural!"

"Wait!" she shouted back. "I can fix this." Moira retrieved the ear from the sidewalk held it in a rough approximation of where it had been as withdrew her wand from her bra.

"By power of water, wind, sky and sea, I ask the Goddess to stick this here ear back onto thee!" A small jet of shimmering blue light exited the wand's tip and concentrated around the joining of the fawn's ear and skull.

Relief washed over her when she released the ear and it stayed put. "There!" she said, fully aware of the note of hysteria in her own voice. "See? It's okay. It's okay."

And it was.

Until its other ear fell off.

Followed by the small white flag of its tail. And its foreleg below the knee.

Moira sucked in a lungful of air, her throat closing over a sudden sob. "I broke it! I broke a baby deer!"

Her lament was cut short when pain, sudden and sharp, invaded her hand.

She looked down, unable to reconcile what she was seeing and feeling.

The fawn had latched on to the meat of her palm, shaking its head like a hound with a rat.

"Why, you ungrateful little fucker! How dare—"

And then she saw its eyes.

Glowing a putrid yellow, the dark pupils stretching into cat-like vertical strips.

She had seen these eyes before. Had seen this look before. Bubbling with festering hatred.

Lucy.

Agony climbed Moira's arm like shards of ice, robbing her of breath as darkness and despair poured into her heart.

"Ain't no demon deer bites my Moira Jo!" Uncle Sal shouted, barreling toward them, his knife raised high and Cheeto right on his heels. "Prepare yerself to get wrassled, Bambi!"

"Salvadore! Move!" Nick roared. His eyes had become glowing amber, his flaming arrow pointed straight at the deer's flank. But Uncle Sal was directly in the arrow's path and showed no signs of changing course.

They went down in a heap, tangled legs and flying fur and the blinding flash of one of Cheeto's fire balls.

Sal sank his teeth into the fawn's shank and it turned loose of Moira's hand, bleating in pain. "Ha!" Sal said, hooting in triumph. "How do you like it, you mangy-ass sum' bitch?"

Suddenly free of the searing pain, Moira reached up to shift the fawn's unnatural weight from her chest.

The impact had peeled a patch of pelt the fawn's flank, strips hanging down like torn velvet. Silvery white cartilage gleamed from the exposed muscle. And just as she pulled her fingers away from the slick, slimy ribs, Nick's arrow found its mark between them.

The fawn shrieked and writhed, a foul black smoke pouring from its mouth before it jerked and flopped over to the side.

Uncle Sal, five-time champion of the hog wrasslin' pit, gained his feet with surprising swiftness, reaching down to help Moira do the same.

Nick sidled up to them, giving Cheeto a wide berth.

Together, they stared down at the discarded fawn husk. Singed, smoking, and missing several vital parts.

"You realize what this means," Nick said.

"That I ought to throw the deer carcasses I picked up near the dock overboard?" Sal asked.

"It means that Lucy knows," Nick said. "She knows that we know about the prophecy. She knows that you've been chosen."

"You're talkin' about the devil, ain't you?" Sal looked from Moira to Nick as he asked this. His face guileless, his hair clumping with the damp sea air like wet crow feathers.

Moira's heart warmed as she looked at her uncle. Common man that he was, so completely willing to accept the extraordinary. A simple gullibility that people often mocked. Never had there been a human more perfectly suited to fish her out of the bayou. To accept her exactly for what she was. What she would always be.

"Yes," Nick said. "We are."

❧ 22 ❧

"Thank the Goddess!" Tierra rushed Moira, enveloping her comforting, brooding warmth. "We were so worried about you."

Her sisters had been waiting.

A simple walk it was meant to be. Moira taking a quick turn to the dock and back with Cheeto along for protection.

Moira had had no way to call. No way to explain she would be arriving late. Cell phone service had been one of the many things the Apocalypse had readily claimed as of late.

"I ran into Uncle Sal," she said.

"Did you?" Aerin favored her with a knowing smile.

"He went back to his boat," Moira said. "He wasn't much feeling like company tonight."

"I think wrestling with Lucifer took it out of him," Nick reported.

"Lucy?" Claire shot to her feet, a sudden movement that had Dru patting himself down for weapons. "How? Where?"

"Main Street," Moira said. "We were comin' home from Sirens when she attacked. Apparently she's down-graded from humans to woodland critters."

"Sirens," Tierra sighed, rubbing the globe of her

belly. "I'd sell my soul for some fish and chips right about now."

"You might not want to say that out loud," Aerin advised. "All things considered."

"Do you think she knows?" Claire asked. "About the prophecy?"

"Without a doubt," Nick confirmed. "All the more reason to fulfill it as soon as possible." He squeezed Moira's hip in silent encouragement.

"There's something we need to discuss." Julian rose from the chaise longue, his face grave. "About the prophecy."

"We've already worked that out." Nick's impatience bristled behind Moira as he spoke. "I'm good. She's good. Everyone's good. In fact, if you'll excuse us, we'll get working on it with all due haste and expediency," he said, nudging her toward that stairs.

"I'm afraid it isn't so simple," Julian said. "There's a ritual. Well, two rituals actually. One to summon the Bringer of Light. The other, The Dark One. Before anything can happen, we need to know which entity you and Miss de Moray might potentially be—" he cleared his throat, casting about for the least offensive word "—conceiving."

"The Dark One." The sound of her own voice surprised her. Moira hadn't known she knew that.

Because she didn't know it.

But Lucy did.

And had somehow passed it along when she bit her.

"I knew it!" Tierra leapt as well as someone as heavily knocked up as she was could. "I knew I was having the light one."

"But Tierra got knocked up without a ritual," Moira pointed out. "How do you figure that happened?"

"If I had to wager a guess," Julian said, his tone suggesting that he'd never guessed at anything in his life, "it would be that because the Goddess had already departed from this plane, the other Miss de Moray conceived her replacement by default. But because Lucifer yet inhabits this planet, a willful and specific displacement will be required."

"Wait just a damn minute." Moira took a step toward Julian, memory washing her in the scent of parchment and port wine. "I thought you said that this wasn't about good and evil?"

"It isn't."

"But you're saying that Lucy was the Dark One or whatever you called it. And she's more evil than wool knickers on an August afternoon."

"Correct." A strange sadness darkened Julian's glacier blue eyes. "Just because she's evil now doesn't mean she began that way. With patience, kindness, and proper guidance, perhaps the next Ceann Dorcha, wouldn't go so far afield from the intended purpose."

This thought dropped the room into sudden quiet.

"All right," Moira said holding her hands out to Aerin, who had retrieved the Grimoire from a nearby end table. "Show me the ritual."

Aerin snagged glances with Julian and drew the book closer to her chest—a first, given its cover was basically a patchwork quilt of leathery human skin and squicked Aerin out something fierce.

"What?" Moira asked, her stomach growing heavy even as her head grew light. "What aren't y'all tellin' me?"

Julian cleared his throat. "There is perhaps one detail we ought to discuss before proceeding."

"And that would be?" Moira folded her arms, her sandal-clad foot tapping expectantly.

Aerin looked to Tierra and Claire who in turn cast nervous eyes to their respective Horsemen. Dru and Bane continued the chain by turning to stare at Nick.

"Would y'all quit eye-ballin' each other and just spit

it out?" Moira asked, sweat beginning to accumulate in places the sun didn't shine.

As was typically the case when some destiny-altering bit of information was to be shared, the task fell to Julian. "The Ceann Dorcha can only be conceived by those whose souls are one."

Moira blinked at him, the words rattling around in her head like Scrabble tiles in a bag. All at once, they landed in order with a clarifying clack.

Nick Kingswood.

In order to bring forth the Ceann Dorcha, she was going to have to soul-bond herself to Nicholas Fucking Kingswood.

❧ 23 ❧

All the air in the room miraculously turned itself into cement. The weight of it pressed against Moira's chest even as she struggled to drag it into her lungs. Faces blurred. Walls swayed and bulged, and before she knew it, she was shuffling backwards.

"I...I need a minute."

With Cheeto on her heels, Moira sprinted up the stairs and down the halls and didn't stop until she burst through the small access door to the widow's walk crowning Maison de Moray. Just a small, rectangular patch on the roof of the sprawling Victorian home, but it had become the place where each sister in her turn seemed to come when heavy contemplation was required.

Moira wandered over to the wrought iron railing, the night air settling on her skin like a humid cloak and her ankle warm where Cheeto leaned against her. She'd often wondered why it was people always came to high places when they needed to think. Like somehow the elevation might shrink their problems just like they did the trees and cars and houses from this vantage.

Her eyes drifted out to the sea, dark and heaving, the moon's reflection a boiling cauldron of blood red on its surface. For the briefest of moments, Moira imag-

ined that beyond it, she could see the fires, the hurricanes, the ash-choked sky. Moira didn't think there was
a cricket's chance in a chicken house there was any
place high enough to lessen the trouble at hand.

Bringing forth potentially evil offspring was one
thing. Moira guessed if Rosemary could love her yellow-
eyed, black clawed, cloven-hoofed infant, she could
probably manage to form some kind of bond to whatever it was she and Nick would create.

But to bind herself to Nicholas Kingswood for all of
eternity? Eternity was an awful long time. Hell, it wasn't
time at all. It was the absence of time. No beginning
and no end. Just now. Forever.

Moira shivered.

Before she'd even known exactly what she was, before she'd known about her sisters, and the Horsemen
and Lucy, she'd had an often unadmitted daydream of
herself as she would be when her hair had gone silver
and her tits migrated towards her knees. Sitting in a
rocking chair on the porch of an equally old house,
snapping the stems off green beans and shouting at the
pack of feral bayou kids to get the hell off her lawn.
Well, it wouldn't have been a lawn. Not really. Nothing
so manicured and fussy as all that.

A vegetable patch maybe. Wildflowers and ivy.

Her own kids had never figured in. Nor the presence of an old man in a matching rocking chair next to
her. Of course, Nicholas Kingswood would never be
old. And if Tierra's experiences with Bane were anything to go by, neither would Moira if she went through
with this.

In this particular moment, she couldn't say with a
surety that she planned on doing so.

She leaned forward against the railing and damn
near jumped over the edge when someone cleared his
throat behind her.

Moira turned, half expecting to see the Horseman

in question hunkering in the shadows. The silhouette she saw instead helped return her heart from her throat to its normal position in her chest.

"Uncle Sal?"

He stepped forward, swiping the trucker's hat from his head and holding it against his chest in an oddly touching deferential gesture. "Hey, darlin'."

Beside him, the lithe and unmistakable figure of Julian Roarke bowed. "I'll leave you two to your counsels."

Moira sent Pestilence the warmest smile she could muster before turning to her uncle. "I thought you'd gone back to the boat."

"I had, but when I got there and told the boys about what happened with that devil deer, they thought maybe we oughta come back and keep an eye on things." He scratched his gray-black neck stubble with his calloused fingertips, the resulting sound closely resembling sandpaper on wood.

Alarm jangled down Moira's nerves. Keep an eye on things was usually a code for looking for an excuse to shoot the shit out of and/or set fire to anything that moved.

She thought about her uncles outside, then Sal's presence on the roof, and realized for the first time that this meant he would have had to come through the house. "Did y'all meet everyone, then?"

Uncle Sal's weathered face screwed up in surprise and consternation. "You mean your...kin?"

"My sisters," she said. "Yes." She'd sent him letters over the months, having disclosed her discovery of previously unknown siblings, but hadn't gotten into the particulars about their being identical and prophesied to end the world and all.

"That's about the strangest thing I seen since that time when Pervis Morton tried to make his pecker bigger hookin' it up to an industrial strength shop vac."

Moira could have gone the rest of her life—however

long or short that might be—without the recollection of that particular experiment.

"Truth to tell, I think the boys mighta took a shine to your sister."

"Which one?" Moira asked.

"The one what looks like someone up and pissed in her coffee every morning since the day she was born."

"Oh, you mean Aerin!"

From the pop of recognition on Sal's face, Moira got the impression that the boys may or may not include one Salvadore Malveaux.

"Anyhow," Sal said, "After everyone was introduced, the boys excused themselves for their evening constitutional."

Evening constitutional. That was an interesting way of saying drinking themselves rubber-legged on moonshine and playing a round of Who Can Piss the Highest?

"How come you didn't go with them?" Moira asked.

"That young man of yours suggested I might should come up and talk to you," Sal said, wringing the cap in his hands. "Said you might be feelin' a little out of sorts."

Moira let out a gusty sigh as she turned her back to him. "He ain't wrong about that."

Sal closed the distance between them, seating himself cross-legged near the railing and patting the space next to him on the cement. "Why don't you set yourself down and tell me all about it."

And she did. Finding her sisters. Opening the Seals. Meeting the Horsemen. Battling Lucy. Tierra's pregnancy. The prophecy. Her choice.

When she'd finished, Sal sank back against the railing and whistled his astonishment. "Damnation, Moira Jo. You got yourself quite a conundrum."

"That's so," she agreed, wrapping her arms around her legs and setting her chin on her knees.

They sat together in the silence as lightning forked across the sky in the distance.

Sal ran a hand through his unruly black and silver streaked hair. "Can I ask you somethin'?"

"'Course."

"Which is it that's got your tail twisted more? The idea of bein' a momma, or tyin' yourself to a man?"

Moira sat up straighter. In her time away from bayou, she had forgotten about the canny ways of men bred to survive lethal animals by quickly reading their mood and movements. About how her uncle could cut straight to the bone of her most tangled thoughts and feelings. She felt a pang of sadness for the girl she was when she'd been on the receiving end of this surprise.

"I can't rightly say." This was true. She'd been standing up here, the wind whipping her hair and the thoughts speeding in ever-tightening circles. Just as soon as she'd convinced herself she might just be able to raise a baby, she would remember who she'd be raising that baby with. Which brought her right back to...holy shit! She'd volunteered to get knocked up.

Sal repositioned himself across from her, his bony knees in their faded overalls touching hers. From this vantage, he reached over and took her clammy hands, sandwiching them between his big, warm, leathery ones. The simple and familiar comfort in that gesture plucked her heart like a harp string, releasing a single, mournful note of longing. Moira was transported back to that creaky old fishing shack. Her single bed. Her simple problems. The knowledge that after Sal relieved her of whatever burden she'd been carrying, she could shuffle into the kitchen and make them celebratory biscuits.

She'd find no such solace now and that was the price of seeing what she'd seen.

Of knowing what she knew.

"Moira Jo, you been motherin' everything with a

heartbeat since you's tall enough to gnaw the kitchen table."

Despite the leaden heaviness in her chest, Moira felt one corner of her mouth tug into a smile. Sal had always loved to tell that story. How, absent the fancy rubber teething toys favored by more civilized folk, Moira had cut her teeth on any piece of household furniture with wooden legs.

"This is a little different than nursin' a three-legged goat back to health," Moira pointed out. "Or rescuing a baby pig from the carnival freak show." As if on cue, Cheeto, who had settled himself into her lap, hiccupped, releasing a little puff of smoke.

"Actually, I think it's exactly like that. Well, just look at me and the boys. Half the time I think it wasn't us that raised you, but you that raised us."

Truthfully, Moira had had the same thought more than once.

"You got a talent for lovin' critters that are different," Sal continued. "And it sounds like that child's gonna need all the love it can get."

"Lookin' after y'all was one thing. We're talking about a baby. A human child."

"Beggin' your pardon, but given who's going to be its daddy, I don't know if that's safe to assume."

Moira blew hot air from her nostrils. "Don't even get me started on that subject."

Wind whipped the of Uncle Sal's hair into an unruly halo. "He ain't all bad."

"All evidence to the contrary," Moira scoffed. "You don't know Nicholas Kingswood."

"I know he went to a lot of trouble to get me and the boys here. Buyin' that ratty old bait shack and tradin' the old pontoon for the Moira Jo. A man doesn't do them kinda things unless he's ass over hooch bottle in love, in my experience."

Love.

She felt her body tense up in an instinctive flinch.

That word again.

Was Nick even capable of love? He certainly knew a brand of adoration and obsession, but as far as Moira could tell, it was mostly reserved for himself and certain kinds of Italian cars.

"How about you?"

"How about me what?" Moira asked, aware she was deliberately trying to buy herself time.

"Do you love him?" Sal asked, his obsidian eyes boring into hers with startling focus.

Well if he didn't have the most irritating habit of getting straight to the goddamn point.

Moira looked from the man in front of her to the small, warm bundle in her lap. Until recently, this was everything she'd known of love. And then she'd met Tierra, and Claire, and Aerin, her heart expanding effortlessly to include every one of them. Hell, even Aunt Justine, who she'd wanted to kick down the stairs a lot less lately.

Then, there was Nick.

Nick with his whisky in the firelight eyes and his hair the color of earth after a heavy summer rain.

The man who'd stopped her from flinging herself into the sea only to shoot her through the heart with his flaming arrow when she'd asked. The man who had brought her the greatest pleasure and greatest pain she'd ever known.

She remembered the first time she'd seen his face. A glance stolen beneath the fringe of dark lashes as she pretended to sleep in the airplane seat she'd stolen from him. She'd seen his mouth. His beautiful, sensitively carved lips drawn up in a smirk.

A smirk that informed her in no uncertain terms that she was in big, big trouble.

She had loved him then.

She loved him now.

She'd loved him every minute in between.

Loved him the way the sea loves the shore. The only thing large and solid enough to not recoil from the full force of its wrath.

Which explained why she'd tried so goddamn hard to drive him away.

"Shit," Moira said, her face dropping into her hands.

Understanding this for the admission it was, Sal reached out and patted Moira's knee. "You two are gonna be real happy, Moira Jo. I mean, provided the world ain't reduced to a heap of smoldering ash directly."

Big fat tears dripped from her chin, darkening the cement like the first drops of rain.

Moira sniffed and wiped at her salty lips. "Because I finally met a man who can tame me?"

"Because you finally met a man who won't try."

With those words, the catch in Moira's chest released.

For the first time in what felt like weeks, she took a deep breath, the mingled scents of ash and salt air filling her lungs. "Well, I suppose there ain't no sense in drawing this out any longer." Tucking Cheeto under her arm, she ungracefully maneuvered her way to her feet.

From somewhere down below, Moira heard a hearty shoooeee and looked over the railing to find Mookey and Little Earl holding the bottom of a violently wobbling ladder and Red halfway up it, clutching a rung with one hand while wildly waving his trucker cap like a bull rider in the other.

"What in the Sam Hill do you fools think you're doin'?" Sal shouted down at them.

The ladder came to rest against the side of the house with a resounding thump and all three men glanced around guiltily.

"We were just out in the yard and we heard somethin'." Red called up. "We thought we might should investigate."

"What the actual fuck?" The outraged cry followed the unmistakable crash of Aerin's window being thrown open.

"Now!" someone hissed from below.

Red pressed his cap to his chest, the other reaching upward with all the gravitas of a preacher at the pulpit. "What light through yonder winder breaks? 'Tis the beast! And Aerin is the sun!"

"You dipshit!" Little Earl barked. "It ain't beast, it's east! We done talked about this!"

His soliloquy interrupted, Red cast a baleful glance downward. "I'm improvizationalizin'! And anyhow, I didn't see you bein' the one offerin' to haul your lazy ass up the ladder, Earl!"

"Don't you call me lazy, you skunk lickin' chicken fucker!" With this, Little Earl gave the ladder a threatening shake.

"First of all, I ain't ever licked a skunk and second, it wasn't a chicken, it was a—"

Moira's eardrum puncturing whistle dropped everyone into a sudden silence. "Uncle Red, you're gonna climb yourself down from that ladder right this second, then you all are going back to your boat."

Mookey shoved his hands in his pockets and scuffed at the dirt like a little boy just sent to his corner as Red descended, a cloud of creative expletives hovering around him like gnats.

"Don't be too sore at 'em," Sal said with something like fondness on his face. "They just never seen a woman with all her natural teeth before."

"You all right to keep an eye on them while I...while we..." Moira paused, searching for the right consolidation of the business ahead. "Do what needs doin'?"

Sal nodded sagely, dropping a hand on Moira's shoulder and giving it a squeeze. "You're the bravest woman I've ever known, Moira Jo. And no matter what happens, I am so proud of you."

Moira's nose stung as she saw the matching sheen of tears gathering in the weathered folds at the corner of Sal's eyes. She let him draw her into his bony chest, resting her ear against the reliable engine of his heart. She thought of the storms she had weathered with this sound as her compass and anchor. Simple steadiness inside the storm's very eye.

Fortified, she released him, turning her face to the chaos to come.

One last time.

$\maltese$ 24 $\maltese$

"Are y'all sure this is strictly necessary?" Moira stood in the center of the room, the circle of flickering candles around her making dancing ghosts of the shadows. Naked save for a plain white cotton shift that someone had hauled down from the attic, Moira waited, her arms held out like a scarecrow.

With more ceremony than Moira would have figured her globe-bellied sister capable of at this point, Tierra approached her with a wooden bowl of some suspicious-looking green goo held in one hand. In the other, a paintbrush. Slightly behind her and to either side, Aerin and Claire followed with bowls of their own, the contents of each the symbolic hue of their respective elements.

"The instructions in Grim were very specific," Tierra said, eyes glowing golden with flames' reflection. "We each have to paint a different part of you with the symbol of our element and bless it before saying the spell."

"I'm pretty sure Nick knows where to find everything. We've done this a couple times before, you know." Moira shivered as a draft from the window found its way right up under her shift.

"That's a fucking understatement," Aerin muttered

under her breath, stirring her bowl of silvery liquid with equal parts suspicion and disgust.

"Tell me about it," Claire echoed.

"All right," Tierra said, marshaling an air of matronly authority. "Off with the shift."

A bead of nervous sweat crawled from Moira's armpit down her ribs like an insect. "Can't y'all just... you know. Reach under it?"

Claire snorted. "You parade around in jean shorts no bigger than a thong most days and now you're getting bashful?"

"I mean, we're identical," Aerin added. "If I've seen mine, I've seen yours."

She had a point, Moira supposed. With one swift movement, she shucked the shift over her head and let it flutter to the floor.

"Remind me to put you in touch with my waxer when this is all over," Aerin said, eliciting a snicker from Claire.

"You guys." Tierra glanced over her shoulder to fix her sisters with a reproachful look. "You're not taking this seriously."

"Excuse the everlasting fuck out of me." Aerin swiveled in her still (miraculously) perfectly creased pantsuit. "Playing paint by numbers on my sister's body so she can conceive some weird immortal baby capable of preventing the destruction of the world as we know it wasn't exactly in my day planner."

"Would you rather you did the conceivin' and I did the paintin'?" Moira asked, her hand planted on her bare hip.

"Nope," Claire answered, a little too quickly. "We're good."

"Well, all right then," Moira said. "Slap some paint on my ass and let's get this over with." She resumed her arms in the out position, all traces of levity falling from Aerin and Claire's faces.

A rare silence held them, filling the room like billowing smoke.

Tierra stepped toward her, dipping her paintbrush in her bowl, her many bracelets tinkling, and she reached out. Moira's stomach shuddered as the cool liquid came in contact with her skin, watching as the rudimentary shape of a tree branched over her navel. "By the power of the Goddess, may your womb be as fertile as the damp, rich earth."

Stepping back, Tierra made room for Claire, sleek in a black tank top and buttery leather pants. The crimson liquid looked like nothing so much as blood as with quick, cascading movements, she conjured the shape of flames over Moira's stomach. "By the power of the Goddess, may your belly be filled with the fire of life, now and always."

Aerin approached next, her eyes taking on the liquid mercury glow of the bowl before her as she walked behind Moira. With the precision she brought to all such tasks, Aerin drew a billowing coil over each side of Moira's back. "By the power of the Goddess, may your lungs be filled with breath everlasting."

They stepped back, leaving her in the circle alone. Moira glanced down at the small bowl of deepest cobalt they'd deposited at her feet.

"The last one you have to do yourself," Tierra said gently.

Her body a running rainbow, Moira bent to pick it up.

Brush in hand, she looked at her sisters, feeling their love vibrating through her every pore. Feeling the protective space they held for her. The measure of their power they had so freely given her.

In that moment, she knew that what remained would somehow be the hardest.

The love she had to grant herself.

Dipping the paintbrush into the azure pool, she

lifted it to her heart, where, in loose, liquid strokes, she brought forth the shape of waves. "By the power of the Goddess, may my heart be brave and boundless as the ocean's tide."

Setting the bowl back down, she nodded to Tierra, who held out her hands to Aerin and Claire.

In a voice trembling with both emotion and fear, Tierra spoke the words they'd read in the Grim.

By the power of earth, air, fire and sea, let the Ceann Dorcha be born of thee.

Moira brought her hands to her navel. No longer cold and clammy, but vibrating with heat as she repeated her portion of the spell.

By the power of earth, air, fire, and sea, let the Ceann Dorcha be born of me.

❅ 25 ❅

Dread roiled in Nick's gut as he listened to the murmured voices from the room next door, where, presumably, Moira's sisters prepared her to sacrifice herself to their shared fate.

And he had no doubt that's what this was. Moira had made it exceedingly clear that she had about as much interest in soul-bonding herself to him as she did setting herself on fire and throwing herself in front of an eighteen wheeler.

Which, he supposed, was a pretty good metaphor for what she had decided to do.

Nick thought of the look of strange, steely determination he'd seen in her oceanic eyes when she'd come down from the roof. He'd been overcome by an impulse to go to her, to tell her that she didn't have to do this. That they didn't have to do this.

They could let the world burn. He would hold her in the flames.

But they hadn't even had a chance to make eye contact before her sisters whisked her away.

He, Killian, and Dru had taken up residence in the room next door, waiting to be called into battle. Julian had made himself scarce, insisting that there was something else he needed to research.

They'd sat in stifling silence for what seemed like for-fucking-ever before the door opened and Pestilence entered, a glass of mud colored sludge in one gloved hand and a book in the other.

"Shall we proceed?" he asked, setting both down on the antique table nearest the door.

"Proceed with what?" Dru asked, combat boots propped up on the steamer trunk in front of the chair he slouched in. "Nick's the one who's got spawn to shoot."

Julian reached into the pocket of his blazer and withdrew a folded sheet of parchment, which he set next to the glass. He flicked a glance to Killian, who seemed to be summoning shadows to his dark, hulking form.

"We have a ritual to do too," Bane rumbled. "To improve your chances of...success."

"Come the fuck again?" Nick asked, incredulous.

"Precisely," Julian said. "The ritual and concoction are meant to ensure your virility."

"My virility is just fucking fine, I assure you."

"It isn't me that needs assuring." Julian passed a hand over his neat, dark queue, his icy blue eyes skating once again to Bane.

"Give me a break," Nick said, hands contracting into fists at his sides. "You knock up the earth witch first time you bust a nut and all of the sudden you think you're fucking Johnny Apple Cock?"

"All I'm saying is, you banged the water witch like a screen door how many times with nothing to show for it?" Bane challenged. "Tierra said that we can't afford to take any chances."

So, the glass full of ass had been the earth witch's idea.

Crossing her meant crossing Death, and, perhaps for the first time in his unnaturally long life, Nick couldn't seem to muster the desire to argue.

How fucking weird was that?

"What is it exactly that we're supposed to do?" Nick asked, his face growing longer and his stomach heavier by the second.

Julian cleared his throat and picked up the parchment. "We are each to recite a phrase which will allow us to imbue the concoction with our respective abilities so that they may serve you in your endeavor."

"She made him a baby batter shake?" Dru whooped out a laugh.

"Not exactly." Julian paused, a fine crease appearing between his dark brows.

In the millennia of their acquaintance, Nick had gotten pretty good at interpreting the fine and subtle shifts in Julian's facial expressions. What he read there now was enough to send a white-hot bolt of panic shooting through him. "What do you mean, not exactly?"

Julian plucked nervously at the ornately embroidered cuff of his dress shirt. "A shake would imply that this is intended to be ingested orally, which, alas, is not the case."

Nick snatched the parchment from Julian's hand, his eyes sweeping fast down the page of Tierra's looping script, arriving at the words just as Julian spoke them.

"The solution is mean to be applied topically."

The parchment fluttered to the ground as Nick held up his hands and backed away. "Forget that shit. No way am I rubbing that on my junk."

Julian cleared his throat. "That's the other thing."

"What other thing?"

"The poultice cannot be self-administered."

At this, Nick turned his heel, prepared to quit the room. The house. The state. The planet.

Death caught him by the shoulder, spinning him roughly around. "Now is not the time for your hubris," he thundered. "If there is even the smallest chance that this will improve the odds of this working, you are fucking doing it."

"And which one of you assholes is volunteering to do the applying?" Nick asked,

In unison, Bane and Julian looked at Dru.

"Fuck all the way off," Dru said, surging to his feet.

"Think about this logically," Julian advised. "Neither Death nor I would be a desirable candidate to address the—area—in question, our abilities being such as they are. Whereas you—"

"Would rather fucking cut my hand off," Dru insisted.

"You fought with the Roman legions," Bane argued. "Don't act like you never crossed swords."

"I don't like it any more than you do," Nick insisted. "But what fucking option do we have? We have to end this."

Dru's hulking shoulders sank. "I swear to the gods, if any of you breathes a word of this, I will find each and every one of you and remove your bowels through your nostrils."

Abruptly, the voices next door stopped, the sudden quiet swarming through the wall.

It was time.

❧ 26 ❧

He saw her first in silhouette.

A blinding flash of lightning burned into his retinas the shape of her nude body against a backdrop bleached bluish white. Thunder chased it into darkness, and then she reappeared in the warm wash of candlelight.

Moira.

She looked like a Celtic warrior queen. Naked and defiant, paint finding each dip and hollow in her waist, sliding down the tender skin of her inner thigh. Cherry wine hair spilled over her shoulders and breasts, the waves in it wild as the sea.

She didn't move. Didn't speak.

Only waited for him within the circle of runes and candles.

Nick went to her, making quick work of his own clothing, wanting no barrier between them. He paused when he came to the circle's edge, knowing that his whole long life came to this line. To his decision to cross it.

Warmth from the candles licked at his ankles as he stepped over them, and into a new world.

Within its confines, they were the only two people alive.

163

He looked into her eyes. Flames played over their shining surface, making a kaleidoscope of azure and gold.

For no reason he could think of, he reached out, tracing with the tip of one finger first the tree at her navel, then the flames on her belly, and last, the waves over her heart.

He watched the gooseflesh rise beneath his touch and wondered at it, at the pure loveliness of her reaction to him.

Continuing up her collarbone, the curve of her neck, the delicate ridges and curve of her ear. The soft, vulnerable indentation of her temple, her cheekbone, her nose, her lips.

He was simultaneously drawing her and discovering her.

Nick slid his hand behind her neck, but did not pull her to him as he had so many times. He waited for her to come.

To his eternal wonderment, she did.

Moving slowly, erasing the distance between them, until her skin was on his skin and her mouth was on his. Searing lust rose up in him, demanding that he consume her, dominate her, make her his own. His hands tightened on her arms as he waged the internal war against himself. Against his very nature.

He wanted her.

He wanted her to want him.

Need me, he silently willed her.

Choose me.

Make me yours.

No sooner had the words floated through his brain than she grabbed a handful of his hair, bit his lip, dragged her fingernails down his back. Delicious pain surprised him, sending a bolt of pleasure from his scalp to the soles of his feet.

And where before they had been silently, liquidly

drinking from each other, tongues and lips entwined, Moira now drew from him, pulling him closer. Deeper.

Hungry as a baby bird, innocent in her single-minded insistence.

Her hand found his, guiding it down the flat plain of her stomach, down to the part of her already wet and wanting.

A moan rumbled up from his throat and he knew she felt him, hard as marble against her stomach, his knees weakening from that simple friction.

She guided him down onto the wood floor, straddling his hips. Her hair was a corona of flame, her cheeks flushed. Pure, animal lust in her eyes.

"I love you." Nick hadn't known the words were going to come from his mouth until they did.

Whatever spell that had held them until now evaporated and she looked down at him, shock and surprise warring for supremacy on her features.

"I do," he said, ready to welcome whatever reality his admission had brought into being. "I love you, Moira de Moray."

MOIRA FROZE, POISED ABOVE HIM, MILLIMETERS FROM joining their bodies with one downward thrust of her hips.

He'd said it.

Nicholas Kingswood, apocalyptic Horseman, destroyer of nations, Conquest himself loved her. Loved her.

She looked the man below her, his face appearing decades younger in an expression of naked vulnerability.

The question in his eyes.

She answered him not in words, but in movement. Keeping her gaze locked with his, she sank down on him slowly, deliberately, not stopping until she had taken him, all of him, into her body.

Only then did she lean down until her breasts were flat against his chest and her mouth was by his ear. "Nicholas Kingswood," she whispered, even as she began to undulate her hips in a rhythm she knew he would find maddening. "I love you more."

She felt a jolt of electricity as his body tensed and sat up, keeping her in his lap. His hands cupped her shoulders so he could push deeper, deeper into her while looking her in the eye, his breath warming her already flushed cheeks.

"I belong to you, Moira de Moray." He punctuated each word with an upward thrust. One hand migrated from her shoulder the back of her neck while the other one found her aching nub. "You own me. Body and soul. Heart and spirit."

"I am yours," she said breathlessly, pleasure stalking her like a great dark cat, ready to drag her spinning over the cliff.

"And you are mine," he answered, with another thrust of his hips.

Those words vibrated through her, and she felt him. Felt him in her heart, her bones, her soul. They were one, and there was no end to her, no beginning to him. Pleasure like bolts of silk, unfurling, expanding, from the place where they joined.

She was lost. Blind with endless bliss.

She felt him join her there, headless of the animalistic roar that tore from his throat.

Somewhere in that vast nowhere, she felt something else.

Small but bright, with the secret promise of a seed.

Life, within her.

MOIRA WOKE THE FOLLOWING MORNING WITH sunlight shimmering across her eyelids, spent candles hardened into wax puddles dotting the room all around them.

She stretched languidly, her muscles deliciously exhausted by the night's exertions.

Peeling back the silky sheets, she rose, walking nude over to the antique full-length mirror.

And screamed.

There, where her wallpaper-flat abdominals had once lived, was a round, bulging belly.

A basketball.

A beach ball.

A goddamn planet.

Nick shot up out of bed.

"What? What is it?"

Moira had meant to say look, but what came out instead was another inarticulate scream as she gestured at her belly.

Nick came up behind her, his hands tightened into wedges, which he brought down to the precise angle of her hipbones as he said one word.

"Boom!"

Just then, the door flew open, three sisters and three Horsemen piling in, filling the room like an old fashioned bedding ceremony.

Moira snatched her discarded tank top from the back of her vanity chair, clapping it to her lady bits as her arm covered her swollen and tender breasts.

Nick, on the other hand, stood there with his hands on his hips and his business swinging in the breeze.

Tierra, a colorful paisley dressing gown knotted over her own distended middle, took one look at Moira and gasped, her hands rising to her mouth. "Oh. My. Hell."

Bane scowled.

Claire grinned.

Aerin gagged.

Dru, shirtless and clad only in rumpled athletic shorts, looked from Moira's belly to Nick and back again. "For fuck's sake. Did you squirt a whole baby out of your dick?"

Moira looked to Julian who, in his smoking jacket and dark slacks, had become an odd tether for her in a sea of uncertainty. "Well done, Moira de Moray," he said, his lips drawing back from beautifully shaped white teeth. "I believe you've conceived the devil."

❧ III ❧
CLAIRE
By Cindy Stark

27

Claire de Moray's excitement quickly faded as she stared at Moira's belly, now swollen with child. "I have a bad feeling about this," she whispered to no one in particular.

The walls of Moira's bedroom closed in around the eight beings who'd attempted to bend the fate of the world by encouraging Moira's pregnancy. Oxygen fled from Claire's lungs, leaving fear in its wake. This was no longer about becoming an aunt again.

What had they done?

Moments before, the entire household of witches and Horsemen had woken in the early morning hours and rushed into Moira's bedroom. Claire had learned that her very own sister had conceived the devil, and a foreboding as dark as the clouds currently hovering over Port Townsend weighed heavy over her.

The previous night, the four witches and the Four Horsemen had agreed that one of the women needed to conceive a dark-souled baby to balance Tierra's angel baby. In the shadows of the night, their idea had seemed completely reasonable. But now?

Good Goddess, that baby in Moira's stomach was almost as big as the one Tierra carried.

Overnight.

Everything about the conception and the child seemed wrong. Nothing good grew that fast. Yesterday, the baby had been a thought, and now look at it.

A chill colder than an arctic wind blew through Claire and threatened her fire, leaving her with a shiver. She'd lost her fire once, when Dru had convinced her to give it up, and she never wanted to experience that again. "I have a really bad feeling. Maybe we shouldn't have messed with babies and prophecies."

All eyes in the room focused on her, and Moira's face turned ghost white. The newly pregnant mom accepted a secondhand blue terrycloth robe from Aerin and donned it. She tied the sash tightly above her bulging belly and then placed a protective hand over the baby. "Don't go saying that now, Claire. This little one went straight from tadpole to full-fledged bullfrog overnight, and I can't—"

Aerin coughed. "You mean whale," she said under her breath.

Moira clenched her fists. "That's just about enough. We decided this needed doin' and I was the only one willin' to do it. So, hush your mouths and start believing that he's gonna restore the balance to the world. Just because he's fixin' to take the devil's place don't make him bad. I thought we were clear on that point."

Her hefty stomach rolled like an earthquake across the land, and Moira gasped.

Claire dropped her jaw. It was too bad Moira hadn't bonded with Nicholas and become immortal like Tierra. Claire would feel a lot better about things then. Still, Claire had bonded with Dru, but she didn't know if she'd been blessed with immortality or not, either. "She sure is a strong one."

Nicholas snorted. "Would you expect otherwise from my offspring?"

Dru and Killian chuckled, but Julian stepped forward and took Moira's hand with his gloved one. He searched her eyes and offered a kind smile. "I'm sure everything will be fine. Would you mind if I touch your stomach?"

Moira seemed grateful to have someone on her side. "I don't mind none if you do, Julian."

Pestilence reached out with a gloved hand toward Moira's stomach.

"Stop!" Tierra said before he could touch her.

Claire turned a surprised gaze toward her earth witch sister. Tierra's face had also blanched, and she clutched her stomach. Her breaths came shallow, and the terror in her expression mimicked that in Claire's heart.

Killian wrapped a possessive arm around her. "What's wrong, my gazelle?"

Tierra panted. "I don't—"

She released a cry of pain and doubled over. "It's the baby," she managed. "Get me to my bed. I need to lie down."

Claire searched her sister's features, looking for evidence of her well-being. "Are you okay, Tierra?"

She blew out a measured breath and gave a short nod. "I will be."

Killian scooped her up faster than he stole a soul and whisked her from the room.

The rest of them looked at each other wide-eyed.

"Did she mean *her* baby?" Aerin finally asked. Then she pointed a manicured fingernail toward Moira. "Or that one?"

Claire pushed her hair, messy from sleep, back from her face. "I don't know. But..."

Aerin caught her gaze and held it. "You're thinking what I'm thinking."

Claire bit her bottom lip and nodded but remained silent. No one would speak the obvious.

Moira's child wasn't natural.

Moira glanced furiously between her sisters. "What

in the Sam Hill are you going on about? Don't you try to keep anything from me. If there's a problem, I have a right to know."

Claire sighed, not wanting to tell Moira the unhelpful bad news. "I don't know what it means, Moira, but as long as history has recorded, the de Moray women have never given birth to...a son."

Aerin lifted questioning brows. "Are you sure it's a boy?"

Moira glared. "All's I know is whatever's in here don't feel feminine. You don't believe me, come put your paws on my belly."

Claire glanced to Aerin who gave a small shrug and moved closer. Claire did the same, though she wasn't at all comfortable touching a pregnant woman's belly, even if it was her sister's.

Aerin and she placed their hands onto Moira's plump stomach. Immediately, loving sensations reached out to Claire, soothing her soul. Warm waves of happiness washed away any doubt she had.

Claire exhaled in relief and smiled at Moira. "You're right. He's okay."

Aerin removed her hands and stepped back. "Agreed. Nothing ominous growing there."

Moira snorted, and a happy smile tipped up the corners of her mouth. "Ominous. How could you even think that? Day needs night, ya know, to keep things balanced and such. Just because something is dark doesn't mean it's bad."

A scream of pain echoed through the house, and Claire cringed from the intensity. "It looks like things are good here, but some of us should check on Tierra."

Julian lifted his chin in acknowledgement. "Yes, let's."

Claire held up a hand. "How about if Dru and I go? You all should stay with Moira and care for her. Waking up with a..."

She paused, at a loss for words to describe the enormity of Moira's stomach and what it contained.

"A baby," Moira said firmly.

Claire nodded. "A baby. Waking up with a big baby. A big, *good* baby must be a shock. We'll let you know how Tierra is."

Another cry of agony sent Claire and Dru hurrying from the room.

When they were out of earshot, almost to Tierra's bedroom, Dru wrapped his hand around hers. "I have a bad feeling about this, too."

Claire cast him a worried glance, nodded, and then hurried faster toward her sister.

❧ 28 ❧

Unimaginable disturbances radiated outward from Tierra's closed bedroom door. Her sister's screams had quieted by the time Claire and Dru had arrived, but Claire felt in her very bones that life had changed significantly. She paused half a second to gather her fire, prepared to battle whatever lay beyond the barrier. She just prayed her sister wasn't hurt.

Dru held his mighty sword in one hand and flung open the door with the other.

Claire gasped at what she saw.

White and black feathers flew through the air as Killian lunged and bounced off walls, trying to capture a small flying enemy that moved so fast Claire couldn't make out the features. Tierra's eyes were wide with shock, dancing back and forth as she followed the skirmish. Otherwise, she seemed okay, huddled beneath a forest green quilt that haphazardly covered her.

Dru lifted his sword to take down the enemy should it fly in their direction. *"What the hell is that?"*

The little pixie or fairy barreled headfirst into Killian's chest, knocking him back against the wall. He quickly brought his hands together and sank to the floor. "Gotcha."

The creature squirmed and fought against Death,

but he refused to let go.

Tierra placed a frantic hand on her chest. "Oh. My. Goddess."

Claire glanced between Killian and her sister, unsure if they were all still in danger. "What in the name of Hell's fire is it?"

Killian tucked whatever it was beneath his wing and struggled one-handed to get to his feet. He drew great breaths and jerked his chin upward toward Dru. "Grab that blanket."

Dru reached for a soft ivory throw that had been draped across the bottom of the bed. He kept his sword out as he approached Killian and the unruly captive.

Death snorted. "Put that thing away, man, or you're going to kill my daughter."

Dru halted, and Claire's mouth fell open. "Daughter?" she muttered.

What kind of monster had Tierra birthed? A demon child sired by Death? Worse, if this was the light-souled baby, what kind of hellish thing was Moira growing?

"Blanket, man," Killian demanded.

Dru sheathed his sword and held out the blanket, looking as dazed and confused as Claire felt. She cast a quick glance toward her sister, who seemed to have lost her ability to speak or act.

Killian snatched the soft throw and tucked it beneath his wing. He fussed and struggled for a moment and then produced the sweetest looking cherub of a baby that Claire had ever seen. Killian had bundled her tightly, and she now stared at him with wide-eyed wonder.

With a dusting of dark red hair, pink cheeks, and a soft cooing sound coming from her cupid's bow mouth, she couldn't possibly be the wild thing that had threatened them all moments ago.

A proud papa's grin nearly split Killian's face, and his happiness filled the room. He strode close to the side of the bed where Tierra lay and held the bundle out to her. "Your princess, my gazelle. Isn't she beautiful?"

Tierra choked out a sob and put a hand over her mouth. Tears streamed from her eyes, and then she held out her hands. "Oh, my sweet Goddess. She's the most beautiful thing I've ever seen."

Killian gently placed the babe into Tierra's outstretched arms and chuckled. "I hadn't realized she'd be able to fly so soon after birth."

Claire raised her brows and glanced to Dru, who shrugged. "I guess we shouldn't be surprised since her daddy has wings as well," she said.

Tierra blinked back her tears and smiled. "Hello, beautiful. I'm your momma."

The baby's face lit up, and she released a soft sigh.

Tierra ran a finger lightly over her cheek, earning another cooing sound. She slipped her hand into the swaddled blanket and produced a soft, pudgy hand. The baby immediately wrapped tiny fingers around one of Tierra's.

Claire stepped forward until she stood next to Death. The baby's face drew into a frown that nearly broke Claire's heart. "Oh, honey. Don't be afraid. I'm your Auntie Claire here to welcome you into the world."

The baby hesitated a moment, and then Claire swore that she smiled. "Look! She likes me."

Tierra nodded. "She does. I can sense it. Dru, you need to come here, too. Little Violet needs to know that you're okay. She was so frightened before, not knowing what had happened when she came into the world. Please, let her know that she's safe."

"Violet," Claire said. "That's such a beautiful name."

Dru shot Claire an uncertain look but then moved forward. He crowded next to Claire and slipped an arm around her. He probably thought she would think it was a protective gesture toward her, but Claire recognized that he was the one who needed emotional support.

He cleared this throat. "Hello, Violet. I'm…"

Claire leaned into him as she stared at the angelic baby. "He's your Uncle Dru."

Dru nodded. "Uncle. That's right. I'm your Uncle Dru."

She tilted her head to regard the Horseman who'd stolen her heart. "I get the sensation that you've never been this close to a baby before."

He snorted. "Got that right. In my line of work, the last thing I want around is a child."

Claire supposed he had a point. She turned her gaze to Killian. "What about you?"

His face fell, and she realized the error of her question. "Far too many times," he said.

Claire shook her head. "Of course. I'm sorry. But look at that beautiful face. This time, you'll get to experience all the wonderful things about a child."

Killian's smile returned, and he sat on the edge of the bed where he could place an arm around Tierra and be closer to his baby. "I swear here and now that nothing will hurt either one of you."

She half-wondered if Tierra would argue, since his possessiveness had been a point of contention between them in the past, but she only snuggled closer to him.

Claire leaned against Dru and nudged him. "We should go and let the family have some time. I'm sure the others want to know everything is okay."

Dru stepped away from the bed so fast that Claire had to restrain a chuckle. Killian might have fallen gracefully into fatherhood, but it appeared that Dru had no intention of doing the same any time soon.

Which was completely fine with her. She liked the idea of being an auntie.

But mom?

Not so much.

❊ 29 ❊

The following day, bright sunshine washed through the old Victorian's kitchen windows, bringing with it a sense of a pleasantness and hope. Tierra had asked the witches to convene in the kitchen, and they were all eager to see the newest member of the household.

Claire eyed Aerin and Moira, who both watched her with expectant looks on their faces. "I'm sure Tierra will be here any minute. She's probably dragging after the birth. I can only imagine how hard it must be."

Aerin glanced at her Cartier watch, sighed, and lifted the lovely Cassius Basaltic black clay mug, hand-crafted by Tierra. She sipped and set it back on the table, leaving a perfect red-lipped mark along the rim.

Moira groaned and pushed on one side of her stomach as though adjusting the position of the baby. "Thank the stars that this one won't squirt out of me and go tear-assin' around the room like one of them murder hornets. I can't even imagine such a thing. That ain't natural."

Aerin slid a sideways glance toward Moira. "But having your child grow overnight is?" she muttered.

Claire sent Moira a reassuring smile. "I'm sure your baby will be perfectly healthy and happy."

She knew Moira still worried about her child, and, of course, both of her sisters had reservations about Tierra's baby. The new mother had asked for recovery time, but everyone wondered what might happen when Violet met Aerin, who'd practiced dark magic and who'd been temporarily inhabited by Lucy, and when Violet met Moira, who currently carried the dark-souled baby who would bring balance to the world.

They hoped.

Moira sighed and glanced about the kitchen. "I'd give my right elbow for some buttermilk-battered frog legs right now."

Claire half-swallowed, half-choked on her coffee. "Gross," she managed.

Aerin turned her face away and held up a hand. "Please. Let's never discuss that again."

Moira frowned. "Don't y'all go turnin' your noses up. Amphibians are practically their own food group back in the Parrish. Used to make hoppers for Uncle Sal every Sunday. They're all crispy on the outside and tender on the inside. Lots a protein, too. Just what a growin' boy needs."

Claire took another swallow to clear the bile in her throat. "I'm with Aerin on this. Enjoy them all you want, but I don't want to see, hear, or smell them."

Aerin pushed back from the table, the chair legs squawking as she did. She stood and looked down at her sisters. "I don't have time for this. If Tierra doesn't want us to meet it, that's fine by me. Babies smell, and they cry."

Moira admonished her sister with a stern look. "She's not an 'it'."

Aerin met her gaze head on. She pointed to the ethereal blue blouse she wore that looked as if it had been spun from clouds. "See this? It's made from the finest mulberry silk, and it can't just be tossed in the wash if one of those things pukes on me. You, your self, told me that Port Townsend's former dry cleaners is now a haven for lonely zombies looking for a hookup. Don't think you'll catch me anywhere near there."

Moira widened her eyes and slyly placed a finger on her lips as though to shush Aerin.

Claire's instincts jumped into overdrive, and she glanced back and forth between the two of them. "What? What aren't you telling me?"

Moira tossed a peeved look in Aerin's direction and then turned to Claire. Her features softened. "I wasn't going to say anything...but Nicholas spotted Tommy hanging out on the street there, flirting with a girl...er, zombie girl with purple hair."

Claire frowned. "His succubus bitch girlfriend doesn't have purple hair."

Aerin lifted her brows and sent Claire a blunt look. "That is correct."

Claire's heart gave a small twitch. "He broke up with his succubus, and now he's seeing someone else?"

She didn't know why she cared, but she did. After all, she had Dru who was ten times the man Tommy had been. More like a hundred times now that Tommy was dead. But Tommy had been her first love, and a small part of her wanted him to always love her, to never be able to move on and be happy without her.

Moira shrugged. "Sounds like it. I say good for him. He might be missing a few parts, but his pecker ain't one of them. Just because he's dead don't mean he doesn't like to play bury the boudin."

The sound of movement coming from the hallway was a grateful distraction. Claire stood. "I think she's coming."

Tierra peeked into the room that had always been a gathering place for the sisters. She glowed, vibrating health and happiness, and Claire was grateful to see she'd fared well since Violet's birth.

She stepped into the room, holding tightly to a bundle of pink. "Hey there. Good morning."

Moira stood and lifted her chin as though that would give her a better look at what Tierra carried. "'Bout time, Tierra. I swear you're slower than a three-legged tortoise. Whatcha got there?"

Tierra beamed and walked closer to Moira. She tugged back the blanket to reveal Violet's sleeping angelic face. "This is Violet Mirelle de Moray."

Moira released a sigh of longing. "Well, if she ain't the most beautiful thing on earth. Look, Aerin, look at that tiny fist."

Aerin cautiously stepped closer and peered at the baby with reserved interest. "Congratulations, Tierra. She's...lovely."

Tierra glanced at each of her sisters, and her smile grew wider. "After the way Violet reacted when Lucy had inhabited Aerin's body, I've been a little worried that my girl might have issues with some in the household, but she seems to like everyone just fine. Would you like to hold her?"

Aerin waved both hands in front of her. "Oh, no. That's okay. I'm..."

"She's not good with babies," Moira finished for her. "But I am. Give her here."

Claire held her breath while Tierra handed over Violet, wondering if the baby would freak out when she realized her mother no longer held her, and that instead, the soon-to-be-mother of darkness did.

But little Violet sighed softly and continued to sleep.

Moira ran a fingertip down Violet's cheek. "We're going to get along just fine."

Which was a huge relief to Claire.

Tierra filled a tea kettle with water and put it on to boil. She returned to the table, sat with her sisters, and smiled at Moira holding her child. Then she sighed. "I returned Aunt Justine's call last night. She and the Coven are eager to meet Violet."

Moira snorted. "I bet they are."

Claire looked to Tierra. "Do you think that's a good idea? I mean Aunt Justine hasn't always been the greatest supporter of any of us, and she's better than the rest of them. Do you really think they're going to accept a child of Death?"

Especially when they discovered she had wings and a powerful disposition.

Tierra shrugged. "Violet's a de Moray, a family of witches who've been around for centuries. Possibly since time began. They can't very well snub her."

Aerin flashed silver eyes in Tierra's direction. "Don't be so sure."

Tierra lifted calming hands. "I understand your concern. Trust me. No one worries about Violet more than me. I wouldn't even consider letting them around her except there's going to be a day when Violet's old enough to have friends of her own. If no one in the Coven accepts her, she'll be an outcast."

"Like us," Claire finished.

Tierra sent her a consolatory look. "I didn't want to say that, but, yes. In order for her to fulfill her role for all mankind, she'll need the support of everyone, including the Coven. I don't want her to start out on the wrong foot and struggle."

Moira kissed Violet's little head. "I agree, Tierra. It ain't fun having everyone look down on you."

Tierra glanced at each of her sisters in turn. "Aunt Justine wants to hold a baby shower."

Aerin straightened. "A fucking *what* shower?"

Claire laughed, though she did understand Aerin's reservations. Polite tea parties weren't their cup of tea.

Tierra chuckled. "A baby shower. She wanted to hold it at their place, but I said, no. If I'm allowing a multitude of people around Violet, it will be here, where all of you and the guys can protect her."

Violet squirmed and opened her eyes, staring at Moira with a most-interested expression.

Moira grinned with obvious affection. "As much as I'd like to tell some of them biddies to kiss the north end of a south-facin' mule, I'd say this little one deserves all the gifts she can lay her chubby paws on."

"Good," Tierra said. "The more the Coven believes she's a normal baby, the more likely they'll accept her. It's traditional for all witches to be introduced this way into their coven."

All but them, Claire thought.

The tea kettle shrilled, and Tierra stood. "I'll let her know that she can go ahead then. We'll make sure the house is heavily warded and that no one who's not invited can enter."

Great, Claire thought. A house full of witches who hated her. What could be more fun?

❃ 30 ❃

Early afternoon, several weeks later, one by one, members of the Port Townsend Coven arrived at the quaint, nineteenth-century home sitting on the hillside above the Victorian seaport village. Witches young and old came dressed in their finery, sporting silk skirts and a variety of crystal encrusted jewelry like any respectable witch would. They chattered as they ascended the steps carrying pink or purple gifts in a variety of sizes, prepared to celebrate the arrival of Tierra's child.

Claire and Aerin flanked the front door, supposedly to welcome their guests, but really to assess everyone entering the house. Claire had warned Aunt Justine to only invite the witches who personally knew Tierra well.

Considering the number of guests arriving, either her sister was a popular lady, or Aunt Justine hadn't listened at all, which was a potent source of frustration for Claire.

Moira had been willing, but not happy, to be banished to their mother's special room in the attic, where they all hoped no one could sense Moira and the dark-souled baby that she carried. Even Aunt Justine thought it was better to introduce the Coven to one world-changing infant at a time.

Honestly, Moira didn't know how lucky she was, not having to deal with the mostly unpleasant witches. Plus, Moira had Nick there to entertain her, and Claire had no doubt that he would.

Aerin and she received several dull looks from the haughty witches as they passed. Although Aerin in her expensive pantsuit far outclassed them, neither she nor Claire, in her red silk shirt and leather pants, won their approval. Likely never would.

Not that she cared.

A lull came between arriving guests, and Aerin sighed with impatience as they waited for the next party of guests to make their way to the house. "This is such a shit show."

Claire groaned. "You're telling me. If I have kids, and that's a big 'if', I don't care if the whole town disowns me. I'm not subjecting myself to their ridiculous trivialities."

Aerin grinned. "Truth. I have better things to do than entertain the lot of nasty women. They don't care about us, don't care about Tierra or little Violet. They've sensed the power and light she's brought into the world, and they're here to witness her firsthand, to judge her power, and to plan the future of the Coven based on what they see."

No doubt Aerin was correct. "Still, who in their right mind would subject themselves to silly games and mindless chatter, all for the sake of a baby they don't even know? There are other, better ways of gaining information."

Aerin snorted. "But this is the easiest way. They *know* she's not just any baby. How could they not? She was born of one of the four who were never supposed to live. They know who we are, know that we've opened six out of the seven Seals, and I'm sure they're wondering who the hell Violet is. Or should I say, what she is."

A tendril of fear snaked through Claire. "This was a mistake. We shouldn't be letting anyone close to the baby. Not until she's old enough to protect herself."

"Yeah. Though I'm not entirely sure Violet can't do that already. She has extremely strong powers."

True enough.

Claire reached out to Dru with her senses, needing to feel him near in case anything went wrong. His presence reassured her, and she knew the other three Horsemen weren't far away. Out of sight, but not too far should they need them. Death would be the nearest, of course, closed up in a room just off the parlor where the baby shower would take place.

Personally, she could care less if the Coven accepted little Violet, but she supposed if there was going to be life after the Apocalypse, the sisters would all want Violet to be accepted by her peers, something Claire, Aerin, and Moira had been robbed of.

Two witches approached the house, one dressed in a flowing purple skirt and the other in a flaming orange Victorian dress and matching feathered hat, and they strode through the white picket gate. The hat partially obscured the orange-clad woman's face until she looked up to climb the front porch stairs.

Gwen.

"Here comes the bitch squad now," Aerin said.

Every time Claire encountered Gwen, half of her wanted to run, and the other half wanted to smash her face into the dirt until she screamed. If it had been up to Gwen, Claire would have been dead before she'd ever had a chance to escape from Dru or meet her sisters.

Luckily, fate had intervened, and Dru really did have a heart.

To make matters worse, Gwen hadn't taken kindly

to the fact that Claire had stolen Dru's heart, something Gwen had always wanted for herself but had never obtained.

Claire steeled her gaze on the ghastly woman.

Gwen forced a smile as she reached the top step. Most likely, Gwen thought if she didn't, she might be denied entrance. Claire would have loved to push her backward and watch her land on her ass in the dirt and grass. But Tierra would have her hide for ruining the party and for any damage to Tierra's garden.

"Welcome to the de Moray Mansion," Aerin said coolly.

Both women responded with thanks to Aerin and completely ignored Claire as they passed into the house. Claire sneered after them. "If this wasn't Tierra's special day…"

Aerin chuckled. "But it is. However, if you'd like, I'll help you search our grimoire for a noxious spell to get even with Gwen once this is all over."

Claire grinned. "Deal."

When the last of the Coven had gone inside, Claire and Aerin closed the doors and double warded them. Honestly, the place was locked down tighter than the Gates of Hell. No one was getting in who wasn't supposed to be there.

Claire and Aerin hovered at the entrance to the parlor. The second Tierra spotted them, she waved them in. "Come on in, guys. We saved spots for you."

Tierra patted the folding chair next to her. "Aerin?"

"Goddess, help us," Aerin muttered and stepped farther into the room.

Tierra pointed toward a couch near her that was already three-quarters full of two plump, older ladies. "Claire, you can sit next to Martha and Hattie Mae."

Claire pasted on a friendly smile for the sake of her sister. Great. Martha and Hattie Mae.

"Hello, ladies," Claire said and sandwiched herself

between a severe-looking black woman who narrowed her eyes at Claire in distrust and an older blonde who reminded Claire of a faded version of Marilyn Monroe who'd refused to age gracefully. Hattie Mae's stifling, cheap perfume brought tears to her eyes, but at least she emitted a friendly vibe.

Aunt Justine stood, looking like she was years closer to the grave than she had when Claire had first arrived in town. An apocalypse could do that to a person. The older woman clapped her hands together. "It's so wonderful to see everyone together. My friends," she said, and then glanced at Claire and her sisters. "And my family. In times like these, we must stick together."

Claire was certain she couldn't get any closer to members of the Coven than she was right now. At least not with Martha and Hattie Mae.

Murmurs of agreement echoed throughout the room, but Claire sensed the disharmony between the Coven members and wanted to call bullshit. Ever since Lucy's short stay with the Coven, dissension amongst the group reigned supreme.

Martha sniffed loud enough to draw Claire's attention. "I noticed that your sister Moira isn't here, and I wonder where she could be on such a momentous occasion."

Claire gave a half-smile. "She's a little under the weather today and didn't want to share her germs."

Hattie Mae scooted closer to the edge of the couch as though Claire might pass along whatever Moira had. Claire grinned inside, appreciating the extra space on the couch.

Aunt Justine looked toward the kitchen. "Sunny? Do you have the bottles ready?"

Sunny strode in, all turquoise hair and piercings, with a huge smile on her face. She carried a tray of baby bottles, each half full of different colored liquids. "Hi guys. I'm helping Justine with the shower, and she put me in charge of the games. So, this first one is called Drink Up, Baby. The goal of the game is to be the first to finish your baby bottle."

❦ 31 ❦

C laire choked on a breath. "Wait. What?"

Sunny wanted her to drink from a *baby bottle*? Uh...no.

Aerin shook her head. "There's no fucking way I'm drinking from a nipple."

Tierra nudged her. "Come on, Aerin. You have to join in. It'll be fun."

Sunny strode to Aerin first. "Don't worry. It's not that bad. I filled them with wine so that everyone will relax and have a good time. You can pick from rosé or pinot grigio. Or for those who aren't up for drinking alcohol, we have a selection of Tierra's teas."

Aerin lifted a defiant brow. "I would like my wine in a glass."

Tierra shook her head. "Nope. You have to play along."

Martha lifted her hand and called out. "I'll take the pinot."

"Same," Hattie Mae said.

Sunny gave Aerin one last chance and then headed toward the couch where Claire and the two witches sat. She handed bottles to the two elderly women on either side of Claire and then looked expectantly at her.

Claire quickly waged an internal battle. Wine to

help her manage this insane affair...or dealing with these lunatics sober. "I'll have the rosé."

Aerin shot her a traitorous look, and Claire shrugged. "It's wine."

Sunny handed out bottles to the rest of the ladies and set the remainder on a side table.

"Wait," Aerin called out, and Sunny turned to her. "I'll have pinot," she said, her words dripping with irritation.

Tierra grinned as Sunny selected a baby bottle for Aerin and strode toward her. "It's not bad," Sunny said. "I tried it out last night and got a little wasted."

Aerin accepted the offering with much distaste. "Wine should be consumed slowly so that one can savor the flavor."

Sunny chuckled. "We have more in the kitchen if you'd like to savor some later."

Aerin shifted her gaze to Claire and shook her head, letting her know the depth of her disappointment that Claire had caved to social pressure.

Claire grinned. Aerin had done exactly the same. Sisterhood had far more influence than either one of them obviously expected.

Sunny glanced about the room. "Everyone ready? When I say go, start drinking. As soon as you're finished, hold up your bottle. The winner will receive a fantastic prize chosen by me."

Claire lifted the bottle close to her mouth and studied the nipple. How long could this possibly take?

"Go!" Sunny yelled.

Claire stuffed the nipple in her mouth and began to suck. Not nearly enough wine came with each attempt. She glanced about the room and choked on a swallow at the ridiculous sight before her. Witches of all ages drank from their bottles as if their lives depended on it.

She shifted her gaze to Aerin who'd unscrewed the lid from her bottle. Aerin raised a saucy brow, lifted the bottle in a toast to obviously how foolish Claire must look, and took a sip. Leave it to her air witch sister to rebel.

But Claire wasn't one to ignore a brilliant idea. She unscrewed the nipple and took a drink. When she finished, she held up the bottle.

Sunny berated her with a pointed finger. "No, Claire. You have to drink through the nipple, or you're disqualified. Keep going, ladies."

A few minutes later, the woman in the purple skirt who'd arrived with Gwen thrust her bottle into the air. "Done!"

The other ladies lowered their bottles, and Sunny strode toward the purple clad witch with a small bag in hand. "Here you go, Melody. Nice job."

Melody accepted the gift bag and stuffed her hand inside. She pulled out a gorgeous amethyst necklace that Claire suddenly coveted. She so should have stuck with the nipple.

Sunny followed with a "guess the baby items inside the diaper bag" game, which Claire and Aerin didn't even attempt to win. Claire opted for a second baby bottle instead.

Afterward, Aunt Justine stood. "We'll pause now for lunch. Sunny and I will serve. But get your gifts ready, ladies. We'll let Tierra have a bite to eat and then start opening them."

At least Aunt Justine was sticking to the rushed party schedule.

"What about seeing the baby?" Martha asked in a loud voice.

Tierra's face flushed. "She'll join us after her nap. I promise."

Aunt Justine and Sunny served Tierra's famous tea and Moira's spicy, fried chicken pó boy sandwiches. Claire hoped their guests also appreciated the fresh fruit and vegetable trays since Tierra's garden was the last dependable source of produce on the Olympic Peninsula.

After fifteen minutes, Aerin gestured to Claire to follow her, and they regrouped at the entrance to the parlor. "Time to open gifts, wouldn't you say, and finish this farce?"

Claire wholeheartedly agreed. "Yes. The sooner we can get them out of here, the better."

Claire headed to the kitchen and snagged the pink gift bag with sparkly polka dots and returned to the party. She leaned close to Aerin. "I'll go first. We'll have these bitches...I mean witches out of here in no time."

Aerin laughed out loud, obviously not caring who heard.

Claire approached Tierra who sat in a circle with many of the party guests. By the look of sheer happiness on Tierra's face, it was clear to Claire that Tierra had had a good relationship with many of the ladies, some of whom she'd likely known her entire lifetime.

Claire eyed the circle, wondering how many of them had known their mother, Mirelle. She also wondered how many had turned away, refusing to help their mother when others had sought her out for evil purposes. How many of these women might have helped, but didn't, with the hunt for the poor woman about to bring four prophesied daughters into the world?

Also, how many of them had outright agreed the babies couldn't live? And who among them had conspired to kill her and her sisters?

Claire couldn't think of that now, or she'd likely lose her head and do something stupid. "Hey, sis," she said brightly to Tierra. "Let me be the first to give my gift."

Claire handed the bag to her sister and offered a warm smile. Claire's cheerful interactions with most of the guests might have been phony, but her love for Tierra and baby Violet was as real as it came.

Tierra blinked back several tears of happiness. "Thank you, dear sister."

She opened the bag and lifted out a frilly spring green dress with matching shoes and headband. "Oh, my Goddess, look. The shoes have amethysts on them."

Claire smiled. "To signify my love and commitment to caring for little Violet."

Tierra turned to her guests. "I'm not sure how many of you have met Claire, but I want you to know she's a wonderful person and one of the fiercest fire witches I've met."

Some in the circle smiled, and Gwen coughed into her hand.

Claire ignored her.

Tierra stood and pointed toward Aerin, who quickly shook her head. "Over there is Aerin, an awe-inspiring air witch. She's unbelievably amazing and runs her own highly successful corporation."

Aerin gave a half-hearted smile, while whispers circulated the room that some believed Aerin had learned to fly.

Jealous witches.

"My water witch sister, Moira, couldn't be here today," Tierra continued. "But she's as gifted as these two and has the biggest heart I've ever known."

Martha cleared her throat. "Your sisters are very lovely, I'm sure, but we'd really like to meet your new daughter. I hear she's gorgeous, with astonishing eyes."

Tierra's pure joy faded into nervous happiness. "Of course. I know everyone's eager. I've been waiting for her to wake from her nap. We don't want a cranky baby."

Some of the guests chuckled, but waves of expectation filled the rose-wallpapered room.

Tierra looked toward Aerin with a hesitant expression. "Would you mind checking on her for me and bringing her here if she's awake?"

Aerin lifted perfectly-shaped brows and panic splashed across her face. "Me?"

Tierra smiled and nodded.

Aerin turned to Claire, silently pleading for help. Claire shook her head, not wanting to have to fetch the baby, either. Besides, if anything went wrong, Aerin was the one who could transport them both to safety in an instant.

❧ 32 ❧

The second Claire sensed Violet's presence growing closer, all of the guests quieted. Claire assumed they must know the baby was nearby as well.

Aerin stepped into the room holding sweet Violet. The witches released a collective gasp, followed by comments on her beauty, how much dark cherry red hair she had, and how big she was.

The baby surveyed them all with the same intensity, but she didn't make a sound.

Tierra stood and held out her arms. A brilliant smile lit Violet's face, and Claire knew she'd spotted her momma.

Once the child was in her mother's arms, Tierra turned so the guests had a better look at Violet, and she beamed with pride. "This is Violet Mirelle de Moray. Named after my mother."

Melody, drew her thick eyebrows together, giving her a unibrow. "She's only a few weeks old, you say? Looking at her, she seems much older, much more..."

"Alert?" Justine added from where she held court, sitting in the prominent pink Queen's Anne chair. "Perhaps wise? Yes, she's very aware of her surroundings."

Claire had feared the witches' reactions concerning

how fast Violet had grown. But what could they do about it?

Tierra shrugged. "Violet's been a surprise to us all. A very happy surprise."

Aerin started to walk away, but Tierra quickly grabbed her by the elbow. "Would you sit by me while I open gifts? Violet would love you to hold her."

Aerin gave her a curt nod. "Of course."

"Claire," Tierra said. "You can pull a chair next to Aerin and help me remember who to thank for which gifts."

Tierra was obviously nervous having Violet in the room. Claire sent her a reassuring nod and moved closer.

Tierra relaxed her shoulders, but apprehension still tinted her green eyes a darker shade than normal.

Claire wondered if there was an undercurrent that Tierra sensed that she could not and wanted Aerin and her close by, just in case. Claire glanced across the gaggle of guests, doing another sweep for anything that might seem suspicious.

She stopped on Aunt Justine, who'd slumped against the back of her chair with her mouth wide open.

Good Goddess. They must have worn out the older woman.

Claire snickered and leaned to whisper to Aerin. "Oh, my Goddess. *Aunt Justine fell asleep. In the middle of the party.* She can try all she wants to hide her age, but it's showing."

Aerin chuckled and turned her gaze toward their older aunt. Claire watched her sister, waiting for her smile to grow, but it dropped completely from her face. She quickly glanced to Tierra who hadn't noticed and then back to Claire. *"Look at her. I don't think she's breathing."*

Alarm dove deep into Claire, and she straightened. She didn't want to ruin Tierra's shower by announcing their aunt may have died, but there wasn't much she or Aerin could do otherwise.

Claire hurried to Aunt Justine and knelt next to her. She gripped her wrist to feel for a pulse. Aerin joined her and shook their aunt's shoulders to try to get a response.

The older woman slumped forward, and Claire reached out to stop her from toppling to the floor. *"Dear Goddess."*

No pulse.

Words of worry from their guests flew about the room. "Someone call for emergency services," Claire said, and then she wondered if ambulances were even operating any longer.

Tierra stood, her face ghostly white. "Nooo!" Her cry came from across the large room.

Tierra clutched Violet and rushed forward. When she reached Aunt Justine, she dropped to her knees next to Claire. "What's wrong? What happened?" she asked breathlessly.

Claire shook her head, feeling certain the woman had passed to the other side. Emotion closed her throat, and she had to force out an answer. *"I don't know. She was fine, and then she wasn't."*

Tierra jerked her gaze around. "Where's Killian? Is he here? Has he taken her soul already?"

Violet released a soft giggle that seemed so out of place that Claire couldn't help but look at her. The tiny child clung to her mother's arm with one hand but held the other in the air, one finger extended. She twirled her finger around and around as though swirling the atmosphere.

Tierra handed Violet to Claire and jumped to her feet. "When I find that Horseman..."

Claire gasped. "Wait, Tierra. Aunt Justine's not gone. She's not with Killian."

She caught Tierra and Aerin's glances and furtively raised her gaze upward.

An ethereal form of Aunt Justine floated above them, translucent and peaceful.

Tierra scrunched her face into a frown and then turned to her baby. She held Violet's cheeks between her fingers, so that the baby would look at her. "Violet Mirelle de Moray. You put Aunt Justine's soul back right now."

The little girl dropped her hand.

A second passed, and then another, and then Aunt Justine sat upright, inhaling a full breath of air. She blinked a few times, obviously surprised to find everyone circled around her. She gripped the arms of the chair and dropped her gaze to her body.

Several long seconds later, Justine lifted her head, looking slightly dazed. "What's going on?"

"Great Goddess," someone in the crowd whispered. *"The baby stole Justine's soul."*

Gwen pinched her lips together and shook her head. "A sure sign of ominous things to come. This is dire. Very dire indeed. We can't allow this abomination to exist."

Abomination? Good Goddess. Gwen was talking about a baby. Claire and her sisters had to do something and fast, or the whole coven would be after Violet.

Claire stood and started laughing. She eyed Aerin who caught on and did the same. Claire grinned at the crowd. "I'm sorry we had that laugh at your expense, but we couldn't help it. Everyone in town has been so concerned that Tierra's baby wouldn't be normal that we simply had to play a joke."

The group remained stoic and unconvinced, and Aerin's and Claire's laughs faded into grim reality.

Then Aunt Justine began to giggle, and the mood of the room turned to confusion. She laughed so hard that tears formed in her eyes and, slowly, others began to chuckle along with her.

"As you can see," Tierra said over their joviality. "My aunt is just fine, and my lovely daughter is perfectly normal."

"Just fine," others murmured, but Gwen narrowed her gaze.

Martha moved closer to Aunt Justine's chair and glanced between Aerin and Claire. "I have to admit you got me with that one. You two witches might be okay after all."

Claire gave a weak laugh and smiled. "Thanks."

Tierra waved her hands as though to clear the atmosphere, and her bracelets tinkled in response. "It might be a while before they forgive you for that one, sisters."

The party continued, and Aunt Justine didn't seem to be the worse for wear. Claire wondered if the older woman had any idea of what had really happened. If so, she'd played her part well.

Aerin and Claire made their way to the edge of the room again where they could watch everyone. "Did that *really* happen?"

Claire exhaled a year's worth of anxiety. "It must have. Didn't you see Aunt Justine floating?" she whispered.

"I don't know what I saw or what just happened, but we need to get these people out of here before something else goes wrong."

Aerin picked up a small, classic black and white striped gift bag from a side table. She held it out as she strode toward their sister. "Last but not least, here's one from Moira and me."

Tierra bounced Violet on her lap as Aerin approached, and then she held out her daughter to her sister. "A trade?"

Aerin sighed heavily and took the baby. She stood in

front of Tierra holding Violet away from her while Tierra opened the bag. Tierra slid out a small jewelry box and flicked a quick glance toward Aerin and Violet. "Should we see what's in here, honey? Something from your aunties."

With a gift that size, Claire imagined whatever her sisters gave Violet would need to be put away until the little girl was much older.

Tierra opened the box and inhaled a strangled breath. She jerked her gaze upward to Aerin and quickly snapped the box closed.

Aerin frowned. "Don't you like it?"

Tierra blinked several times, obviously confused. "It's...it's lovely. Thank you both so much."

Aerin's frown turned into confusion. Claire sensed that both had more to say, but it was obviously something they couldn't speak of in front of guests.

Undeniable tension filled the room, and Tierra stood. "Thank you all for coming."

A belch worthy of a drunken seaman erupted from sweet little Violet, and Aerin yelped in surprise. She shoved the baby at her sister, who wasn't prepared to catch her.

Little Violet bounced off her mom's arm and fell toward the floor. Tierra gasped and lunged toward her daughter.

But Violet didn't land hard like Claire had feared.

Instead, little white wings fluttered out from behind her. She giggled as she rose once again to her mother's height. Tierra, with her face as white as morning mist, snatched her out of the air.

Claire glanced from guest to guest, finding all the women with wide eyes or open mouths. *Oh, shit.*

"Unnatural," someone whispered.

"Can't be good," said another.

Then the chaos began. The Coven witches squawked and pushed in their attempts to leave the parlor and escape before the house came down upon them and the abomination who lived there.

Aerin nearly flew to the door and jerked it open as their guests rushed outside into the fresh air and supposed safety. Claire brought up the rear, following Gwen, who paused just outside the door. "This kind of evil can't be allowed to exist," she hissed.

Claire snorted. "If that little baby is anything, she's an angel."

Gwen straightened. "Try to hide it all you like, but I saw her steal Justine's soul. Nothing you can say will convince me otherwise. I shouldn't need to remind you, but angels don't steal souls."

"Fuck off," Aerin said and promptly closed the door in Gwen's face.

❈ 33 ❈

With the last of the guests gone, Claire and Aerin turned toward the parlor just as Moira hurried down the stairs as fast as she could considering she had a full-size basketball in her stomach. "What in the hell just happened? The vibrations I was getting upstairs were muddier than a crawdad's poop chute."

Aerin shrugged. "Overall, I think things went rather well. The party ended right on time."

She strode into the parlor, and Claire and Moira were quick to follow.

Tierra hugged little Violet tightly to her chest as tears streamed down her face. Aunt Justine soothingly patted her back. "It will be okay. They'll get over it."

Moira put hands on both her hips. Her ocean-blue tank slid higher up her abdomen until her belly completely poked out, and she glared at her sisters. "From the looks of Tierra, I'd say things didn't go right at all."

Aerin lifted a brow and regarded Moira's exposed tummy. "I know times are tough, but I bet we could shop for maternity clothes somewhere online."

Moira glanced down at her protruding stomach. "Why? It would be a waste since I'm fixin' to push this puppy out any day. And stop tryin' to change the subject. I wanna know what happened."

"The shower was a big, freakin' disaster," Claire said, and Tierra cried harder.

Aunt Justine shot a look of reproach toward them. "You're not helping."

Tierra drew a knuckle beneath her eye, wiping away tears. "They hate Violet. They called her an abomination."

Moira gasped and then looked from Claire to Aerin and back again. "Say it ain't so."

Claire sighed. "We had a few issues. A few, slightly problematic issues. It seems Violet has taken after her father and can steal souls."

"Took Aunt Justine's right in the middle of the party," Aerin added.

Moira's eyes grew wide, even as a smirk creased one side of her mouth. "You don't say."

Aunt Justine chided them with a grunt. "She didn't really. That was a joke."

Claire snorted and shook her head. "It was no joke. She had you swirling around the ceiling."

Aerin nodded to confirm. "You don't remember any of it?"

Aunt Justine put a hand to her throat. "I...I... Oh, my stars. I do remember feeling lightheaded and like the room was spinning, but the same thing happens when I stand up too fast."

"Except you weren't standing," Claire added.

Tierra hugged her baby tighter until Violet squeaked a complaint.

Moira strode to Tierra and held her arms open to Violet. "Come see Auntie Moira."

Violet reached for her, and Moira scooped her up and propped her on a hip, while Tierra wiped her eyes. Violet placed a small hand on Moira's stomach, and her cheeks pushed out in a wide grin.

"That's right," Moira said. "You love your little cousin, don't you, and he'll be here soon, and the two of you can catch lightning bugs and chase frogs all the live long day."

Moira switched her gaze to the adults in the room. "If those dusty-crotch lemon-sucking biddies have a problem with this little one, I can only imagine what they'll think of what I got cookin'. Don't matter, though, Tierra. We got everything we need in this house, and if they want to throw a hissy-fit, we'll let little Violet steal all their souls."

Tierra blinked wet lashes and sniffed. "That's not all. Violet burped. Aerin freaked out and tossed her."

"I didn't toss her," Aerin interjected. "I gave her back to you. In a hurry. She burped, and I thought she was going to puke all over me."

Tierra sent her a look of disagreement. "That doesn't mean you can just throw her."

Aerin glanced from Violet to Tierra. "I'm sorry. I...I panicked."

Things were rapidly declining between her sisters, and Claire felt the need to intervene fast. "Long story short. Aerin caught Tierra by surprise when she handed over Violet, but instead of falling to the floor, Violet sprouted adorable, little white wings and flew, which sent the witches into a panic, and they all rushed out of here. The end."

Moira raised her brows high enough to wrinkle her forehead and gazed down at Violet. "You flew in front of them?"

Violet giggled.

Aerin lifted a forefinger. "You're forgetting about Gwen's threats at the end."

"Her threats?" Tierra cried.

Claire shot Aerin a look that said she wasn't helping matters. "No one cares what Gwen thinks."

"Some do," Tierra argued. She exhaled a shaky breath. "There's worse than that, too."

Her statement surprised Claire and apparently Aerin as well.

Tierra looked toward Aerin. "Your gift. I don't know if you meant it as a joke or what. But if so, it wasn't funny."

Moira frowned. "What in the Sam hill are you talkin' about?"

Tierra reached for the small box from Moira and Aerin. "You gave Violet a piece of brimstone."

Aerin strode forward and thrust out her hand. "What the shit?"

Tierra dropped the small box into her hand and then shooed Aerin away from her.

Aerin took several steps and then carefully opened the box. Her eyes widened in horror, and she quickly snapped the box shut. "I promise you that is not what we got Violet."

Moira shook her head. "No, ma'am. It was one of them Tiffany rattles, only Aerin and I fixed it up with a teething spell."

Claire glanced at her aunt and sisters. "Someone must have switched them out. But who?"

Killian strode into the room. "I've stayed away from the hen party and minded my own business as long as I could. My guess is Lucy brought the brimstone."

Tierra hurried to Moira and pulled Violet into her arms. "What do you mean, Lucy? She wasn't in the house."

Killian folded massive arms across his chest. "That's what I originally thought, too. I sensed her a couple of times and figured she was nearby somewhere. But she's pretty much wasted into nothing, so I wasn't too concerned."

Tierra inhaled a sharp breath. "Not concerned? How could you not worry about our child?"

Killian moved to her side and spread one wing around his woman and baby. "I'll never let anything happen to you or Violet, okay? We've proven you're immortal, and with my blood flowing through Violet, she is, too. You can't die, and if someone were to take either one of you, I'd search to Hell and back to find you."

Tierra blinked wet lashes several times and leaned into him.

He lifted Violet from her mother's arms, held her close to his to face, and grinned. "Look at you stealing souls already. Papa's proud of you."

Violet cooed, obviously a daddy's girl.

Aerin rolled her eyes. "Now that we have all that sappy bullshit out of the way, we need to think about what the hell we're going to do with Lucy. Her reign is over, and she needs to come to an end. I say the sooner, the better."

Claire couldn't agree more. "Let's give Tierra today to settle. The rest of us can think overnight and meet tomorrow with possible solutions."

Moira brightened. "I could cook up some jambalaya for dinner tomorrow night. I promise you'll love it."

Aerin regarded her water witch sister. "As long as no frog's legs are involved."

❧ 34 ❧

Dru woke the next morning to find Claire slumbering next to him, his arm draped across her waist, and he smiled. Their naked bodies fit together like two halves of a whole.

He couldn't believe almost a year had passed since he'd first caught sight of her at the airport. She'd been so attractive...and also his target. He'd been born to kill her.

He wondered if she'd known that day how lethal he was and how many men he'd killed, if she would have confronted him as she had, or if she would have high-tailed it out of there.

Wouldn't have mattered, he decided. He would have tracked her down until he got what he wanted. Fortunately, what he ended up wanting was *her*.

He couldn't imagine what life would be like if he'd listened to his head instead of his heart. He wouldn't be bonded to her as he was, he forever hers, and she forever his.

Hell, he couldn't have imagined having a woman in his life period. Now, here they were entwined after a heated night, where their bodies and hearts had melded them into one.

Claire stirred, and he quickly closed his eyes, lest

she catch him with emotional tears in his eyes. *War* did not cry.

She trailed a fingertip across his thick forearm, and he struggled to keep from reacting to the rush of power he received from her touch. She'd told him once how hard it had been for her to grow up without family. A lost orphan who'd searched desperately for someone to love her.

And Dru had found her, bringing an end to loneliness for both of them.

Yes, he'd had his Horsemen brothers, along with countless women who temporarily filled the void. He'd seen and done many things throughout the centuries, but none of it compared to how Claire filled that bottomless ache in his soul.

She lifted a finger to his lips and lightly traced them. Resulting shivers coursed through his veins and left him hard with need.

Unable to pretend sleep any longer, he cracked an eyelid. "What are you up to, fire witch?"

"Nothing," she replied in a teasing tone that still held the dregs of sleep.

Dru shifted, slipping a muscular thigh between her legs and against the warmth of her core. She squirmed, and he sighed with satisfaction as he propped himself up on one elbow.

Her gaze traveled to the tribal tattoo on his bicep, and her finger followed. She drew along the thick black lines, rekindling the low fire smoldering in his veins.

"Am I immortal, Dru?"

Her question jerked him from the sexy place his mind had wandered, and he resented the distraction. Her thoughts, on the other hand, appeared to be somewhere other than her bedchamber and him.

She frowned. "Exactly how long will I live, Dru? We're bonded, so does that make me immortal like Tierra?"

Hell if he knew. "Uh..."

"I don't feel any different," she said, not waiting for more of a response from him. "So maybe I'm not. Though Killian had said Tierra wouldn't have known either if her life hadn't been challenged."

She shifted her gaze to him, and he worked to formulate an answer that would satisfy her. "Truth is, I don't know."

She huffed her frustration. "Then how do I find out? I need to know, Dru, and I need to know now. We're burning a course straight for the Apocalypse, and I would be helpful to know if I could die or not."

He cupped her chin and kissed her gently on the lips. "I wish I knew, too. I waited so long to find you and can't live without you. But this is all new to me."

She drew her brows together. "There must be a way to find out."

He snorted. "Short of receiving a deadly blow of some kind and having you die or not, there is no quick way."

She caught his gaze and gave a small shake of her head. "How am I supposed to judge what risks I take when the last Seal is broken?"

He smiled. "That's easy. Take no risks. Let me take them for you."

She began to argue, but he trapped her mouth with a kiss. Instantly, the spark between them ignited. It caught hold and burst into massive flames inside him.

Her fire. Gods, he loved her fire.

He kissed her until she was breathless, and he burned with need.

She inhaled a deep breath. "You remind me of a tiger."

He chuckled. "A tiger? Never been compared to a cat before."

Claire smiled. "You're fierce and strong. Smart and

cunning. If you have an enemy in your sights, he won't likely get away."

Dru snorted. "Likely? You mean never. I always complete my missions."

And that was a fact.

She studied his face and grinned. "Except me. I got away."

A flash of fire, *her fire*, grew the flames into an inferno. "Only because you bewitched me. And, I might add, you only temporarily got away. In case you haven't noticed, you're trapped in my lair right now."

She laughed and drew her hands over his powerful shoulders, sending a frisson of powerful sensations rushing through him. "Uh, excuse me, but I believe you are in my lair. This is my house."

He pushed hair from her shoulder and laid a kiss on her sweet flesh. "Only because you blew mine up."

She sent him a look of sarcasm that he found entertaining. "Manresa Castle wasn't yours," she said.

Dru slipped the sheet down and exposed her breasts. Her nipples pebbled and begged for his touch. "The cabin was mine," he said, his focus turning elsewhere.

A growl, fueled by intense need, rumbled from deep in his throat. Unable to deny himself the pleasures before him, he claimed a nipple with his mouth, and he swore her eyes rolled back from pleasure.

"Sorry about your cabin, but really, that was your fault," she said breathlessly.

He paused for a breath. "Mmm-hmm."

Holding her gaze, he slid a hand down her thigh and brushed her nether regions.

She tensed in response. "Are you trying to distract me from our conversation?"

Damn straight. "Distraction should never be underestimated when planning an attack."

He slipped his fingers inside her, and her groan of pleasure nearly undid him.

"Is this an attack, Mr. War?" she whispered.

He hovered above her, maintaining a position of power, but they both knew who was in charge. "It's an all-out war, if that's what it takes."

He held her gaze and pressed his manhood against her. "Are you prepared to surrender, my fierce warrior?"

She grinned and shook her head. "Never surrender."

Dru lifted his brows, enjoying their teasing. "Never?"

He pressed closer, and she lifted her hips.

He took her response as an invitation and buried himself inside her. She gasped and squeezed his shoulders with her fingertips.

"I'll never tire of that," she whispered.

He paused, sheathed to the hilt and whispered an ancient expletive that didn't come close to explaining the fierce emotion their joining drew from him.

She took his cheeks in her hands and tugged him closer. He lowered his weight to his forearms, bringing himself close enough to feel her breath on his face. Her expression of love and passion mirrored what burned in his heart, and she kissed him with sensuous lips that would forever own him.

He could not, would not deny her anything.

His heart thundered in his chest as he rested on one arm and claimed her breast with his other hand. He massaged her soft mound and pinched her nipple. She tightened in response around him, and he growled. "Felt that."

She gave him a dazed smile. "Did you now?"

He smiled, savoring this moment together.

She arched against him and pushed at his hips with her hands as though to move him. "Don't you want to feel that again?"

More than he could say, but her body wasn't enough.

He wanted all of her. "You must surrender, Claire. Surrender your life and love only to me. Always."

Curiosity lit in her eyes. "I already pledged myself to you when we bonded."

"Yes, but I want to hear again that we'll always belong to each other."

A softness fell over her features. She placed her mouth against him and kissed him. Without moving away, she whispered. "I surrender to you, my love. Always and forever."

That was all he needed. He slid out and pushed deep inside again, over and over, until she cried out from the pleasure. *"Oh, Goddess."*

He thrust harder. "It's not the Goddess who's making love to you."

She gripped his shoulders hard and accepted him again and again. "No, but I'm forever grateful that she sent me to you."

He ceased talking then, and she must have lost herself in the pleasure of their joined bodies. Blinding white bliss grew to a crescendo. Suddenly, her body convulsed around him once again. He growled with pleasure and plunged forward to find his own satisfaction.

Pounding on their bedroom door brought their lovemaking to a screeching halt, with him only seconds away from achieving the ultimate bliss.

Dru growled his frustration. *"What the fuck do you want?"*

Death opened the door, took in the sight before him. "Sorry, man. Sexy times are over. We've got a fucking mob outside, and I need your help."

At that moment, if his brother Horseman wasn't immortal, Dru would have killed him.

✻ 35 ✻

Dru cursed Killian's interruption, and Claire held back a smile, feeling only slightly bad that Dru hadn't found ecstasy like she had. Poor man. She silently vowed make it up to him later.

Killian grinned. "I need your help, man."

Dru shook his head and tugged the sheet over Claire. "Get Nick to help you and leave me alone with my woman."

Death acknowledged Claire with a nod.

She smiled in return. Despite the fact that Death broke hearts daily when he stole loved ones from friends and family, she admired the man and the way he cared for Tierra and their baby.

Killian flicked his gaze to Dru. "Sorry, but Nick's not here."

Dru turned over fully in bed, not bothering to cover himself. "Where the hell is he?"

Killian shrugged. "Moira's craving turducken and some...boudin sausage thing. He's gone on the hunt looking for it."

Dru scoffed. "We're facing the end of the world, and Nick's out looking for turducken? What the ever-living fuck?"

Death shook his head as though he commiserated

with Nick. "You don't understand. You think battling a hundred demons is bad, try living with a pregnant woman craving something ridiculous, who absolutely won't take no for an answer. Tierra ate bacon for hell's sake."

Dru slid his gaze to Claire, and she recognized a hint of fear in his expression.

She laughed. "Don't worry. I have no plans of getting pregnant anytime soon, if ever."

Dru scrubbed the stubble on his chin and climbed out of bed. He reached for the jeans he'd left in a pile on the floor next to Claire's lacy red bra. "Why can't you take care of them yourself?"

Killian thumbed over his shoulder. "If it's left up to me, there will be bodies in the street outside the house. Pretty sure Tierra would have my hide for that."

Probably, Claire thought. But Tierra would have to understand if the crowd left them no choice. "Won't Dru kill them, too?"

Dru slid a black t-shirt over his head, and Claire watched with appreciation as the fabric hugged his muscles. "Not necessarily. I could send them home bruised and beaten if I wanted."

She supposed that made sense. "Then I guess Julian is out of the question, too."

Killian lifted his hands in defeat. "Again, hundreds of bodies dead in the street."

The actual number of people he mentioned caught Claire by surprise, and worry burrowed deep into her heart. "Hundreds? Really? I don't hear them."

"That's the weird thing," Killian said. "They're being all respectful and shit. I don't get it, and I don't trust it. That's why I need my buddy there as a backup."

He'd have more than one person there. There was no way she was going to miss this, either.

Claire circled her finger in the air. "Turn around, Killian. I'm coming, too."

He nodded toward the doorway to her bedroom. "I'll wait out there."

Before Killian had finished closing the door, Claire was out of bed, reaching for her own pair of jeans.

Dru regarded her with a cautious look. "I don't suppose you'd stay in the house if I asked."

She pulled a black silky tee from her closet and slid it over her head. "Nope."

He nodded solemnly. "You still have access to my sword if you need it, you know."

Claire wiggled her nails in a wave motion, and fire shot from each tip. "I can take care of myself."

Dru held up her red bra. "Aren't you forgetting something?"

She rolled her eyes. "Don't have time for that right now. Let's go."

He gave her the once-over. "Okay, *Moira*. But if I see even one dude checking you out, he's dead."

And she knew he meant it. A drawback to bonding with a Horseman, she supposed.

They descended the stairs and met Killian. Something brushed against Claire's leg, and she looked down to find Kai had joined them as well, always her fierce little protector. He rubbed against her, and she sensed his concern. She reached for him and pulled him close against her chest. "It's okay, buddy. Nothing to worry about."

Before Dru could reach for the front doorknob, Aerin called out as she hurried down the stairs, wearing light blue silk pajamas. "Have you guys looked outside? What the shit is going on?"

Killian lifted his chin in greeting. "We're about to find out."

She regarded the three of them. "Then I'm coming, too."

Killian and Dru opened the door, blocking Claire's view. On purpose, she was sure, because it also blocked the crowd's view of her and Aerin, thereby protecting them.

A chorus of cheers raised into the atmosphere, like angels praising the heavens, and Claire shared a questioning look with Aerin.

"What the hell?" Killian said, sounding bemused.

Dru and Killian stepped out onto the porch and scanned the crowd. "I don't see any weapons," Dru said.

Claire and Aerin pushed out behind them. "Can't sense anything evil, either," Claire said, but Kai bristled in her arms.

Dru strode to the edge of the porch and down the steps. "What's going on?" he said in a loud voice to the growing crowd. "Why are you all here?"

A bunch of people spoke at once, drowning out each other's words.

Aerin leaned close to Claire. "Do you feel it? The calm peacefulness in the air?"

After months of Port Townsend declining into the dark depths of despair, the world seemed somehow lighter. Claire looked to the sky, and the brilliant rays of sun caused her eyes to water. She nodded. "I feel it, but I don't trust it. Neither does Kai."

Aerin agreed with a quick nod. "Agreed. It's a little too peaceful. Too hopeful."

Dru cast a quick glance back toward Killian and then proceeded to the front gate. The cheers grew louder, and Dru leaned to talk to a woman and man both garbed completely in white. He nodded a few times and turned.

The bewildered expression on his face as he returned to them puzzled Claire. The second he stepped onto the porch, she hurried to him. "What is it? What do they want?"

He puffed up his cheeks and blew out a breath. "They want to see Violet."

"What?" Aerin exclaimed. "No fucking way."

"Apparently, some in the Coven spread the word that Violet has white wings," Dru continued. "Now, people believe she's an angel, here to light the way for the second coming of the Lord. I think they want to worship her."

The four of them stared at each other for a long moment. Then Killian cleared his throat. "She's an angel, all right, and worthy of their worshiping, but she's here to bring about the Apocalypse, along with Moira's baby. They're not going to like it when they learn that part."

Dru whispered a string of cuss words. "We need a meeting. Right now. Between the eight of us. Can't wait until evening. Someone call Nick and tell him to get his ass back here."

Aerin's eyes grew wide. "I hope you all understand that something big has shifted in the world. Likely caused by Violet's arrival. While it seems all rosy and shit, I believe we've entered the eye of the hurricane."

36

C laire waited in the secret room in the attic, entertaining little Violet while her parents took a brief rest until Nick returned. No one needed to tell Claire that parenthood wasn't all it was cracked up to be. Long nights with no sleep didn't appeal to her at all.

Kai rested next to the door, keeping guard Claire supposed.

Violet grew nearly as fast as Moira's baby. Born only a few weeks ago, Violet now looked more like a toddler and had no trouble sitting upright.

Claire bounced the fussy baby on her hip while she pointed out various jars of herbs and crystals resting on a bookshelf in the room. She pointed to a six-inch purple tower gemstone pointed toward the sky. "This is an amethyst. It's violet like you," she said in a sing-song voice.

The little girl quieted and widened her violet eyes to stare at the stone.

Encouraged, Claire continued. "Did you know that purple and violet represent the future, imagination and dreams? Just like you."

Violet turned her gaze to Claire in wonder.

An odd feeling of connection ran straight through Claire, and she pondered the meaning for a moment.

"You understand everything I'm saying, don't you? You might not be talking yet, but you're fully aware of what's happening around you."

Violet grinned and clapped her pudgy hands together.

Maybe children weren't so bad after all.

Claire shifted her gaze to the fist-sized rose quartz ball displayed on another shelf. "Would you like to try playing ball?"

"Baa," Violet said.

Claire blinked in surprise. "Oh, shit. I hope that wasn't your first word. Don't tell your mommy or daddy. They'll be so disappointed that it wasn't one of them."

Violet's cheeks grew pinker, and she grinned.

Claire hugged her. "You're just a cute little thing, aren't you? Wait until you get older, and Auntie Claire will teach you all kinds of things like how to ride a bike, a real one, and how to throw knives. All kinds of important stuff."

Things her mother wouldn't need to know about.

Claire retrieved the rose quartz and carried the small child toward an ancient wooden chest. She set her down, anchoring her against the chest, and tucked her frilly, rose-print dress so it would be out of the way. Violet complied when Claire pushed her feet outward for balance. "Okay, you sit here, and I'm going to sit across from you."

Violet didn't squawk even once.

Claire sat on the hardwood floor with her legs open and her feet touching Violet's so that they formed a diamond shape. This way, the gemstone ball couldn't escape. "I'm going to roll it to you, and then you roll it back to me, okay?"

She hoped the little girl understood and that the quartz wasn't too heavy to push.

Gently, Claire sent the ball rolling in Violet's direction. Violet released a squeal of delight. She caught it and quickly pushed it back to Claire.

"You are such a smart girl. Your mom is going to have her hands full with you."

They rolled it back and forth several times, and each time it was Violet's turn, she giggled. When she rolled it the next time, however, the ball didn't make it to Claire, but ended up hitting their shoes where they met. "That's all right, Violet. I can get—"

Before Claire could finish her sentence, the ball rotated and rolled in her direction. She caught it and eyed the little girl. "Very clever girl. Does your mom know you can do that?"

Violet only smiled.

Claire held out her arms, and Violet crawled to her. "I guess if you're capable of stealing Aunt Justine's soul, then moving a ball isn't any big deal."

The moment the words left her mouth, inspiration struck. Violet had taken Aunt Justine's soul... So, did that mean it was possible that she could do the same with Claire's? If so, that had to be considered dying, didn't it?

If Violet was able to take her soul, then Claire would know she wasn't immortal. The question burning in her soul would be answered.

Plus, odds were that she wouldn't ultimately stay dead because Violet would probably play with her spirit like she had with Aunt Justine's. And Killian certainly wouldn't accept it. Dru would never forgive him if he did.

She pondered the idea for several moments, and then decided that it might be irresponsible to leave her lifeless body with a child who could get into all kinds of trouble if she wanted.

What she needed was a co-conspirator. Someone to watch over everything.

Kai lifted his head and sniffed the air as though sensing her plan.

She snorted. He certainly wouldn't help her.

And she knew damn well no one else in the house would be willing to take the small, very teeny, tiny chance that she might not be able to re-inhabit her body.

And that was only if she died at all.

And now she had a mostly-solid plan to prove her immortality one way or the other, with only a small risk. Some would call her crazy for even attempting it, but she'd always lived life on the edge.

Claire stood and scooped up Kai. He protested when she set him outside the door and closed it. She snatched a notepad from the antique writing desk and quickly jotted down her plans and wishes to see her soul rightfully returned should Violet manage to extract it.

She slipped the phone from her pocket and texted Aerin, asking her to come to the attic in five minutes. Her experiment shouldn't take any longer than that. And if Violet did remove her soul, five minutes wasn't long enough for her body to reject it when Aerin told her to put it back.

Claire scooted until they were both propped against the old trunk. "Violet, I need you to do something for me. Do you remember how you took Aunt Justine's soul?"

Violet giggled and nodded her head several times. Claire hoped her nodding was from understanding and not excitement.

She looked the little girl straight in the eyes. "I want you to do that to me. Do you understand?"

The cheerfulness slipped from Violet's face, and her expression turned serious.

"Just take out my soul," Claire said in encouragement. "And then if you can also put it back, that would be great."

Violet continued to stare, and Claire kept her gaze trained on the child's purple eyes.

Do it, she thought. *Do it*.

Knowing if one was immortal or not was nothing to be trifled with. If she couldn't die, then that changed everything.

The door to the attic burst open, causing Claire to shriek and Violet to wail. Dru strode in looking wild-eyed and angry with Kai hot on his tail. "What the hell is going on here?"

Kai marched forward and stared at her with accusing eyes.

Claire pulled the crying child to her chest. "Look what you did? You made Violet cry. You big bully."

She kept her head down, unable to look Dru or Kai in the eye for fear she'd give herself away.

Dru crouched next to them. "Claire. Look at me. Tell me what you were doing and don't lie because I'll know."

She steeled her gaze and tilted her face upward. "I was playing with Violet until you barged in."

"No," he said in a commanding tone. "You were in danger."

She wrinkled her brows in disagreement. "Violet wouldn't hurt me, and there's no one else here."

"Tell. Me."

She huffed and turned Violet toward her so she could pat her back. "Fine. I thought maybe Violet could try to temporarily borrow my soul like she did with Aunt Justine. If she managed it, then I would know if I'm immortal or not."

Dru shook his head in disbelief. "Are you insane, woman?"

She frowned at his insult. "No, I am not. No harm came to Aunt Justine when it happened, and I have a safety measure in place."

Just then, Aerin appeared in the doorway. "If you're

wanting me to take a turn babysitting, sorry. Children and I have a mutual dislike."

Violet sniffed and turned to Aerin. Her face immediately split with a huge smile, though tears still stained her cheeks.

Claire frowned at Dru but answered Aerin. "No, I wasn't going to ask you to watch her. I needed your help with something, but Dru showed up instead."

Dru held her gaze, his own expression supremely unhappy.

Aerin's phone rang, startling Claire all over again. Aerin answered and then shifted her gaze to Dru and Claire. "Nick's back. I'll get Tierra and Killian and meet you guys downstairs."

Claire headed for the door, but Dru blocked her way. "Promise me that you'll never attempt anything like that again."

She huffed in disgust as Kai pressed hard against her leg as though admonishing her, too. "I can't live my whole entire life not knowing if it is my entire life."

"And you won't have to," Dru said. "But it might take ten years before you realize you're aging or not."

"Ten years? Think of all the crazy things I'm going to miss while riding my bike."

He snorted and shook his head. "Promise me."

She stared at him for a long moment and then sighed. "Fine. I promise not to ask Violet to steal my soul again. Now, let's get downstairs. We have more important issues at hand."

Though she wasn't about to promise that if another viable opportunity presented itself, she wouldn't take it.

37

By the time Nick arrived, the crowd outside had lost their patience and the ability to maintain the peace. Cries of *Angel Baby* echoed into the house as the four Horsemen and four elemental witches gathered in the parlor. The Horsemen, with the exception of Killian, remained standing, while Claire and her sisters sat.

Claire had returned Violet to her mother, and she'd dozed within minutes. The precocious baby lay sleeping in her mother's arms, oblivious to the commotion outside, all because of her. Killian sat next to Tierra, holding them both closely.

Worry glistened in Tierra's expression as she glanced to each of the occupants in the room. "I don't like this. Not one bit. I don't feel Violet's safe."

Killian hugged her tighter. "She's safe here, my gazelle. Look around you. The power that resides in this room is unmatched by anything they have out there."

Moira crossed her arms protectively over her belly. "I agree with Tierra. They're creepier than a two-headed clown. I can handle the negativity we've been living with. But back home, when someone started bein' all nice and stuff, that's when I knew it's best to beware."

Nick dropped a hand to Moira's shoulder, and she leaned her head against him. "I don't have the patience for this madness. Dru and I have taken out bigger armies. I say we let loose and dispense with them."

Julian shook his head. "This is not a matter of conquering the believers, Nicholas. Aerin and I discussed this at length upstairs. We believe the issue is that Lucy has lost a significant amount of her power, which has left the world unstable. The last time any of us saw Lucy, she'd lost half her face and was barely more than a corpse."

Aerin stood and took Julian's gloved hand. "With the world having very little dark power now, the light has tipped the scales. While light might seem better than dark, a world out of balance is detrimental either way. If we dispense with everyone outside, others will replace them."

She pointed at Moira. "We need that baby now, too."

Moira rubbed her stomach. "You're preachin' to the choir on that score. I feel like ten pounds of possum crammed into a two-pound sack."

Dru claimed Aerin's space on the couch and draped an arm around Claire. "Maybe we need something to induce labor. If he gets any bigger, Moira's gonna burst."

Moira sighed and dropped her head. "Been trying everything I can think of to break my water, but nothing's workin'. I thought about asking Uncle Sal to take me out on his boat when the water is really rough."

Nick shook his head. "Not happening."

Claire shot her a sympathetic smile. "If anyone could cause her water to break, a water witch should be able to."

"Unless," Julian said, "the baby can't be on earth at the same time as Lucy. Maybe he has to wait for her departure before he can completely enter this realm."

Nick walked to the cabinet and poured a glass of

scotch. He downed it in one swallow and refilled the glass. "Looks like we have one option. Remove Lucy from this planet."

Tierra frowned. "I thought you guys weren't supposed to say her name. That doing so would draw her attention."

Killian shook his head. "With as diminished as she is now, I doubt she can do much more than crawl. Even if she could hear us, she wouldn't be a threat. Her reign is over."

Tierra shook her head. "You say that, but someone switched out Aerin and Moira's gift and replaced it with brimstone. You're the one who said it was Lucy. She has to have some power, or one of the Coven is working against us and with her. No one was hurt, but I feel like it was a warning. We need to be careful."

Claire considered Tierra's thoughts. "Maybe Lucy somehow convinced another witch to do her bidding. It wouldn't be the first time. Or maybe she overtook someone's body like she did with our sister."

Aerin eyed the group. "We definitely need a plan to get rid of her. Then if there's still a threat remaining with one of the Coven members, we'll move on to that."

Moira shifted and then rubbed her belly where it protruded from her tank top. "If we could somehow get her inside the Standing Stones, I bet she'd be even weaker there."

Claire liked the idea, but... "She's not dumb enough to go there. The bait to lure her in would have to be something she's desperate for."

Aerin turned to Tierra and focused on the baby sleeping in her arms. "I think she might risk it if she could gain control of Violet."

"No!" Killian and Tierra said in unison, and Killian jumped to his feet.

Julian looked to his brother Horseman. "Hang on a

minute, Killian. Let's consider this more fully. Obviously, we're not going to put Violet's life in danger."

Insight blew through Claire's mind. "No, but there is the portal between the Stones and our mother's room upstairs. Lucy can't enter that room."

Tierra tilted her head to the side. "So, you're thinking of luring her there with Violet, but Violet doesn't stay. She goes immediately through the portal to the room."

"That's an interesting idea," Aerin said.

Moira blinked in surprise. "I can't believe y'all are considering it, Tierra."

Tierra flashed a quick look in her direction. "Then you obviously don't know how badly I want Lucy gone. Until then, Violet will never be safe. Your baby won't be either."

Nick agreed. "Lucy will go after Violet until she no longer has breath in her lungs. If she has Violet on her side, she'll be unstoppable."

Moira lifted a questioning gaze to Nick. "If y'all think she's weak, how could she even consider attempting this?"

"She'll grab another body," Dru said. "Just like when she took over Aerin. She doesn't have much strength physically, but I'm sure she's still mentally capable. Another reason why we need to eliminate her before she figures out a way to get stronger."

Tierra nodded solemnly. "If we were to somehow get the word out that I'll be going there with Violet, to go visit my mother's grave..."

Killian growled his disapproval. "The only way you'll go is if I fly you and Violet there. I'm not letting you out of my sight."

Aerin shrugged. "I don't think that would scare Lucy away. Not if she wants Violet bad enough."

"I agree," Tierra said.

Seemed like a brilliant plan to Claire. "You and Killian go, but the rest of us women will wait just inside the portal. You arrive, pass the baby to us *mortals.*" She was really beginning to hate that word. "Moira can hold Violet and protect both babies. Aerin and I will be close by, doing what we can to fight her, too."

Julian nodded, excitement glowing in his eyes. "Nick, Dru and I will wait a fair distance from the Stones, but not so far that we can't get there quickly. If Lucy shows, she'll have to reckon with all five of us. An impossible feat, I'm sure."

Moira studied the rest of the group, and Claire could see she still had reservations. "I think we should all consider what might possibly go wrong before we agree to do this."

Nick squeezed her shoulder. "Thinking like a Conqueror now."

Claire wracked her brain for anything they might have missed. "I think it sounds pretty solid. Aerin? Tierra?"

Aerin shrugged. "I'm on board."

Tierra nodded. "Seems good to me. I can use Aunt Justine to put the word out. I'll say I'm taking Violet to her grandmother's grave. Aunt Justine never could keep her mouth closed, and I'm certain Lucy is still in contact with some from the Coven."

Dru scanned the room. "Solid battle plan. Let's make preparations."

❧ 38 ❧

The moment Killian lifted off from the widow's walk, carrying Tierra while she held little Violet, the sparks in Claire's nerves roared to life along with voices from the crowd outside. Though sunshine glared brilliantly upon Port Townsend, when Claire peeked through the portal to the Stones, everything was cloaked in deep shadows.

Calming scents of earth and flora filtered through to the room in the attic, belying the turmoil bucking beneath the surface. Claire scanned the faces of her two sisters. If anyone could take down the devil, it would be them and the Horsemen.

Their familiars also paced restlessly, nervously waiting what was to come, with the exception of Dr. Lecter who fluttered about the room, sending off waves of anxiety.

Claire released a long exhale, trying to slow her heart rate. "How long will it take for them to get there?" she asked quietly.

Aerin glanced at her watch. "No more than a couple of minutes, I'd guess."

Claire tapped a nervous foot on the floor. "There is the possibility that she might not show."

Though she prayed to the Goddess that Lucy would.

The whooshing of powerful wings stole their attention. "Killian," Aerin whispered.

A moment later, Tierra peeked through the opening and quickly passed her child to Moira, where she'd stay safe. Claire shoved the clothes-stuffed baby blanket meant to look like Violet into Tierra's arms. She met her gaze for a brief moment. "Good luck, sister."

Tierra gave her a confident nod and disappeared.

Aerin paced the room from side to side, waiting for Lucy to arrive, while Moira cooed and kissed little Violet.

Claire stayed close to the opening, listening for signs of Lucy so that she could send Dru a mind message and alert the other Horsemen to close in.

Aerin paused and released a heavy sigh. "This is going to drive me fucking insane. It's times like this that I wish I hadn't given up smoking."

Moira bounced Violet on her hip. "Try not to worry none. This little girl isn't worried, and you know how she can be when danger is around. She must have faith in her parents."

Claire shushed them. "I need to be able to hear."

She leaned her head closer to the opening and closed her eyes, hoping to give her other senses a greater advantage.

Something sharp tore through Claire's soul like a dragon breathing fire, and she gasped. She didn't need to hear Lucy to recognize the evil that lurked nearby. Claire jerked her gaze to her sisters, and they nodded. They'd sensed her, too.

Violet whimpered.

Aerin nodded to Claire. "Let's go."

Claire sent the message to Dru and grabbed her wand. Together, she and Aerin slipped through the portal.

But they didn't find Lucy in the circle of stones with Tierra and Killian.

Instead, Gwen stood, regal in all black, with her platinum hair tightly coiffed on her head. She held her arm out straight, with a manicured finger pointing directly toward Tierra and Killian. Tierra clutched the fake baby tightly to her chest.

"Don't you two move," Gwen called over her shoulder. "Or I will remove your sister and her precious baby permanently from this earth."

Her threat only angered Claire more. Lucy thought she had them fooled. The Devil had to know she was up against serious power. With the eight of them now united, they harnessed far more strength than Lucy, even with her inhabiting Gwen's body. "We know it's you, Lucy. We know you've taken over Gwen like you did Aerin. We sense your vile presence."

Lucy chuckled and flicked a gaze at Aerin and Claire. Bright yellow eyes burned in place of Gwen's icy blue ones, and Claire realized she'd also underestimated their opponent.

"Yes," Lucy said, her voice echoing, giving off vibes of power. "But I didn't have to force my way in. Gwen, the beautiful, graciously allowed me to take the driver's seat. She willingly gave her body to me like a good servant would, reviving my powers. I don't think she expected she'd lose so much of herself in the process, but that's hardly a concern now."

Maybe not for Lucy, but her power was of great concern to Claire. She tried to reach out and warn Dru, but her thoughts hit the Standing Stones and bounced back. That knowledge burned through Claire's confidence.

Lucy must have created a barrier of sorts. If it was strong enough to keep out the Horsemen, the rest of them might be in more danger than they'd realized.

Killian stepped forward so that he partially blocked

Tierra and drew Lucy's gaze away from the rest of them. "You're finished, Lucy. Your time on earth has ended."

"Certainly, you must sense that," Tierra added. "There's a new baby, about to be born, who will control the dark power in the world. Power that once belonged to you, does so no more."

"You've so little left now," Aerin added. "I know because I lived with you."

Claire put on a brave face and nodded in solidarity with her comrades. "Soon, you'll have none."

Lucy eyed each of them and then the baby-substitute in Tierra's arms. Then bright red lips peeled back from perfectly white teeth. "You think to trick me, don't you? You think I don't realize the baby is no longer here? You think I didn't already know about the dark one growing inside your sister, Moira? You're wrong."

Before any of them could respond, a violent wave of black bats surrounded them. Wings flapped in Claire's face and bodies slammed into her, causing her to shield her eyes, blink, and duck. She tried to see the others, but the bats blocked everything.

Moments later, when the attack stopped as suddenly as it had started, Claire sucked in a huge breath of air and realized her wand was missing. She glanced around and found Aerin and Killian as bewildered as she was.

Lucy had pinned Claire's wand beneath one foot and had a chokehold around Tierra's neck with the other. "You, of all people, Killian, should know not to mess with me," she hissed. "Or have you forgotten there's a reason the Four Horsemen of the Apocalypse have lived in fear of me for so long?"

Killian flicked his gaze between Tierra and Lucy but didn't respond.

Claire knew he was calculating his next move, and

she wished she could read his mind as well as Dru's. Killian wouldn't be worried about Tierra's life, so she wasn't sure why he held back. Maybe for her and Aerin's sake?

A rush of heat from behind warmed her, and she caught sight of Kai hurrying through the portal, his tail high in the air. A gentle flap of wings flew overhead, announcing Dr. Lecter. Jinx brushed her leg, and Claire experienced a huge sense of pride as little Cheeto passed all their familiars and walked bravely into the center of the stones with his curly little tail quivering with energy.

Moira must have sent their familiars in to help as well, and Claire silently thanked her sister for being so wise.

Lucy released a chuckle and then all-out laughed. She turned her gaze to Killian. "This is it? This is the army you think to use to defeat me? Has love addled your brain?"

Death opened his wings to their full breadth, sweeping bits of dust and leaves into the air. He gazed down at Lucy, every bit the formidable Horseman, causing Claire the slightest tremble. *Your reign is over.*

Tierra dropped the fake baby and whipped out her wand. Claire focused on the fire inside her until it was a swirling mass of flames. She was certain Aerin called upon her power as well, and the ground began to shake with Kai's fury.

Lucy glared at Killian. "Always remember, you brought this on yourself."

She uttered unintelligible words, and all hell broke loose.

Claire launched a fireball. Aerin's vicious wind thrust it at Lucy with a mighty force. Tierra's vines sprouted from the ground, twisting around Lucy's ankles.

Dr. Lecter tore at the Devil's hair, while Jinx jumped onto her back with claws out, and Cheeto shot off his own form of fireballs.

Lucy lifted her arms, deflecting their attacks and flinging vines and familiars into the air. Kai landed roughly at Claire's feet, fueling her rage.

Lucy directed her gaze at Tierra and a black mist shot from her fingers and straight into Tierra's heart.

Tierra gasped and fell to the ground.

A flare of panic gripped Claire, even as she reminded herself of Tierra's immortality. Killian flapped his wings, sending an unseen wall of power toward her, but the force of it bounced off Lucy and knocked everyone to the ground.

Lucy seemed to grow taller, and she focused her gaze on the ground. "I call all that is dark and powerful, the night and its shadows, the darkest of forests, the deepest of oceans, and the burnt embers of those who have passed, to give me all that is mine."

She thrust her hands outward, and the Standing Stones shuddered and shook. Pieces broke off and fell to the ground. The large slabs began to rock. Killian scooped up Tierra, and Aerin made a mad dash for the portal, with the bat, cat and little pig rushing along beside her.

Claire frantically searched for Kai and found him limp on the ground next to a large rock. She dove for him as Lucy's fury unleashed around them.

One of the Standing Stones fell and then another.

Claire wrapped her hands around Kai's still-warm body and stood. Through the gaping holes in the Standing Stones, she caught sight of three imposing figures galloping toward them on red, white and black magnificent horses.

Dru's thoughts slammed into her. *Run!*

Before she could, something impossibly heavy and

hard struck her in the head and brought her to the ground. Her vision blurred, and everything turned black.

$$\text{❧ } 39 \text{ ❧}$$

Hours later, Claire left the safe confines of the de Moray Mansion, carrying the lifeless body of her precious fox now wrapped in a red silk scarf. Untamed grief flowed like molten lava through her veins, boiling her blood and singeing her soul with a mark that would forever remain with her.

She'd woken not long ago, tucked in her bed, with a headache raging like an untamed forest fire. Dru had handed over her wand that he'd retrieved from the battleground, and then with a voice softer than she'd ever heard, he'd imparted that her faithful companion had not survived the crushing blow, one that she shouldn't have, either.

She'd proved her immortality but lost one of the true loves of her life. She couldn't imagine a tomorrow without him.

Claire headed toward the hillside where she intended to honor her precious familiar with her fire and cremate his remains.

Kai.

The thought of him brought a fresh wave of pain rolling over her.

Her familiar. Her baby. The one being who knew her very soul. The one who'd worshiped, no, loved her unconditionally. He'd been her constant companion, always keeping a watchful eye on her. There to protect her and love her as needed.

They could raise the Standing Stones, but nothing would bring her baby back.

Her heart folded in on itself, and a raw sob escaped her.

She'd taken his presence for granted. She'd naively thought he'd always be with her, and she hadn't truly cherished him like she should have.

Now, he was gone.

Forever lost to her, with memories of the love they shared left to haunt her every thought.

Dru and her sisters had offered to come with her to honor and bury him, but this was something she needed to do alone.

Heart-wrenching pain left her legs weak, but she pressed on.

When she reached the top of the hill, she gathered logs and tree limbs and created a pyre. She held Kai to her chest one last time and struggled to breathe past the crushing pain. "I love you, little buddy. Run free now and know that you'll forever be in my heart."

Claire squeezed her eyes shut, forcing tears down her cheeks, and she remained that way until she could catch her breath. Then she gently set his body on top of the pyre and took several steps back.

She lifted her hands, and the strength of her fire jumped to life. "Rest in peace, Kai," she whispered.

Unbridled anger and brutal grief exploded inside her, and a massive ball of fire jumped from her hands and landed on the pyre. Brilliant flames leapt into the night sky, sending red hot sparks swirling into the air.

She stared at the wildfire that grew bigger and bigger until it was a massive wall of flames that roared in the night, screaming out her fury.

When she was beyond exhausted, she fell backward

onto the grass and sobbed while the heat of the fire cradled her in its arms.

An hour later, the flames had died back. Little remained in its wake.

Claire rose and realized she hadn't brought anything to dig up soil to cover the ashes. She looked around for something that might help and then sensed a presence behind her.

She whirled, not sure if she would find friend or foe.

Tierra approached, walking softly on the grass, the bells on the bottom of her skirt tinkling softly. "Hey," she said.

Claire started to cry, and Tierra strode forward and wrapped her in an embrace. "I forgot a shovel," Claire said, her breath hitching.

Tierra stepped back. "Here, let me help you with that."

With a wave of Tierra's hand, dirt piled onto the burned mound, suffocating the remaining smoke and burying her beloved Kai's remains with dark, rich soil. "The circle of life," she whispered.

Claire nodded but couldn't speak.

They both stood silent for another few moments, and Claire allowed the softly blowing breeze to cool her cheeks.

Tierra squeezed her hand. "Aerin and Moira would have come, too, but it's not safe for them to be out of the house right now."

"I know," she said softly.

She blinked wet lashes and looked to her sister as another wave of grief rolled through her. "The Standing Stones."

They'd been destroyed, too.

Tierra gave a small smile. "They were built once a long time ago and can be built again."

Claire attempted a smile but failed. "Let's go home. I need to be with my family."

Tierra nodded and linked her arm through Claire's. "Everyone else is in the parlor. They're discussing what we'll do next. This vicious rampage of Lucy's will not go unanswered."

Claire shook her head, trying to hold back tears. "No, it won't."

Vengeance burned strong in Claire's veins. Lucy would pay with her life for what she'd done. Claire had immortality now, and nothing would stop her from extinguishing Lucy's presence from the earth.

When they arrived home, Tierra headed into the parlor, and Claire excused herself to freshen up. She needed a few minutes to gain what composure she could. She wasn't sure she could ever find the person that she'd been before Kai's death, but she'd cling to revenge until she found another source of strength to carry her forward.

In the bathroom, she splashed water on her face until her cheeks cooled. She opened the window, breathed several measured breaths of cool night air, and allowed sounds of the ocean to comfort her.

Then she steeled her heart.

Halfway down the stairs, she realized that the front door stood open, and everyone had congregated there. She frowned, not seeing anyone on the porch or any reason why the group talked excitedly.

Dru glanced over his shoulder as she approached. "Claire!"

He turned to face her, and she realized he held a beautiful red fox with a bottlebrush tail against his chest.

Her legs buckled beneath her, and she dropped to the stairs in disbelief. The moment the fox's eyes connected with Claire, he pushed from Dru's arms and dashed toward her.

She grabbed him, and her soul instantly connected

with his. "Kai?" she said half-laughing and half-crying as she brushed dirt from his fur. "What? How?"

Moira wiped tears from her own cheeks. "I guess he's your little phoenix fox risen from the ashes."

"That's a perfect description, Moira," Aerin said.

Claire cried happy tears this time as she petted him and kissed his head. "My little phoenix fox."

Moira suddenly bent forward and gasped, drawing everyone's attention.

Nick grabbed her to keep her from falling. "What's wrong, Moira?"

He glanced to the others with a panicked look on his face.

Moira breathed deeply and turned to them all. "The baby wants out, and he's gettin' pretty insistent, but my body won't release him. I'm not sure I can manage this for much longer."

Nick scooped her into his arms. "I'm going to take her to the bedroom and stay with her until she's settled, and then I intend to fucking conquer this town until I find Lucy and end her."

Claire looked up to find Dru watching, and she nodded. She would never have a happy life with this man and her fox until their enemy was destroyed. It would take all of them to achieve it, but the time had come to end Lucy or risk losing her sisters, her home, and possibly the world.

IV
AERIN

By Kerrigan Byrne

❧ 40 ❧

"I have a bad feeling about this," Tierra said as she tracked Aerin's marching progress across the ever-verdant lawns of the de Moray Mansion. "You look irate."

Aerin's ears pricked to the chime of Tierra's bangled wrists as she patted and bounced the fussy baby.

Claire finished wrapping the last lock of Moira's black cherry hair around a curling iron before she paused to look up. "You look *mad*. Real mad. Like, *hold on to your knickers, there's about to be a hurricane,* mad."

"You'd better stow that stirring wind until after the weddin'" Moira warned in a voice meant to carry over the diminishing distance between her and Aerin's advance.

Moira sat at a makeshift vanity constructed from a gilded mirror and rustic desk, dragged out of doors and propped in the gazebo that had become the *de facto* bride bower. A cobalt silk robe shimmered in the autumn sun, seeming to waterfall around her. The effect was only slightly hindered by the enormous belly she had to rest on her own lap, on top of which a plate of half-consumed pork cracklins surrounded a small lake of Louisiana hot sauce balanced.

The first absurd thought that burped through

Aerin's mind was that she could only imagine what poor Nick's first "you may kiss the bride" kiss would taste/smell like.

The second was evoked by the actual eruption from the infant's esophagus that competed with the concerning volcanic rumbles that were, even now, stirring noisily beneath Mount Baker, Mount Rainier, and Mount St. Helen's, respectively.

Forget the methane farting cows, vegans should start protesting the gasses emitted from a one, Violet de Moray.

With Tierra's layered sage gown flowing in the—admittedly—increasing breeze, and Claire's silky scarlet number draping from her hot curves, they looked like the elemental goddesses they were.

Aerin would have taken the time to appreciate the tableau...

If she were not so fucking pissed off.

With some deft sewing skills and no little bit of magic, Tierra had turned a circus-tent sized cream bolt of lace they'd found in the attic into a wedding dress. The gown hung from a railing beam above them, waiting to be donned once Moira's coiffeur was in place.

Aerin slapped the gown aside as she, quite literally, stormed up the steps, letting it swing like a pendulum back into place behind her.

"Irate?" She gritted from between teeth fury had fused together. "Mad?" The hairs at her neck prickled and crackled with dark, electric magic, and awareness of the entourage of four distinct men she trailed in her wake.

Dead men all, if she had anything to say about it.

"I get *irate* when Tierra laces my coffee with some peat moss tasting herbs for my health," she seethed. "I get *mad* when a shit-eating she-Satan wears my body like a meat suit and tosses me into the darkest corners of my own psyche. But *this*!"

She thrust the abomination forward for all of them to behold.

"There are no words for the rage. There have not been languages evolved upon this goddess-forsaken earth to encompass the *wrath* I am about to unleash...if..."

She could not finish the sentence. Words escaped her brain like scattered marbles. Her throat closed off.

Oh Goddess. It wasn't a cliché. You could *actually* be choked by rage.

Claire released the final perfect ringlet from the curling iron so Moira could turn to observe the carnage cradled in Aerin's hands.

Heavy boots announced the arrival of the cadre of men into the women-only gazebo without a by-your-leave. Of course, they went ahead and fucking barged in and made themselves at home. Because that was just the kind of primeval, barbaric, insolent ass clowns they were.

"Just what the *hell* have you four gone and done?" Moira demanded in a deceptively even voice.

"'T'wern't nothing, Moira Jo," hee-hawed a hillbilly from behind her. "All's I did was cut the heels of them alligator shoes so she wouldn't fall off 'em they's so high. She might sprain one of her delicate ankles." The cretin in question pulled up alongside Aerin, looking down at her ankle as if he might start gnawing on it at any moment.

If looks could wither a man, Aerin tried her best. "These shoes are Alexander McQueen alligator sling backs. They cost me eight hundred dollars on *sale*."

Even though the man had showered that very morning at the mansion, he still somehow managed to have a pall of engine grease on him. He went beet red. Then purple as he gawked up at her in open-mouthed astonishment.

Aerin counted two missing teeth before he regained his wits enough to talk.

"See now, this is why you need me," he said wagging a stumpy a finger at her. "I got all sortsa colors of gator skins back home. I think I even have some cobbler's nails somewhere." He tugged on his ear as if that could help him remember. "I coulda made you them shoes fer a fiver." He eyed her thoroughly. "Question unrelated to said nails: Is yer tetanus shot up to date? Nah, you don't have to answer. Classy gal like you, course you come vaccinated." He reached out to pat her arm approvingly, but Aerin shrunk away. "We'll talk about that later, on account of the government nanobot tracers y'all have swimming in yer blood now, though I suppose what with the apocalypse and everything that's sort of a non-issue—"

"Moira," Aerin clipped, feeling on the verge of a meltdown that would make Katrina seem like a spring breeze. "Your uncles Stinky, Salty, and Surly need to go back to their boat—"

"That's Sal, Mookey, Red, and Little Earl." Moira pointed to them in the line, identifying the shoe murderer as Mookey.

"I don't fucking care what their names are, Moira," Aerin exploded. "You tell them to keep their fucking hands off my shit before I—"

"Aww, don't be too sore at 'em," Moira said, hiding a smile behind her hand. "He was just trying to help. Besides, I think they got them a crush."

Didn't she fucking know it? They'd been her constant weird shadows since they'd decided to take up residence at the Manse yesterday in preparation for the wedding.

Tierra paused in her pacing to glance at Moira. "Don't you think it's a bit creepy, them being sweet on Aerin, seeing as how she looks exactly like you?"

From somewhere behind her, Red snorted, horked,

and spat his disagreement. "Y'all don't look a thing alike. She has class where Moira's got sass. And she's taller, for one."

"No she isn't," Tierra argued. "She's just usually in three-inch heels."

"Well, not the fuck anymore," Aerin bitched, waving the remnants of her beautiful, beautiful pumps.

"She has purty silver eyes and her skin ain't seen the sun like you, Moira," Red chimed in. "And her mouth has these...regal lines at the corners where they turn down on account of her scowlin' all the time."

"You take that back!" Aerin bent down to check the mirror for frown lines.

"And," Mooky decided to add. "She smells like that one time Pervus Mcfee tried to ferment all that vanilla moonshine in the cedar chest. Juss look at 'er," he held his hands one high and one low to frame her silver-blue Zuhair Murad slip gown and gauzy wrap. "She dresses real el-gant."

"Elegant?" Claire supplied helpfully.

"Glad y'all agree."

"Also," Red cut in, "Her tits are way up here." He hefted imaginary breasts past the "I got crabs at Boudreau's Fat Boy" slogan on what must have been his Sunday-best tank top.

"That's due to the gravity defying efforts of a very secretive Victoria," Claire snarked, biting the inside of her cheek to contain her giggles. "And Moira's lack of one."

Aerin whirled on him. "Listen here you slack-jawed yokel, if I catch you looking at my tits—"

"You can catch me at anything, my lady," He swiped his trucker hat from his balding pate and held it over his heart. "I'd wrangle a gater for one of your smiles." Red had taken to addressing them all directly as "my lady" as he figured a coven of powerful, Goddess-blessed witches as noble as any title-holding royal on the entire flat earth.

Just then, a hum of energy glided across Aerin's senses like a smooth, silken breeze feathering over naked flesh, which could mean only the arrival of one individual.

Julian Roarke approached looking alarmingly gorgeous in dark Brioni Vanquish Bespoke suit. He'd the stride of an immortal, languorous and long. His pale skin and Byzantine bone structure cut a sharp contrast to the dark hair shot through with threads of silver. His was not a brutal beauty, but a haunting one. She was instantly so struck and aroused by him, she almost forgot to be angry.

"Are you going to do anything about this?" she demanded of the Horseman.

One dark brow arched. "Is there a reason to?"

For a man who put Einstein, Plato, and Aristotle to shame, he could sure be a dumb-ass.

"They're hitting on your..."

His other eyebrow joined the first. "My what?"

They hadn't DTR'd, so to speak. Her inner feminist wouldn't allow her to say "your woman" even though she was. "Girlfriend" wasn't strong enough. Soulmate sounded trite and stupid. Wife...well she couldn't let her mind go there. And they hadn't technically soul-bonded yet. The "L" word was often said against a pillow in their more intimate moments.

Though not broached in public.

Amusement danced in his Baltic blue eyes. "While your coterie of knight's *errant* leave much to be desired in their comportment—and hygiene—their loyalty is commendable and their veneration of you unequivocally comprehensible. Moreover, if your affections toward me were endangered by them, we'd have more dire augury calamities than the impending Apocalypse to occupy us."

"If I find out you were just insultin' me..." Mookey shoved his sleeves up his forearms.

"I don't even think he's speaking American." Little Earl shook a mallet-sized fist at him.

Ignoring them, Julian said, "I've been sent to inform you ladies that the garden arch has been prepared, and we're ready to begin at the bride's convenience."

"Not without me," Sal jumped to. "I'm officiatin'." He leaned down to drop an air kiss on Moira's temple before scurrying away. "Come on, boys, if you want to get all the good seats afore these towering jack-holes steal the front row."

No one bothered to tell them that the only guests at the impromptu wedding were, in fact, the wedding party.

Aerin's particularly favorite 'jack-hole' executed a bow that would have impressed at the court of Queen Elizabeth I, and with a fond look in her direction, he strode away.

Damn, but the man was smooth.

And his ass was just so, *so* fine.

Moira took in a deep breath before letting it out between two pressed lips with a decidedly equine sound. "I feel so crazy stopping in the middle of an apocalypse to get married. Especially when it's sort of a moot issue what with being soul-bonded and all. But... it's worth a try, I guess. I just wish I didn't have to fit *that* dress over *this* mess." She gestured to her midsection.

Though she'd been pregnant for less than a handful of weeks, she was big enough to make a person wonder if there weren't four babies in there. The consensus was she should have given birth days ago, and the fact that they'd failed to kill Lucifer, the Princess of Darkness, herself, was the cause for the delay.

Sal, ever the helpful hillbilly, posited—well more like insisted—that her living in sin with the "baby daddy" was "Not right with the Lordt," and decided a shotgun wedding was imminently necessary.

So here they were.

Moira struggled to her feet and reached for her dress. "I'm so desperate I'll try anything. I've been following all the online advice. Hikin' my ass all over town. Scarfin' food hotter than the devil's nutsack. Riding Nick like a rented mule. If this wedding don't work, I'm going to find me a pogo stick."

"Even if this doesn't work," Claire said, helping Tierra wrestle with the dress, "it's nice to have something to celebrate during a time like this. Some hope to cling to."

Aerin had to agree. She reached over to help, and realized she was still clutching her ruined shoes. She'd overreacted, she supposed. But when she had to keep her shit together about so much tragedy. When it was all out of control and crazy...her emotions seemed to go volatile over the other things.

"Aerin, would you go tell them we'll be ready in ten minutes?" Moira asked, her gaze gentle with a knowing —an understanding—that made Aerin want to squirm. Here it was Moira's wedding day and Aerin was the one acting like Bridezilla.

"Yeah," she muttered, sufficiently chastised. "It'll give me time to change my shoes."

	land;

TO EVERYONE'S ASTONISHMENT, NICHOLAS Kingswood, the first and arguably most insolent of the Four Horsemen of the Apocalypse, he who conquered the world from atop a horse the color of his bloodlust; *Conquest* his own big dick-swinging, over-ruling, civilization-wasting *self,* took his almost farcical wedding ceremony as seriously as if it were held in all the pomp and ceremony of Westminster Cathedral. With his dark hair slicked back and his powerful frame clad in a tux that might have been tailored for Gieves & Hawkes, he looked like a hot Bond villain.

Standing in the garden's arboretum, framed by a trellis strewn with autumn foliage in every earthen shade, he claimed Moira's hand in front of a teary Sal.

The de Moray Mansion's spires reached for a sky in which large, happy, lazy clouds were tugged in all directions by fragrant sea breezes. The trill of songbirds and the soft percussion of deciduous tree leaves in the gentle wind had been the only melodic accompaniment of the bride down the aisle. And even though Salvadore Malveaux's "dearly beloveds" sounded nothing like anything civilized society would recognize, the ceremony had been charming and, blessedly, short.

Moira had practiced her lovely vows with her sisters that morning, but by the time she had the third sentence out, the pregnancy hormones had taken over, and, sobbing, she shoved the paper she'd written them down on into Nick's hands. He'd read them quietly with features softer than Aerin had ever seen them. Then, he folded them up, and tucked them into the pocket next to his heart.

His fingers shook when he slid a diamond the size of the Rock of Gibraltar onto Moira's hand, and his voice rang strong and resonant as he recited his vows.

"I'd like to say I chose you, but there was never any chance of that. You exist. And so, I am conquered. Thank you for teaching me how to smile. How to appreciate the quiet moments and simple pleasures. My protection is unequivocal. My devotion is absolute. My love and commitment are unconditional. The future, while uncertain, belongs to us, to our family, and my only reason for existing now is to fight for the chance for an eternity with you at my side. You have given me your hand in marriage this day, and in return I give you my life, my very heart to keep."

A crisp, perfectly folded handkerchief appeared in Aerin's hand, pressed there by long, elegant fingers.

"I don't need this," Aerin sniffed. "I'm not crying." She cleared her throat. Then blinked the burning away, which only made the tears fall faster.

"I know, darling." Julian's shoulder leaned more heavily against hers as he pressed a soft kiss into her hair.

She clutched the handkerchief and brought it to her nose and did not blow. But inhaled. He smelled of bergamot, ambergris, and that indefinable perfume only found in the pages of well-loved books. Aerin breathed in, and in, and in, wanting to lock the scent of him inside of her lungs and never release it. To keep him.

Always.

But, even though some of her tears were happy ones, she mostly wept for what they might not have for much longer.

For what they might all lose in the end.

"And now!" The twang of Uncle Sal's patois jarred her into the moment. "By the power invested to me by the Highway 90 Holy Serpent Mega Church of Stumps Bayou, Orleans Parrish, Louisiana, I pronounce you two hitched! You may kiss your bride."

Nick and Moira's kiss was full of teeth, as they were smiling too hard to properly pucker.

Red, whose bald spot in the back of his head had been staring at Aerin through the entire affair, turned to Little Earl and queried. "Speakin' of serpents, how come there ain't none at this here ceremony?"

"Dunno," Little Earl shrugged a big shoulder. "I offered to go catch us some, but Moira Jo said we can't."

"Hardly seems like a legal weddin' without 'em," Red tutted, swiping his red, sweat-ringed trucker cap from his back pocket to return to its eternal perch over his ears. "Maybe it's on account of that one-time Mookie's pecker done near dropped off when one of them fuckers got 'im in the biscuits."

Mookie tensed as straight as a divining rod. "You shut your whore mouth Redford Alouicious Meredith Mcgillicutty or I'll gut you like a pike and pickle your innards in mason jars." He turned in his chair to glance shyly back at Aerin. "Don't mark them none, all my dangly business is right where it ought to be."

"Congratulations," she said with a sour smile.

Julian leaned forward, bringing his aquiline nose close to Mookie's porcine one. "If you want your pendant glands to remain so, you will refrain from mentioning it in the presence of my woman."

Mookie blanched, blushed, and then turned some strange shade of puce, but to his credit he narrowed his beady eyes and said, "I am going to turn around now, but it ain't because I'm afeard of you."

"You should be, mortal, for a creature does not exist as venomous as I." Beneath Julian's near porcelain skin, veins of darkness surged and slithered before disappearing in the blink of an instant.

Each of the men surged to their feet and retreated toward the married couple.

Aerin hoped the shit in their pants was only figurative.

"Neat trick," she muttered.

He merely shrugged.

"Your woman? I never said I was your woman."

"Neither did you deny it," he challenged.

It was her turn to be silent. She looked on as Claire and Tierra rushed to Moira kissing her cheeks and showering her with love and laughter. The uncles were next, lined up like misfit toys to pay their respects to the couple and whoop and holler their happy wishes.

Drustan joined in, back-slapping and elbowing Nick with manly jibes. Killian's deep laughter was added to the din even as he held his daughter, so tiny against his deep chest.

Aerin stood, if only not to be rude, but couldn't seem to make her feet move to join.

Julian unfolded himself from the chair next to her, but slid his arm around her waist to breathe into her ear, "You're troubled."

Aerin made a wry noise. "Don't read my mind, we're not bonded."

"I can read you, Aerin, because you are my favorite thing to study. Tell me what is wrong."

Well... if he wasn't the rightest thing-saying mother-fucker alive.

"I'm not troubled," she admitted, pasting on a false smile as Moira turned to beam at her. "I'm scared."

She'd never uttered those words to another soul.

"Scared of the evil that threatens to take all this from us?"

She shook her head. "Scared to hope we can defeat it."

"I'm assuming the shotgun wedding didn't work," War remarked the next day during a traffic jam on the grand staircase as all seven of them waited with varying degrees of patience for Moira to finish waddling down on her swollen feet.

Aerin almost plowed into her when Moira stopped abruptly and turned to address Dru. "You don't have to assume anythin' as you might use your immortal powers of observation to deduce that I'm obviously still knocked up and wide as a pontoon."

Seven voices clamored in ardent and overblown disagreement as they each filed behind her into the den. They praised her grace and goddess-like beauty, miraculous maternal body, magical glowing skin, and glimmering hair.

"Oh, stuff your pie holes y'all, I ain't blind, I looked in the mirror this morning." Moira, clad a pair of Tierra's yoga pants slung below her belly and an oversized T-shirt that simply read *Y'all need the Goddess* more tipped over than sat down, landing on the overstuffed couch with a moan of relief and an uncouth sprawl. "How does anyone do this for months?" she bitched, glaring at her stomach. "Just get it out!"

Nick, his concession to casual being that he rolled

up the sleeves on his silk Bruno Magli shirt, perched a butt cheek on the arm of the couch next to her. The idle fingers of one hand wound their way beneath Moira's lustrous hair to absently work at knots in her neck and shoulders.

"Put it in. Get it out. Make up your mind woman," he leered at her, receiving a swat on the thigh for his troubles.

Aerin appreciated the joviality their conversation brought to the heavy purpose of their mid-morning meeting. The gist of it being: What the fuck did they do now?

Killian, who was the last to file in the room, planted his boots in a wide stance in the doorway. The leather of his coat creaked as he tested its mettle by crossing his ginormous arms. A man that monstrous needed some give in his seams. Death's own sentinel, he scanned each of their faces with his dark gaze and opened their conclave with all the ceremonious candor of his years, immemorial.

"Sooooo... What the fuck do we do now?"

Crickets.

Aerin looked to a flowy, pajama-clad Tierra, who was usually a fountain of ideas—a few so wild and wide of the mark they had to wade through some hippie crazy sauce to get to the expert ones. She found it deeply un-settling that her eldest sister kept her eyes trained on the antique carpets the hue of Bordeaux, as if silently calling *not it*.

Dru claimed the other end of the couch from Moira, Claire curled up so close to him she was practi-cally in his lap. The couple said nothing, but held some sort of intense, silent court with their eyes.

"Didn't anyone tell you it was rude to mind-meld in public?" Aerin flung herself into the Queen Anne chair opposite them in a fit of pique and adjusted the cuff of her cream blouse.

Claire dashed her a conciliatory glance. "We were trying not to argue out loud, which is also rude."

"By all means, have at it." Aerin gestured for them to continue. "It would be nice to hear just about any idea right now, no matter what it is."

It wasn't that she didn't have all the answers that bothered her, it was that, for once, she didn't have *any*. She was a data miner, goddammit. And, while magic was a code she was learning to hack, what the fuck did she do about fate? Destiny?

Prophecy.

Dru made a growly noise and pulled Claire closer, tucking his hand beneath her hip. "If we agree on any one thing, it's that we are every which way but fucked."

"If I may." Julian, resplendent in a navy checkered morning suit and butter-soft gloves, stood with his hand resting on the high back of Aerin's chair like a monarch posing for a portrait. "I think it's safe to say a cohesive strategy thus far has been woefully—you'll forgive me— preposterously nonexistent. Because we were unable to arrive at an initial consensus regarding how many of us were for or against the apocalyptic prophecy, and accept or decline our part in it, we've frankly buggared the whole business."

"Harsh, bro." Dru shook his head.

"A harsh reality." Killian ran an exhausted hand over his face. "Six Seals out of seven are open, and look what ripe and holy shit has been dumped onto the planet."

Nick scratched at his sharp jaw, a sheepish look sitting oddly on features as brutal as his. "A few government coups and stock market crashes and a global recession. Not something mortals haven't rebounded from before."

"Yeah." Dru straightened a bit. "I mean sure, some warlords are doing each other in, but most destabilizing countries are only *threatening* to go to war. And, I'll admit, a few fingers are fondling nuke codes, but no one's pushed the red button yet."

"Likely because so many of them are starving or infirmed," Julian's bleak and sonorous voice called to Aerin, and she slid his glove off his fingers before entwining them with hers.

"Let's not forget the zombies and zealots and witch hunters." Killian said. "And the She-devil who followed me here."

"The moon turned to blood," Tierra supplied as forlorn as Aerin had ever seen her, the weight of earth's pain curling her shoulders forward. "The oceans are toxic and dying, the earth trembling, fires ripping across entire continents, super storms displacing millions, volcanoes threatening to erupt at any moment. It takes all of our powers, daily, to keep all this from consuming everything and everyone. What sort of place are we making? What are we leaving for our children?"

"Julian's right," Moira said with uncharacteristic solemnity. "Nothin' we've tried seems to have worked."

"What if we stopped trying?" The words escaped Aerin before the next thought had fully formed, her idea needing to be manifested before it slipped away like vapor on the wind.

"Darling." Julian's fingers squeezed hers as he leaned closer. "I know things appear hopeless, but I don't believe we're beyond the pale. Surely not all is lost—"

"No, hear me out." Aerin turned to look up at him, decided she didn't like that one bit, and tugged him down so he crouched beside her chair. "Do you remember what we spoke of that first ride we took to the cliffs? About the Goddess?"

His electric irises warmed to the color of the Mediterranean in July, the fine lines branching from his eyes as he looked into the past with that perfect memory of his. "I told you the Goddess was no longer allowed in the realm, that the feminine divine is lost—"

"Yes, yes, that's the part. Now remember when you explained to me the meaning of the word apocalypse?" She leaned forward, intensity gathering as she saw the spark in his features and the birth of something echoed in her own vibrating soul.

Hope.

"Apocalypse, when translated from Greek, its original language, literally means a revelation or... cataclysm really. I told you that when the Goddess was driven from this, her creation, she left it forsaken, vulnerable for other deities to pick over once the prophecy was complete."

"But she didn't forsake it," Aerin said. "She left us. We could have the power to take over once the prophecy is complete."

"Uh oh," Claire fretted. "Is she evil again? Because when she gets evil, she gets power hungry."

Aerin turned reluctantly away from the fierce, beautiful face of the man who stared at her as if she hung the moon—before it was all bloody and stuff—to face the skeptical gazes of her sister witches.

"This isn't about power this time," she said fervently. "This is about protection. Think about it. When the Druid Malcom de Moray wrote the Domesday Prophecy, he essentially said it would be the end of life as we know it." She gestured widely. "But what is life as we know it now?"

In the most excited tones he'd used since she'd met him, Julian picked up what she was throwing down, quoting himself from that first time they'd met. "The world is an overpopulated, unmitigated disaster. Your governments are all corrupt, incompetent machines run by money and special interests. Humans in the first world are overfed, entitled, heartless bureaucrats who prefer to be blind to the suffering of others so long as they're entertained by screens and buttons and social diseases. They do nothing for those who are still chained by tyrants or starved and abused by those who call themselves holy men. The feminine divine is lost. Wisdom is falling prey to dogma. And fear, greed, and apathy are keeping everyone subservient while corporations threaten entire ecosystems, fish the oceans to emptiness, and turn the planet into their own rubbish heap."

"Exactly." Aerin jumped up in her excited exuberance, a broad smile spilling over every muscle in her face until she felt as if her entire body thrilled with life. Eureka! "Life is meaningless and terrible. Basically, it's the fucking worst. So let's like, end this thingy."

"Uh-oh," Tierra's eyes went owlish as she backed away slowly. "She's not gone evil. She's gone freaking nuts."

Aerin was too electrified with an idea to be irritated. "*Listennnuh*, I'm saying let's save the fucking world by ending it. Not ending people's lives, but the way they live it. Let's get rid of it all. Every imbalance. Every evil. Every suffering. Patriarchy, Oligarchy, Monarchy, other...archies and pave the way for your little cretins to bring power to the light and dark side of the force, or whatever. And then, with our immortal elemental powers of badassary, we can restore the feminine divine and, hell, possibly restore the power of the Goddess to her rightful place."

She could feel her idea take root in Tierra, catch fire within Claire, and wash over Moira.

And then a man opened his mouth.

"That's all well and good, but you're forgetting a few things," Killian said dryly. "Lucifer, for one."

"Well yeah, I mean, we'll have to kill her and her minions, obviously." She gestured impatiently. "And then save the world."

"And how do you propose we do that?" Nick asked.

"Well... I don't know," Aerin said. "We're supposed to be a fucking think tank, I can't have *all* the answers."

"And then there's us," Julian said, his voice dripping with regret. "The fact that we exist mean others suffer. That is who we are, and we are undying."

Aerin whirled on him. "Don't fucking pop my balloon right now, bucko, I'm on a roll. We'll figure that part out, but first thing's first. We go after Beelzebitch."

"First thing's first," Tierra echoed. "To even hope to do that, we need to be at maximum power and you still don't have your crown and wand yet."

"And to get your crown and wand," Moira said. "You'll need to do some selfless act of sacrifice."

At that, Nick started laughing, startling them all. "Oh man," he guffawed. "Aerin has to be selfless? Humanity is well and truly fucked."

$$\maltese \quad 42 \quad \maltese$$

Hours later, Aerin climbed to the de Moray
Mansion's widow's walk and jumped.

I'll show them selfless, she thought as her blood
thrilled to the feeling of her broom catching an air current to lift her above the treetops. *I'll be so mutha fuckin'
selfless and sacrificing, they'll put my picture next to the words
in the dictionary. And magnanimous. And altruistic. And
heroic just because I'm saving the world and shit.*

QUESTION WAS... WHAT DID THE COSMIC
wand/crown decision makers want from her?

A list of things she'd already tried:

1. Donated maybe a bazillion dollars' worth of designer clothes and shoes to charity. Even some of the
shoes the hillbilly herd *hadn't* ruined.

2. Stopped drawing her salary from Windmark Tech,
her cloud company, and disseminated it as bonuses to
the lowest paid, along with offering everyone shares in
the company. Decreased work hours and increased paid
days off.

3. Donated her entire savings to feeding the hungry.
Literally millions.

4. Gave Julian his first blow job. Okay, granted,

not exactly altruistic because she'd enjoyed the hell out of his awestruck ecstasy. Also, if they were counting—which they were *not*—she was still behind him in the oral sex-o-meter because after she'd taken his virginity, he'd become some sort of tongue-twisty vagina junkie. Dined. Out. Ev'ry. Night. Still, she was keeping it on the list because her jaw was tired.

5. She even babysat for Tierra and Killian so they could enjoy some private time. It lasted all of fifteen minutes, but she'd been donzo after fifteen *seconds* of drooling and random screaming, so math told her she was fourteen minutes and forty-five seconds ahead.

And still nothing. No crown. No wand. No dice.

So, she'd decided to take to the skies and see if she could Wonder Woman her way into her powers. Basically, the plan was to fly around until she spotted someone in distress and use her magic to save said person.

Problem was, Port Townsend was a hamlet of maybe ten thousand souls, give or take the summer tourists and the occasional infestation of poltergeists and/or zombies. On top of that, the entire place went to sleep around 9pm. Especially since aforementioned zombies became a thing.

The fifth Seal had called the souls of innocent dead to cry vengeance against the blood of their enemies, or whatever that prophecy was, so really you only had to be worried about a zombie situation if you ever did someone a bad turn and then they died before you made it right.

The first wave had been astonishing, and Lucifer had learned how to, through admittedly impressive necromancer powers, direct the undead rage toward the de Moray witches. But that seemed to calm down once they blew her up and melted her corporeal form, so she had to body snatch.

Felt like a victory until she started body snatching powerful witches.

Hindsight? They could have planned that better.

Man, how awesome would it be to have necromancer powers? Like, to rule the dead? Raise armies? Own the darkness and—

Nope! Aerin slapped herself so hard she almost fell off her broom. Don't go there. Evil. Bad. Darkness. Destruction.

She was an air witch and air powers were cool enough.

Plus, there was always the lightning. Who needed dominion over the undead when you could zap people?

Where was she? Oh, zombies. Zombies had gone back to trying to kill their still-living enemies, and all-in-all people seemed to know what—and who—to expect and how to kill them. Sometimes for the second time.

Zombie killing was pretty basic for anyone with cable TV. Shooting them in the head. Cutting off their head. Squishing, crushing, or shattering their head.

Burning also worked in a pinch.

In the daylight, zombies were generally easy to spot and outrun. Hell, most of Port Townsend's population —which 30% was over fifty-five and still astonishingly granola fit— could powerwalk away from their worst enemy while melting them down with a lighter and some aerosol hairspray.

But at night it was a little trickier to see in a place with so few streetlights, that a body might not notice the vengeful undead until one's enemy was gnawing on one's leg like store bought rotisserie chicken.

That's it! Aerin realized. She could take out the zombies! That would be really fucking nice of her.

She veered toward the downtown square where a bronze fountain drizzled water over a naked lady with eternally marble-hard tits. One would think zombies would haunt the cemeteries, back yards, and out-of-the-way wooded graves from which they sprouted, but no, for some reason downtown by the theater and Alchemy Bistro and Wine Bar was where the undead liked to meet before they broke away to—you know—*meat*.

What Aerin *could* do was clean up the entire town once and for all, securing the streets and saving ten thousand-ish people from facing their own problems.

And hope she didn't run into Gwen/Satan alone, as her sisters and their significant others were holed up at the Mansion trying to come up with end of world battle plans that were contingent on her success in the selfless endeavor.

No pressure.

What she didn't expect, was to show up late to a battle. Below her in the square, a lone man with a sabre sword and a shirt puffy enough to impress Lord Byron, was propelling and reposting lumbering zombie attacks with enough skill to put Inigo Montoya to shame.

Aerin recognized him immediately as the only other man on earth who was not Julian Roarke that could pull off that kind of fashion on the daily.

With a whoosh and dismount onto the cobbled stone, Aerin took in a deep breath, swung her arms back, and thrust them toward the only two zombies left standing who were currently flanking the swordsman. The gale-force gusts she summoned knocked the zombies into the wrought iron fence on the far side of the square, impaling them on the spikes, and also blew Norman Barriston's silvery waxed mustache only slightly askew.

The ostensibly anachronistic keeper of Ye Olde Constabulary Inn was a mere mortal, but no one had the heart to tell him so. A local IT professional, pacifist, and fencing enthusiast, he'd been thriving in the Apocalypse with his signature flare and endless good humor.

"Well, hello there!" he greeted, smoothing down the

curly hair she'd rumpled after sheathing his sword with his characteristic flair. "Congratulations! I do believe you killed the last two zombies in Port Townsend proper."

"Goddammit!" she swore, making a frustrated gesture. "Fucking figures!"

He looked at her askance. "If you'll pardon my saying so, I thought that might be good news. My fencing class and I have been hunting them, as it seemed you lovely de Morays had so much on your shoulders, what with the Apocalypse and everything. Didn't want to be a nuisance."

Aerin sobered immediately. "No, yeah, no. Thank you...for doing that. *So* great." She gave him a thumbs up that she hoped seemed like she meant it.

His smile brightened. "Don't mention it."

They spent an awkward moment admiring the strewn chaos of several bodies he'd re-killed.

Well, Aerin puffed out a deep breath. So much for the zombie plan. Maybe she'd have to go find a town without a resident Zorro.

"So," Aerin opened her hand and called her broom to her palm. "Not to freak you out, but the actual Devil is maybe who-knows-where close by and more than a little pissed off. Do you want me to give you a lift home?"

He grimaced. "I'm no great lover of heights, and I only live a quarter mile up that hill so, there's no need."

"Let me at least walk you," she offered. "Safety in numbers and all that."

His grimace deepened to a scowl that didn't sit well on his cheerful round cheeks. "As a gentleman, allow me to offer you an alternative," he said with ebullience, holding his finger up as if he'd a *Eureka* moment. "*I* can accompany *you* home, for *your* safety."

"I mean, I'm a super powerful elemental witch,

sooooooooo..." She let that trail off leaving the bloody fucking obvious unsaid.

She needed protection like a zombie needed a library.

"Still," he insisted. "As you can see, I'm no slouch myself, and you are still a lady."

Aerin bit her tongue until it hurt before forcing herself to say. "Okay. Yeah." Maybe if she indulged the male ego that would totally count as sacrifice.

Because beyond that she was out of ideas.

They fell into step next to each other in a congenial march up the concrete steps that would lead them uptown where de Moray Mansion hunkered against the bluffs.

Ever the raconteur, Barriston didn't let the awkward silence settle in. "If I may ask, what brings you out here on a night such as this?"

Because Aerin was too frustrated to lie, she told him what she'd been doing. Then she just kept talking. And the talking became ranting, until she'd spilled the beans to him about *everything*. The Coven, the baby shower, her missing wand, Gwen/Lucifer, the children, the broken Seals, the Goddess.

All in all, other than a stress rash creeping from beneath his collar, he took it all in stride. Finally winding down, she let him take a moment to digest, wondering what he'd say.

It was the last thing she expected. "You know, I've garnered a little wisdom in my years, and forgive me if I overreach, but I'm not certain when else I'll have the pleasure of your company. Sacrifice, I've noticed, isn't simply giving something shiny away. Or even putting yourself out for the sake of someone else. That is called service. Or kindness. Virtues that shouldn't be extraordinary, but mundane, do you see what I mean?"

Aerin nodded. "Yeah, I'm following."

"Excellent," He continued. "Real sacrifice, I've

learned, is painful. Often not physically, but on a deeply individual level. It is usually a mechanism for personal growth and change. It often galls you or humiliates you or, at the very least, humbles you. Humility, I gather, is neither of our strong suits." He threw her a cheeky smile, evoking her to answer with one.

"That it is not, sir."

Barriston took in a breath of the fragrant night and peered up at the moon for an appreciative moment, finding beauty, it seemed, even in the blood. "It seems to me, if the Devil is building an army, so must you all. And... it strikes me as odd, that Port Townsend is full of witches who can't seem to work together. Does that seem right to you?"

Gall rose in Aerin's esophagus as she narrowed her eyes and shook her head at him. "I hate you right now."

He grinned. "Because I'm right?"

"Because you're...not wrong."

He leveled her a cheeky wink pairing it with a what-can-you-do shrug. "Sometimes the answer isn't bending the world to your will, but bending your will for the sake of the world."

Drawing up to the Mansion, she put her hand on the gate. "I'm going to go get drunk," she announced, "Would you like to join me?"

"I'd be delighted!" His merry eyes twinkled and he gestured expansively for her to go before him. "Maybe I inquire as to the occasion?"

"I need to fortify myself if I have to go make peace with a bunch of bitches tomorrow."

"Don't you mean witches?" he clarified.

"No, Sir Barriston. No, I do not."

$\mathbf{\mathscr{H}}$ 43 $\mathbf{\mathscr{H}}$

From her hidden vantage, Lucifer watched the de Moray witches approach the Raven Rook Inn where the Coven gathered. They waked in a triangle formation around Moira, as if to shield her gigantic belly from the world.

Human gestation was so disgusting.

They'd come for a reckoning.

She pondered the monstrous book ill-concealed beneath Moira's jacket.

About just how many holy books were full of lies about her.

Except for one thing.

The Devil used to be an angel.

Well, kind of. Not like a wings and seraphim angel, but celestial in the way of the Horsemen and beings of their ilk. An extra creation of the Goddess. Favored. Blessed.

Necessary.

Once upon a time, Lucifer had been a title rather than a name. She was the Morning *fucking* Star.

Until her star had fallen.

She'd only wanted to help, at first. Had looked forward into eternity, locked in a struggle for balance against the original *Tugadh Solas*. The Bringer of Light. She hated their destiny, to be eternally balanced.

Even though he'd loved her.

Adam.

She'd begged him to change, and he wouldn't listen to her. No one listened. No one cared in those days to change or question anything. Humans had been happy frolicking about in their Eden, naked and ignorant. They'd reveled in the light of her lover, basked in it, letting it warm their skin and nourish their souls.

And they feared her darkness. Feared the power she wielded and the way she hid the truth from the light. They hunkered down and covered their heads, turning away from the night and all her beautiful creatures. All her terrible secrets. For the dark is where sins were committed and things were concealed.

And as a woman, as the *Ceann Dorcha*, The Dark One, Lillith had witnessed them all. All their sins. All the things they wished to hide from the goodness of the Goddess, and the mortals twisted her from the light.

Turned her away from Adam.

And so, he'd turned to another. Eve.

That had been the beginning of the end. The balance they'd struck in their love had been disrupted, and she'd known no good would come of it. She'd lowered herself to beg him for his favor.

But Adam had been a man, and he'd insisted that he'd *known* better. He'd wanted something other than a scheming woman. He wanted sweetness and softness and amenable self-sacrifice in a mate. He'd wanted a woman on her knees to accept him. To accept the role she'd been given. To not reach above or beyond her station or her question her destiny.

Because the light could be corrupted, too. The light was often just as damaging as darkness.

If only he'd listened...if only he'd joined her. Chosen her. The balance never would have been distorted. The hurt within her wouldn't have turned to anger, would never have spread the darkness. That darkness wouldn't have obsessed her every moment, overwhelmed her until she gathered enough of it to smother the light.

Only because she could not bear to watch Adam and Eve be happy together.

When Lilith fell from the Goddess's favor, she knew she had to bring Eve down with her, for only then could she banish the light from the world.

It had been almost too easy, coiling as a serpent, leaking poison into Eve's ear. She knew Adam's weaknesses and his wants, she knew the parts of his heart he kept hidden, and the little pinpricks of darkness seeded within him.

She knew how to drag them down with her.

Now she was no longer a Morning Star. She was again that helical serpent. Or a spider. Gathering her resources, her power, sucking it from whatever source she could find and storing it away to expend later. Tantalizing her prey with her shiny web and all the abundance caught within it.

She'd snatched up everything that was supposed to belong to the Goddess. Starting with the Horsemen. They'd been blessed, too. A higher race of immortals tasked with power and the prescience of prophecy to fight for the divinity of the Goddess's creation.

She'd corrupted them over millennia. Corrupted their powers of protection against the mortals they'd been birthed to defend. Turned the divine blessing that was their celestial bodies into her own depraved playground.

And sometimes, they'd begged her to do it.

As the years slid by, she'd shrouded the truth as was her way until they'd forgotten their place. They'd forgotten their Goddess, or had become certain their Goddess had forgotten them. They'd forgotten that

Adam and Eve had borne children. Not two boys, as the story had been changed for the official records.

But girls. Four of them.

And those children, that divine lineage, had been their responsibility to guard.

To love.

De Moray. It meant *the leaders*. *The Lords*. Because language back then didn't have any gender, and as a parting gift the Goddess left her priestesses with one last blessing.

A way to end it all.

For there was never any doubt that this would end, it was now only a question of how.

Lucy scanned the world through eyes that were not her own. Gwen, the poor, deluded soul, battered on the place in her mind that Lucy had banished her to.

They had so much to thank her for, these mortals. Their towers of glass and steel. Their wealth and weapons. Their millennia of progress in both science and skill, entertainment and now, the inevitable entropy.

It was over, their ridiculous, meaningless rule. She'd given them plenty of time to fuel her powers. To feed her stores and to break this world down in a way she'd always known was possible. Dismantling the gift of the Goddess until it begged for change.

For the Apocalypse.

Once the final Seal was broken...she'd give it what it wanted, wiping the last seed of Adam from the planet as she should have done eons ago.

She'd reclaim the Horsemen as her consorts, chaining them to her throne of thunder as she burned the entire world to the ground.

And rule over the ashes.

Aerin sensed the moments the wards went up against them. Wards against evil. Wards against harm. And wards against them, specifically.

Goddess give her strength to deal with bitchy witches.

She had tried to strategize with her sisters last night regarding what would be the best configuration of the four of them to attempt this peace offering. It was settled that it would be just as foolish to leave anyone out of it as it was to bring all of them.

So, they went together.

Situated in downtown Port Townsend, The Raven Rook Inn was a three-story red brick building which claimed a corner of Water Street lined—as so many Victorian towns were—with tightly stacked buildings. Old-timey shingles advertised shops and restaurants beneath their delightful varied edifices and meticulous scroll-work. It was charming as fuck and had been overpopulated with tourists back before the end of days.

The town gleamed in the intermittent early-afternoon sun, barely revealed by this morning's rainclouds. Moisture still dripped off the leaves and sparkled like little gems on potted flowers, assorted awnings, and the oil slicks left by cars in the road.

The Raven Rook Inn was no longer a functioning hotel, but had been conscripted by the local coven as a base of operations during wartime. A war that seemed to be raging just as much within their ranks as without.

The wards vibrated as they approached, and when Aerin lifted her fist to knock on the intricately carved front door, her skin prickled as if being stung by a handful of bees.

Uncomfortable, but not a significant impediment.

They could have forced their way into the hotel in any number of ways. Flown through the rooftop skylight on their broomsticks, for example, or blown the door wide open.

But that was not how truces were made, and they decided that they'd do this as mortals. As women. Nary a wand, broom, nor protective Horseman in sight.

Of course, all were stashed nearby in case the need arose.

They were being nice, not naïve.

Through the textured glass, the distorted forms of two matrons trundled forward and Aerin recognized them from Tierra's ill-fated baby shower as Martha and Hattie Mae.

Once they opened the door, the steel-haired women who stood sentinel might have stepped out of a noir mystery. Martha, a severe-looking black woman in a long, elegant gray dress and perpetually narrowed eyes, and Hattie Mae, a faded blonde bombshell who's lip liner painted an almost comical fiction of her features.

Aerin didn't exactly expect to be invited in, but the open rebuke on the women's faces threatened to damage her calm.

Martha spoke for them both. "You have some nerve coming here," she tutted, sucking at her teeth.

Tierra stepped forward, as it had been agreed that she'd break the ice, seeing as she had a long-standing relationship with these women and, until recently, an exceptional reputation and place among the Coven. "Martha, Hattie Mae, we've come to talk." She pulled her bronze sweater tightly around the ultra-feminine palazzo pantsuit she wore, making a show of being chilly left out in the autumn breeze.

"Okay." Martha planted a fist on her hip, clearly unmoved. "So, talk."

Tierra paused for a moment, notably affected by the hostility on the faces of the women who'd helped Aunt Justine raise her.

"I was hoping to be invited in," she said carefully, maintaining her composure. "We'd like to address all of you."

Hattie Mae, her eyes peeled wide by the magic wielded only by a plastic surgeon's knife wagged a long-nailed finger at them. "We're not stupid enough to fall for that. Did you bring your soul-stealing spawn with you?"

"Justine is watching her. And that's uncalled for," Tierra said in defense of her child. "She only borrowed—"

Claire put a hand on Tierra's elbow. "We're looking to broker peace and foster understanding. We know there is a past and prophecy and fear, but we're hoping to try to move past that. To work together."

Martha shook her head. "We're past that now. Goodbye Tierra, and good luck." She stepped back to slam the door in their faces, and that's when Aerin stepped forward, catching the door against her palm. "We're here to help you idiot biddies, now find your manners and let us in."

"Not a chance." Martha threw her weight against the door, and Aerin was surprised that the old woman's muscle was every bit as strong as her perfume. "We'll do just fine on our own, thank you very much."

"Wrong." Aerin shoved her way past the threshold, gritting her teeth against the pain of the wards until she made her way through, much to their shock and dismay. "Your wards are weak, and your power is waning. You need us. And we want to help!"

Moira, who'd hung back in hopes to make the fact that she carried—in their estimation—demon spawn 2.0, now reached for Aerin's elbow, tugging her back. "Intimidation's no way to broker peace," she hissed.

Hattie Mae blew a puff of her bangs out of her eyes. "No. This air witch speaks the truth; we *are* weakening and it's all thanks to you lot."

Aerin's brows sank in consternation. "*Excuse Moi?*" Were they just getting blamed for all the rando bad shit now?

"That's right." Martha nodded, scalding her with a withering glare. "Ever since *you all* came to Port Townsend and began opening the Seals with your reckless use of magic, the powers of the Goddess retreats farther away from our reach, as *you* become more powerful."

Behind them in the entry way, Aerin could see several of the witches gathering. Drifting from other rooms and down the plush arabesque carpeted staircase. Some of their faces curious, others anxious, a few outright antagonistic.

"It's as if you are stealing it from us," Hattie Mae accused. "For what nefarious purposes, we can only imagine."

Tierra took a step back as if she'd been physically struck. "We'd *never.*"

"How do we know that?" Martha challenged.

"Because you know me!" Tierra cried, holding her arms out to present herself as if that should be answer enough. "I've been a part of your coven for my entire life. That's garnered me some trust, hasn't it? Doesn't that mean anything to you?"

Another woman stepped forward. Younger, pretty, with a wealth of hair streaked a vibrant purple and braided like a Valkyrie. "We thought it did, Tierra, but you sided with *them*."

Aerin recognized the woman as Melody, Gwen's minion from the other day.

The Devil's minion, now.

Tierra shoved inside wards behind Aerin, standing against the two mavens with Q-tip haircuts and all the witches who had appointed them their mouth pieces. "You know, I didn't just side with them because they were my family, I did it because *you* allowed yourself to be infiltrated by the actual Devil. You tried to kill my sisters! More than once! That's just—well it's *mean*, and I'll not stand for it."

Aerin advanced further, partly to crowd the older women farther back into the building, and partly to make room for Claire and Moira to enter behind her. She heard their gasps as they, too, pushed through the stinging wards. But they could all do it.

Which meant Moira's baby wasn't evil. Of course, Aerin had believed that already, but it was nice to have it verified by anti-evil wards.

"Look you guys." Claire stepped forward, attempting to level with them. "The problem here is Gwen—or the woman who is currently wearing Gwen's skin—she attacked us. She tried to hurt Violet, who is innocent in all of this. She doesn't care about anything but power and getting what she wants. Can't you see that?"

Aerin chimed in. "Don't you guys *want* Gwen back? I mean, I'd get it if you didn't. She's kind of a rank bitch, but aren't you worried that Lucifer, *the actual Devil*, was able to worm her way into your ranks in the first place?"

"We all know that the Devil isn't what the patriarchal scripture says it is," Melody preached patiently, with the skill of a woman born to lead. "The Devil is a construct of—"

"Whatever," Aerin cut her off, not in the mood for a lesson in theology or magic, she got enough of that from Julian back home. "We can agree that the entity in Gwen is fucking dark and destructive, and we can prove *she* is the reason the Seals are broken. She's the architect of every magical mistake we've made. And we need to vanquish her so that balance can be regained. Don't you feel the truth of that?"

Hattie Mae eyed them with—well it was hard to name the emotion blunted as it was with Botox. "How do we know you aren't just trying to steal her dark powers?"

"Y'all don't. Because we are." Moira stepped forward, holding in her hand their one greatest hope. The one offering they could give that might bring them all together. "This here is the de Moray Grimoire. We call him Grim."

Martha put her hand to her bosoms. "Lands, is that made out of human skin?"

"Irrelevant," Aerin clipped. "Also, probably. But it contains every magic secret we know. Every origin of power and every answer to your questions. It's all in there, and we're here to offer it for coven use."

"Why would you bring this here?" Melody asked, her eyes gleaming as she stepped forward and ran her finger over the book's surface with reverence and no small amount of lust.

"Because we believe that magic belongs to everyone," Tierra said clearly. "To all of us and all of you. We seek no dominion nor absolute power nor to hold all the secrets or answers. We plan to share it with every witch. With every *woman*."

"Exactly," Claire stepped in. "We shouldn't be fighting. We should be on the same side. The side of peace and power. We should stand together because we are all in this battle. We all, in our hearts, want the same things. Sisterhood, friendship, belonging, peace, prosperity, happiness, and love."

Murmurings rumbled through the assembly maybe fifty or so strong…it was hard for Aerin, in such a tight space, to get an exact read on the crowd. But she felt a disturbance here. A ripple of something…

"Please," She addressed them, identifying what she felt. "Fear and mistrust and anger, they aren't part of the Goddess. They are the tools being used to steal your powers. And not by us. We're here to help you reclaim what you have lost."

"And so you have."

An oily slick of disgust and darkness slithered down Aerin's spine before Gwen glided beneath an archway that led to another room, trailing dark robes behind her like a slithering mist. She held out her hand in silent demand for Grim, and Melody relinquished it immediately.

"What the actual hell, you guys?" Tierra cried.

No one said a word until Gwen spoke.

"Thank you for bringing this to me." She pushed newly colored black hair out of her eyes before she reached down to brush her fingers over the skin of the book. "I shall enjoy studying your secrets…but only after you are dead."

With that, the wards that had let them through the door snapped tight.

They hadn't even been meant to keep them out, Aerin realized with dawning horror. But to cut them off from the Horsemen, and to lock them inside.

❈ 45 ❈

Claire was the first to speak out, kicking her hip to the side and crossing her arms. "You can't kill us, you idiot, we're immortal."

Lucifer's eyes glittered with malevolence as an unhurried smile spread like bitter honey across her lips. "Gwen hates you most of all, Claire" she sneered, apropos of nothing. "She wants to fuck Drustan. She can experience my memories of doing so."

Claire ripped her jacket off her shoulders, ready to throw down. "Bitch, I will slap you into the next apocalypse—"

Tierra held her back as the Devil continued, drifting across the black and white checkered marble floors with an ethereal grace. Her skirts drew a line of darkness behind her, something inky like pitch or tar, cutting them off from the other witches as she spoke.

"Immortal?" She cackled. "You *infants* cannot even begin to fathom the word. I am a being of true immortality. My genesis was so long-ago even *time* cannot remember it."

"'Cept here we are," Moira chimed in. "Consistently whoopin' your ass."

"Shit." Aerin raked the devil with a scathing glare.

"How long do you think it will take your decrepit soul to rot this body, too?"

It was happening already, Aerin could smell the decay in the air. The more powerful Lucifer became, the weaker the mortal shell would be.

Lucifer leered at her, sliding an almost sensual leer down her long black slacks and shock white blouse. "I'm trying on a few, to see what fits until I can decide. You're not off the table, you know. And maybe after you're dead, I'll do things to Julian that will make him loathe the very sight of you before moving on."

Though she'd die before admitting it, a part of Aerin trembled in the presence of such a threat. She remembered the absolute helplessness of being banished into the murkiest corners of her own mind while Lucifer possessed her body.

It was a violation she'd never thought to fear before then, and would never forget so long as she lived.

Also, she was keenly aware in this tenuous moment that she was the only one of her sisters *not* immortal at the moment, and fuck if she didn't feel that mortality in every single one of her breakable bones.

Tierra turned to the coven, hurt and disbelief glimmering in her emerald eyes. "This is what it's come to? Why are you constantly taken in by her? Why can you not see that she's destroying you from the inside and driving you to do heinous things?"

Melody stepped forward to answer, flipping her violet hair from her shoulders. "She's powerful. And she says she can not only stop the Apocalypse, but save those we love. Every time she speaks prophecy, it comes true."

Aerin gestured to Grim. "Because she's prophesying from our own book! It's all in there, if she'll let you read it. And you'll see how she bastardizes it. How she twists it to control you."

Several doubtful gazes swung over to the Devil;

whose knuckles tightened on the book. "Of course, I'll allow it," she crooned. "I wouldn't dream of keeping anything from any of you."

"Except the truth," Aerin spat. "And Gwen."

"I told you at the battle in the stones!" Lucy exploded. "She allows me this coil. She gifted me use of it."

Tierra pounced on that. "So, you admit you were in the stones. That you attacked us."

The Coven, rapt now, swung their eyes to Lucy in search of an answer.

The shadow gathered around the Devil intensified. She boiled with evil, with malice and contempt. "I will do whatever it takes to vanquish you from this earth." A disturbance in the air riffled the tresses at her temples. "Though you consider yourself immortal, there are ways of *unmaking* you. Of dismantling your physical bodies so absolutely that your soul can no longer be considered cohesive. You will exist, and you will rue that existence. You will wish for the oblivion of death. So, help me, I'll—"

"Listen," Moira stepped forward, resting a hand on her alarmingly large belly. "Whatever Cunty McSkin-sack has told you about our prophecy and our children are rank lies. Y'all witnessed Tierra's winged angelic miracle and I think you are powerful enough to sense that she's nothing but a beam of light in this world. And this little'un is fixin' to replace this Mephi-syphilis as *Ceann Dorcha*, The Dark One. Not dark like this satanic taint stain, but dark like the night. Like death and shadow and repose and renewal. Her purpose is bal-ance, but in the way of nature, not the way of power. Read the book. Learn the truth. Summon the specters of the past to bear witness."

Aerin started as Claire nudged her from her place at her right side, gesturing to something behind the Devil. Threads, it seemed. Little dark spools, almost too faint for the eyes to see, wending their way to her from each of the gathered witches.

The Coven saw it too. Their reactions vast and varied as they realized what Lucy was taking from them.

"Better women than you have sought to replace me," Lucifer vowed, "Your spawn will never get the chance." A miasma of black overtook her pupils, her irises, and then the whites of her eyes until her gaze was nothing but unfathomable evil. "I will imprison you here, Moira de Moray with the same chains I used to geld Conquest. I will suck the power from the unborn, and then its life. I am the *Ceann Dorcha* and will forever be."

The threads tying the coven to her became stronger, more corporeal and she undulated like a woman in the throes of ecstasy. Grim dropped to her feet as a black swirling cloud levitated her above the ground. Dark tendrils streamed from her hands, lashing toward Moira.

Without a second thought, Aerin dove in front of her sister, allowing the tendrils to encircle her own wrists.

She knew this spell. She knew this power. She'd read about it in the back of the Grimoire. In the pages that were verboten.

Insatiable Chains, it had been called. A spell used to steal from its victim. Youth, beauty, luck, and, when applicable, power.

Life.

A chilling pain lanced through her as she felt the spell go to work, ripping her away from herself in slow, agonizing increments.

Her sisters rushed to retaliate.

"You will *not*," Tierra drew her fingers into claws and the building shook.

"We'll end you first." On Aerin's other side, flames

ignited in Claire's hands. She could sense Moira draining the air of moisture, could hear it knocking about in the pipes below them.

Claire's fireball hit Lucy in the arm, knocking one of the chains free.

Aerin screamed in agony as a scorching burn blistered her skin.

"Whatever you do to me now, will be done to those in my thrall," Lucy warned, her lips pulled back in a smile of brilliant glee as her sisters hesitated.

Around such putrefying power, Gwen's features, like all the rest, were beginning to disintegrate. "You burn me, you burn your sister. Drown me, imprison me in ice or vines, and so shackled is Aerin. What would you do? Trap all these women in a blaze? The walls are warded and can only be penetrated by darkness. No magical being, witch, nor Horseman can get in or out."

"Maybe," Aerin labored to speak around the unfathomable pain. "But Hillbillies can."

Summoning her dwindling powers, she activated Plan B.

Aerin was barely given time to enjoy Lucifer's almost dog-like glance of befuddlement before the windows to the Raven Rook shattered and four ridiculous humans blew inside, straddling brooms and whooping up a ruckus.

Sal, wearing the armor of an unbuttoned Hawaiian shirt and ratted jeans, crash landed by them and wrestled his broom to the ground.

"Ha!" he hollered. "And they kicked me out of hog ridin' on account of me bein' dumped on my head so much." His victory smile was cut short when he took in their situation. With a motion smooth and strong for a man his age, he scooped up the girl who'd been like a daughter to him, and deposited her sidesaddle on the broom.

"C'mon Moira Jo, time we git the hell outta Dodge."

Moira didn't tear her eyes from Aerin, though she clutched at the broomstick as if afraid to fall. "I can't leave!"

"You're the only one who can," Aerin gritted out. "Darkness. The baby will unlock the wards."

"It's impossible," Lucy screeched.

"No, it isn't." Aerin laughed triumphantly. Or maybe she moaned, it was hard to tell. "You forget that not only did you live in my body, I lived in your mind, too. I know how strong you are...but I know your weaknesses too."

Moira shook her head. "No. I'm not leaving the three of y—" Suddenly she doubled over and clutched her belly, her breath obviously stolen from her.

"Sal!" Aerin screamed, as a pulse of power drove her to her knees.

"10-4!" With a salute, the broom took off beneath them and he steered it toward the window. The entire room held its breath as he approached the window and then deflated as he *wooshed* through without so much as a hiccup. His entourage went *YeeHawing* after him with their legs kicking in the air.

Aerin's relief was short-lived, however, as the three of them turned back to the Devil, who had just had her best laid plans shit-kicked out of her.

And still, she held them prisoners of her wrath.

As Aerin's powers slid away from her, she felt the spell go to work on her life.

"We have something you want." Julian's cultured baritone crashed like a rogue wave over the din, leaving smooth silence in its wake.

The entire room turned to where two of the Four Horsemen stood, each framed by a separate shattered window, unable to advance any closer.

War, enormous and stone-faced, planted his boots on the left ledge. His awe-inspiring sword rested across the span of his shoulders, one hand grasping the hilt, the other hooked over the blade. His eyes blazed with the kind of wrath that had ended entire civilizations.

Pestilence stood two windows to the right, leaving a space in between them. Tall, dark, and impeccable, his expression was so mild as to be enigmatic as he pulled at the tips of his gloves one by one, sliding them from his graceful, masculine hands.

Conquest, Aerin assumed, would be found at Moira's side, ushering her to safety.

There was no sign of Death.

Her heart surged at the sight of Julian, and her eyes drank in every lovely line and sinew of him. She wanted to call to him, to reach for him, but she'd barely the strength to keep her eyes open.

And he barely spared her a glance.

Instead, he addressed the assembly, though the daggers in his gaze were aimed directly at the Devil. "If any of you persist with any part of this endeavor, then I'd caution you not to have plans to leave this inn alive. For it will become your prison and your graveyard. You'd better trust that Lucifer is a devil of her word and will keep the wards intact. Because the moment you fall into our hands, you will learn every meaning, every dark and terrible facet of the word *suffering*."

Anxious glances and quiet murmurs thrummed through the coven as they took in the awe-inspiring sight that were these astonishingly masculine immortals.

Lucifer scoffed, yanking on the dark chain still imprisoning one of Aerin's wrists, tumbling her to her hands and knees on the hard marble floors. "If you're here to offer yourself as trade, you needn't bother. You'll belong to me soon enough."

"I wouldn't dream of it," Julian said blithely. "We're here to offer you something you crave far more than any of us. Something you covet more than victory, revenge, or even power."

"And what might that be?" she scoffed.

"Yourself."

Death descended from the sky, strong and majestic. He landed in the middle window, his eyes burning holy condemnation and his onyx wings drawing in like an archangel.

The limp body of a lithe woman draped over his arms.

Aerin felt the spell draining her slightly abate, as if its attention had gone elsewhere.

"We always knew this would be a last resort, but here we are," Julian motioned to the remains, kept in a strange torpor of shadow. "I sent Bane on a quest to find your body. The only one that will not be rotted by the decay in your soul."

Hunger gleamed in the abysmal wells of Lucifer's eyes, even as her skin began to putrefy. "Why would I trade, when I can kill one of the four and thereby win the day?"

Claire stepped forward, the fire in her palms catching on her hair, in her eyes, igniting her with a beauty so fantastic, even Aerin wanted to cower before the heat.

"You don't have the power to fight us all as you are," she said, the carpets at her feet catching as she began to lose control of her temper. "And if Aerin dies here, so does everyone who watched it happen, including Gwen's body."

"Damn straight." Tierra agreed, plaster pouring from the ceiling as the building shook with her rage. "Try finding a witch to possess *then*. And if you do, we'll keep forcing you out until we figure a way to vanquish you for good."

Whispers and murmurs intensified behind Lucifer as the witches processed what she had done to them. The proof of their pilfered magic. One of them snatched up the Grimoire.

Julian, held in check by the wards, ran his finger across a shard of glass still in the pane. "Tell me, would you rather wither again and again in a shell that will not contain the entirety of your power? Or would you prefer to have an immortal body back?"

Aerin scowled up at him. "Does this...seem like...a shit...idea to anyone else?" she managed.

"Done." Lucifer released Aerin from the spell and lifted her hands to her sides prompting the darkness to levitate her upward toward Killian. "Give it over."

Dru sliced through the air with his sword, creating a barrier. "Lower the wards first."

Aerin felt the magic imprisoning them into the Raven Rook loosen and then fall.

"I've done my part." Lucy reached for the body in Death's hands. "Now keep your end of the bargain."

"Have you guys lost your mind?" Aerin screeched. They were handing Lucifer exactly what she wanted to grow stronger. They might as well be handing her victory.

Death drew Lucifer away through the window, and out of their sight.

"Come on." Claire said, wrapping one of Aerin's arms around the back of her neck so she could stand. "Let's get you out of here."

With a flick of her finger, Tierra blew the sturdy wooden door off its hinges, testing the wards by marching through it.

On Aerin's other side, Martha took her arm, looking over at her with an expression of conciliation. "We're coming with you," she said. "Well some of us are."

They hobbled out onto the porch and sat down in the sunlight, breathing in the air.

Because of the power required of Lucifer to do what she'd done to Aerin, some of the witches had been nearly as drained as she. Claire and Tierra made several trips back inside to conduct a quick assessment of the damage, and spared precious time ministering spells and herbs to those who were pale, drained, frightened, and wounded.

"We never should have doubted. Never should have let fear take root," Martha tutted, laying her hand against the burn on Aerin's arm and murmuring a healing spell. "Not that it is an excuse, but no one is equipped for times like these. No one knows which side is the one with the truth, sometimes until it's too late."

"I understand," Aerin replied, and she did. "I know what it's like to be seduced by the darkness."

Later, by the time all the witches had been led out onto Water Street, Aerin's wound was little worse than a nagging sunburn. With what little strength she had left, she summoned her broom, noting that Claire did the same.

Tierra herded maybe half the coven down the street toward the fountain where they could climb the steps to uptown. "Everyone collect your things and your loved ones. You'll shelter on the de Moray grounds tonight. We'll ward the hell out of it."

The other half...had gone with Melody. Following Lucifer, it seemed.

After a time, Death glided down on his ebony wings. "She's gone for now," Killian said, grabbing Tierra and kissing her. "It'll be at least a full rotation of the moon before she can resurrect into an immortal body. If we're lucky, it'll take her longer."

"Oh, good," Aerin said, her tone dripping with sarcasm. "We have twenty-four hours until all of our hard work is completely unraveled."

Killian's eyebrow lifted. "Uh, you're welcome for saving your life."

Aerin felt like growling. Screaming. Punching him. And thanking him. "I would have given my life if it would have meant the end of her! If it would have meant an end to this." She thrust her hands to the destruction wrought on Main St. "My death would have been worth it if it saved lives."

Lightning crackled across the cloudless sky, causing many of them to jump or cover their head out of impulse. Thunder followed, shaking the ground beneath their feet with the power of a Santa Ana earthquake.

"That wasn't me," Tierra said, glancing around with eyes wide as gooseberries.

"Nope." A smile split Claire's lips ear to ear as she beamed at what Aerin was now holding in her hand.

Aerin closed her palm around what felt like cold, smooth ivory at the top of which a moonstone was cast into the intricate tinges. The gentle pressure of a crown on her head carried the weight of the entire world's demands. Of their destiny to either destroy the earth or save it.

Her wand. Her crown.

She'd earned it.

For some reason, she had thought that she'd feel something like victorious after such a momentous achievement. But instead she felt humbled. Grateful. Determined.

She needed to earn this honor. To deserve it.

Returning Claire and Tierra's congratulatory hugs, she lifted her head and looked for Julian to share in this moment with her.

He was nowhere to be found.

Frowning she looked down into her hand, considering what she'd done. She was not, at her core, a selfless woman. Her entire life she'd only had herself to look after, to rely upon.

To care about.

And in such a short time, all that had changed.

She'd give her life for those she loved. She'd have died for Moira.

Moira! The thought of her bending down and clutching her belly had Aerin hopping on her broom. "We have to get to Moira!" she called to her sisters.

"I was feeling that, too," Tierra agreed, allowing her mate to lift her in his arms and take off with a great beat of his powerful wings.

"Let's go," Claire took a running start and hopped on her broom.

Aerin reveled in the lash of the wind as she blew toward the mansion. She fixated on the spires visible above the rest of the town, knowing exactly which balcony was her sister's.

The French doors were flung wide open as if in anticipation of their arrival. Aerin did a less-than-dexterous dismount onto the deck, nearly crashing into the fresh-water aquarium Moira kept for the rehabilitation of cracked-shelled turtles.

Though it'd been less than an hour since Moira had escaped, she'd done the impossible.

"Holy fucking shit balls." Aerin breathed. "It's a girl."

Looking resplendent from where she reclined in the bed as deep and comfortable as seafoam, Moira speared her with an aquamarine gaze just as censoring as it was sparkling. "Aw man, now those are the first words little Seraphine Morgana de Moray ever heard from the aunt who saved her life."

Had Aerin not been so awe-struck and speechless, she would have pointed out that the kid had almost certainly already heard worse from her father in her blissfully short life.

The man in question stood next to the bed, cradling a tiny bundle wrapped in a cobalt blanket.

He stared down at the child with more grace and love than any depiction of a saint, virgin, or deity Aerin had ever seen. He was a man lost in love and beaming with a heart she hadn't known he possessed.

Justine had been standing beside Nick in a smart pink house frock, allowing Violet to look down into the bundle containing her cousin.

When Killian and Tierra landed, Justine returned the baby to her parents' care. "My soul stayed right where it ought to be the entire time," she said proudly. "And she only sprouted her wings the one time."

Tierra kissed Violet as they all gathered around Moira's bed taking a silent moment to stare in wonder at the being who brought them all full circle.

The *Ceann Dorcha*. The Dark One.

"You should be the first to hold her," Moira said, nodding to Nick to hand her over.

Aerin balked, holding out her hands in protest only to have them filled with a baby.

"Don't drop this one," Tierra snarked. "I doubt she can fly."

Aerin looked down and, for a moment, the entire world receded. She thought she distantly heard Moira and Tierra remarking about how, though being a de Moray witch came with a great deal of pain and responsibility, one perk was near instantaneous labor.

At least when immortal babies were involved.

Two little eyes the color of black sapphires gazed up at her from a tiny face. She knew babies at this age weren't supposed to be able to focus very easily, but their eyes connected instantaneously, and Aerin read from within them a soul as ancient as the cosmos.

And a heart as good as it was dark.

"Don't hide from your darkness little one," she crooned, touching the tiny nose with her fingertip. "We'll help you nurture it into something good."

First, they would have to defeat the Devil who was, even now, gathering her strength. Then they would need to save the planet from their own prophecy. But they'd find a way. Because they had to. For Violet and Seraphine.

Tiny fingers wrapped around her extended one with a surprisingly strong grip.

And with that one motion, she stole Aerin's heart.

❧ 47 ❧

Julian Roarke was not an immortal prone to pacing, yet here he was, wearing a tread in the plush arabesque rug in front of Aerin's white marble fireplace. His heart would not slow, his veins constricted, and his thoughts raced with all the pounding, churning speed of his midnight stallion, Archimedes, at full gallop. Feeling confined by his own skin, he ripped his suit coat off and flung it on a chair before yanking on the knot of his tie, jerking it from his neck.

Freeing a few buttons, he pulled air into lungs that technically required none, wondering if this was what it felt like to drown.

Because it was bloody awful.

The door whooshed open on a fragrant breeze. "Oh my God, Julian, you should see those Kentucky Fried fogeys with the babies. It is hysterical."

The voice from the doorframe planted his shoes to the ground. He was facing away from her and for that he was glad. Because the teasing nonchalance in her voice threatened to drive him certifiably mad.

Aerin.

She continued, her speech a flurry of excitement and warmth. "One of them, Spunky, I think, tried to catch Violet in a pillowcase when she took off. Tierra gave actual birth to a cow and Moira shit an actual brick. I don't think shaken baby syndrome is a thing with immortals though, Killian seemed fine with it—" She paused, seeming to finally take note his discomfiture. "You're—let me guess, I'm getting better at this—Anxious? Irritated? Not angry, are you?"

Julian's fingers curled into fists, and he contemplated putting said fist through the marble, just because he could. "I've searched the vocabularies of every language I know, which is nearly infinite, and I am convinced there isn't a word in existence to encompass what I am currently feeling."

Her heels clacked against the hardwood floors and the door clicked softly as she allowed it to shut behind her.

"I warn you," he growled. "It might not behoove you to be shut in a confined space with me. Not like this."

She joined him on the carpet, close enough to touch him, but deciding not to do so.

"You left after Lucy," she said with more sobriety. "And you didn't come to see the baby. Why? Are you wounded? Did something happen?"

"Did something *happen*?" he whirled on her then. He was not a violent man by nature, but his fingers itched to clamp around her perfect pale throat and throttle some sense into her. "Did something—" The sight of her stole his breath for a dozen different reasons.

Her hair, usually pulled tight into an updo, was loose around her shoulders and down her back, ruffled and windblown by a sprint on a broom, he assumed. Atop the glorious mane was a crown made of an opalescent structure, strewn with the clearest, most brilliant diamonds, moonstones, and mystic topaz. In her hand she clutched a wand made of the same ivory gems, a moonstone set on one side, and Labradorite on the other.

She'd done it. She'd made the sacrifice. He'd watched her do it.

And he was livid about it.

"I'll tell you what happened," he snarled, astonished at the violence in his own voice. "Mere *hours* ago, I was forced to watch from outside dark and impregnable wards as you put yourself in harm's way. For what seemed like an eternity, I stood helplessly by as my greatest adversary drained the life out of the woman I love. That's what happened. That's what *never* should have happened!"

Aerin blinked several times, derision clouding her quicksilver eyes. "I understand that, I do. But I also had to watch the man I love hand over a trump card that will make our next move nigh to impossible. We had her contained to rotting corpses. We had her weakened and now—"

"It wouldn't have worked like that," Julian gritted out. "She would have been slowed, certainly, but never stopped. What we know is that it will take all four elements to vanquish her. All four of you to stop or fulfill this prophecy. And you were more than ready to just throw that away—throw this away—" he gestured between them, her heart and his. "And for what? Some misguided sense of self-sacrifice?"

"I *had* to save Moira's baby from that spell," she explained evenly, as if talking to an overwrought child. "There was no choice. I believe those two are more important than the four of us, hell even the eight of us. And if Lucy's spell had shackled Moira, sure my sister would have survived, but the kid could have died before she had a chance to live."

"It didn't have to bloody be you!" he roared, throwing his hands up in a gesture of all-encompassing exasperation. "Either Claire or Tierra could have withstood that spell. They're soul-bonded. They're immortal. You're—we're—" He whirled away from her again, unable to stand the sight of her, the elation he felt in her presence. The pride he couldn't admit at her tenure of the wand and crown. The desire she evoked. The very masculine, utterly mortal possessive instinct that he'd battled all bloody afternoon.

He hauled in an endless breath fragrant with her calming scent. Citrus and fresh linen and something sharp and pure like snow. "I've lived to witness the destruction of millions," he said upon a sigh. I've withstood untold millennia of pain, isolation, and a burden of guilt that would have crushed Atlas. But watching your life drain away from you was by *far* the worst thing I've been privy to."

She laid a gentle hand on his back, and said the very worst thing she possibly could have.

"I'm sorry, Julian. I didn't mean to put you through that."

She was sorry. *Sorry?* He turned and caught her wrist before flinging her hand away. "I don't want your pity." Realizing he couldn't stay in the room for a moment longer, he retreated toward the door and wrenched the latch.

"Then what *do* you want?" she demanded.

The question hurt him just as much as anything else, and finally, he exploded. "How can you ask me that? I want *you*, Aerin. All of you. I want your past and your future. Your heart and your *immortal* soul. I want you bonded to me like your sisters have bonded to my brothers so that eternity might belong to us. And today you almost sentenced me to a life lived in the same hellish loneliness I've been sequestered to since the fall of man. How could you? How *dare* you?"

Her mouth dropped open, but she didn't utter a word as she reached up and relieved herself of her crown with trembling fingers. She made her way to the mantle and set it and her wand on the ledge before turning back to him.

Her eyes had dimmed to pools of gray as a fathomless emotion stole the vibrancy of her spirit he so adored.

"I thought I was protecting you," she whispered.

His eye twitched and his blood pounded. "You'll have to clarify, because I cannot begin to fathom what would possess you to—"

"It seemed strange to me, all this time, that four Horsemen were sent after four identical quadruplets, and one by one, they fell in love." She rubbed at a muscle in her neck as if it wouldn't release. "It seemed like fate. Like prophecy. Though it was written nowhere. And I thought...I thought...that yet again you drew the short straw."

She wrapped her arms around her own middle as if she could contain whatever she was about to say, or protect her vital organs from whatever threat she perceived. It was difficult to tell. "I didn't want to bond you to me just because it was the expected thing to do. Because the others did it. I didn't want you to love me because I'm the only woman you can touch. Or fuck. Because the novelty of that will wear off eventually, and you'll want someone else."

Julian released the doorknob. "I would never—"

"We're talking about eternity here." She sliced the air with her hand "An eternity with *me*. With my smart mouth and my wicked tendencies. What if we win this, Julian? What if you no longer have to be Pestilence and can walk the earth as a man? You're a living anachronism for Christ's sake. A God's honest gentleman. What if the world of options opens up to you and a gentle*woman* with gentle ways and gentle words captures your heart? It's not fair of me to stand in the way of that. A soul-bond could become your soul-bondage and..." She looked away, seeming unable to watch his expression as she said her next words.

"Julian, I love you too much to put you in chains."

At her admission, Julian felt as if she'd both dismantled him and stitched him back together. His soul flew at the motivation behind her words, and his heart fell at the content.

She loved him. She loved him enough to leave him his liberty. Even at the expense of her heart. Her needs and desires.

Her own life.

Whatever intent she read on his features blanched her skin even paler than normal. However, true to her nature, she did not retreat as he advanced.

They collided like thunderclouds. All electricity and wild, chaotic recklessness.

His mouth claimed hers as her fingers tore at his clothing. The buttons of his shirt clattered to the floor and she purred into his mouth.

The sound vibrated all the way down to his cock.

Julian crushed her to him, knowing he was being rough, that neither of them would come out of this encounter unscathed, unmarked.

Or un-bonded.

He didn't fucking care. He wanted her to score his skin, and he ached to mark her as his own. They belonged together, eternally and otherwise, and as soon as he could tear his mouth away from hers, he'd find the words to tell her that.

He ripped away her blouse and bra, shucking it down her shoulder and pinning her elbows behind her, thrusting her breasts forward. He bent to devour the pink pebbles of her nipples, laving a gentle tongue over them in wet, worshipful glides before using his teeth.

She made a guttural sound that drove him to the very edge of his sanity.

Julian often tempered his supernatural strength, but not this time. Clothes disintegrated in his hands, he rent her leather belt with as much ease as he did her panties until nothing was between their souls but flesh, sinew, and bone.

He captured her lips once again, lifting her against him and splitting her legs around his waist as he explored the recesses of her mouth he might have missed before. He thrust deeper, coiled his tongue against hers, their passions sparking into an inferno.

She hooked her heels around his buttocks as three long strides had her pressed against the wall. And his sex pressed against hers.

He pinned her there, shoving her thighs wider and thrusting inside her heat.

She made a raw sound of astonishment, her fingers tangling in his hair as she pulled him closer. Deeper. Using the wall as a ballast, she met him thrust for breath-stealing thrust.

Suddenly it wasn't enough. He wanted to crawl inside of her, to be a part of her, as deep as he could physically go.

And then deeper.

He rebounded off the wall, to another hard surface, the dresser maybe, he didn't care. Swiping the contents away, he rested her ass on the edge and angled it so he could reach between them, deepening his strokes as he brushed his thumb over the ruffles of flesh above where they joined.

She whimpered his name. Then she called it to the sky as she came apart, her intimate muscles clenching over and around him. There was desperation to her cries, and a pain that melded with the pleasure, wrenching her higher.

He could feel it in his own soul. The clutching, seizing, bruising desperation of it.

"You are mine," he growled.

"Yes," she rasped, her eyes rolling back in her head as her spine arched in a sinuous undulation of bliss. "*Yes!*"

He bent down and caught her hair, weaving his fingers through the strands before pulling it taught. Exposing her throat.

"*Say it,*" he commanded.

Her mouth opened, but nothing escaped.

"You are mine and I am yours," he pounded into her, holding the storm of pleasure rolling down his spine at bay.

She reared up, her hand against his chest, her eyes no longer languid with pleasure, but wide with surprise. "But—"

"I. Am. Given," he said, in time to his powerful thrusts. "Say it."

Her arms wound around his neck, bringing her warm body against him, threading their limbs together. She smoothed her hands down the straining muscles of his back as if they struck her with awe and wonder, before she pressed her lips to his ear.

"You are mine and I am yours," she whispered, and he thought he heard tears thicken her voice. "I am given."

He said her name like dying men pleaded for mercy. It was both a war cry and a prayer. An invocation of forever. Warmth spread through him making way for his release. It lasted for an eternity, seizing not just his body, but his soul, his spirit, the very essence of him. Just as his body fit into hers, so was she a piece of his puzzle. Only she made him whole.

And an eternity without her would be a hell like none other.

After, he pulled away from her and carried her to the bed, cleaning them both before dragging her up his chest to settle over him as he reclined against the headboard.

"I don't want a gentlewoman," he murmured as he traced the brackets of her spine with idle fingers. "I want *you*. The perfect complication. The incredible dichotomy of strength and a softness you reserve only for me." Catching her chin in his hand, he lifted it so she could look into his eyes.

He knew that she could detect a lie, that it was part of her powers, but he still wanted her to read his veracity, to see the undying fervency of his love. "No matter what happens tomorrow, know that I love you. That if we are to be unmade by evil, the torment will be worth it if I am at your side."

She swallowed, her auburn lashes sweeping down to hide a rare glimmer of vulnerability. "Are you not afraid?" she whispered, "Are you not afraid to lose this bliss, afraid to hope that we might be able to keep it?"

He shook his head, a celestial sort of tenderness gripping his heart. "How can I fear anything with a woman as fierce as you to protect me?" he teased, thumbing away a tear as it streaked from the corner of her eye.

"I'm not as strong as they all think," she murmured.

He gathered her to him, wrapping her rather too tightly in his embrace, pressing her ear against his chest so she could hear the heart that beat only for her.

"You're strong enough to save us all, Aerin de Moray. I don't doubt that. You and your sisters are the most extraordinary creatures to ever grace this planet, and I can say such things. I've been here since the beginning, I think. I'm starting to remember..."

Her hand settled on his chest and she yawned greatly, tucking her knee up between his legs. "Remember what?" she murmured.

What the world had been like. What it could be again.

What they were fighting for.

Mortals. No matter the damage they'd wrought. No matter what prophecy contained. This capacity for love was worth fighting for.

Especially with this woman at his side.

❧ 48 ❧

I f someone had asked Aerin a year ago where she thought a battle for the future survival of the human race would be held, she certainly wouldn't have answered "Port Townsend, Washington."

She might have thought somewhere ancient and meaningful. Someplace closer to the cradle of civilization than the last bastion of it.

Why not Stonehenge or on top of various and sundry Biblical ruins? Or like, one of those places where comic book movie battles went down like downtown NYC or LA or London. Not bumfuck USA, this town of ten thousand people surrounded on three sides by the Pacific Ocean, a stone's throw from Canada. *Canada*! She'd be willing to bet her life that no one in the history of *ever* would have thought the Devil would venture this close to Canada. I mean Georgia, sure, but—

"Aerin!" Claire snapped her fingers in front of her eyes, startling her. "What is wrong with you? Where did you go?"

"Canada," Aerin muttered, opening the door to their mother's attic.

"What?"

"Nothing, never mind." She was losing it. Here,

standing in her mother's secret room, the portal to Siren's Cry a shiver at her back, she was realizing she didn't really wanna go do the Apocalypse. She wanted to crawl back into bed with Julian. Or go for a ride on her broom somewhere far, far away.

But she couldn't, even if her conscience would allow it. Because if she didn't stay and do what her birthright demanded of her, there would soon be nowhere to fly to.

The world as she knew it would be lost, and any hope for a better one, an impossibility.

Aerin would have also expected a little weirder pomp and ceremony or... something. Some sort of celestial heraldry or harbinger of hell. But she'd arisen this morning and done what spells she could with her sisters to strengthen and protect the mortals and earth in their care.

Then they did a spell to strengthen and protect Moira's vagina because she'd just given birth, and no one wanted to ride a broom or fight evil with their lady business blown out by an entire tiny human.

After that, they'd made breakfast burritos and ate them with the Four Horsemen of the Apocalypse around their dining room table.

Plus a few extra hillbillies because no one had thought to tell them to leave.

It had been surreal AF.

They introduced the babies to their familiars, and laughed and cooed at their antics. They fought about who made the best coffee (Dru did). And they waited for the Apocalypse to start.

Because what else could they do?

But dread?

And hope?

Reports came in that several volcanoes around the globe blew around noon.

By three PM, the Amazon rain forest was on fire

and Death Valley had flooded. Hail pelted the Sahara and the Alps were beginning to crumble. Locusts feasted on crops in South America and the entire South China Sea turned blood red. Great and ancient rivers like the Euphrates and the Rhine slowed to a trickle, leaving the skeletons of numerous ships stranded in their beds.

And the de Moray sisters knew that when the blood moon began to set over the standing stones at Siren's cry, they would be there.

And so would the Devil.

They'd have this out once and for all.

Their Horsemen had left as the shadows grew long to do whatever it was warriors did before such a battle. Ready the horses, shine the armor, sharpen the weapons, etc. The de Moray sisters each kissed Violet and Seraphine who, even at such a tender age, were ridiculously well behaved, as if they understood the gravitas of the day. Not wanting to bring infants to an apocalypse, they left them once again in Justine's care.

Moira and Tierra helped each other up the stairs, both holding in hiccupping sobs as they retrieved their crowns and wands, and all four trudged toward the attic like women about to face their fates.

And so, they were.

As they spilled into Mirelle de Moray's attic room, they stopped to breathe her in. To look at the book-shelves full of ancient tomes and rows of herbs hanging from hooks. Baubles sparkled beneath the skylight and with a flick of Claire's finger, candles flared to life.

Their flames illuminated four ancient-looking trunks lined up in front of the portal that Aerin was certain hadn't been in this room before.

Tierra went to them, throwing open the lid and staring down at the most vibrant scarlet material. Lifting it out of the trunk she unfurled a long robe stitched of the finest silk and softest velvet. "Look,

Claire," she said, fingering a note pinned to the long sleeve. "It's for you."

Claire allowed Tierra to slip the robe over her usual jeans and black tank, and then she unpinned the note and read it aloud. "These robes are woven from threads of fire and passion and stitched with cords of illumination and creativity. Though it seems the world is burning around you, know that the destruction is necessary for rebirth. You will win the day, so he can light the way. Signed, Kenna de Moray." The robe fastened with tiger's eye toggles that glinted in the candlelight as she fastened them.

"Ugh. They rhyme." Aerin muttered. She thought Claire looked like a goddess and told her so. Noting how the robes shimmered with umber flames when she walked. "I remember reading about Kenna, she was Malcom de Moray's sister. The fire druid."

"That's right," Claire said as she bent to open another trunk. This one contained a robe of cobalt and azure, and she unfurled it to hold up to Moira. "For you."

Tears still leaked from Moira's eyes as she slid her arms into the robes. "How do you think these got here?" She sniffed, tucking her arm beneath her hair to pull it away from the collar.

Tierra put her finger to her chin in thought. "There are torpor spells that can hide things until they're needed," she reflected. "I'm sensing a bit of that sort of magic at work."

"Makes sense," Moira said as she caught at the note hanging from her robe. "These robes are woven with shifting threads of water and dreams and stitched with cords of vision and serenity." she read. "Though floods rage and seas swell, the path of least resistance will serve him well. Signed, Morgana de Moray."

"Aww," Tierra said. "I love that you gave Seraphine her middle name."

Moira fastened her toggles and tucked the note away. "She was there for me when I needed her. She will always be close to my heart."

"Here's yours, Tierra." Aerin flapped a stunning robe of greens and golds underlaid with deep shades of bronze. She held it while Tierra slipped it on and waded around for the note she knew was there.

"These robes are woven from threads of soil and seed, stitched with cords of manifestation and abundance. Though the earth is in upheaval, know that she is the source of our strength, and will always nurture us. You will hold the ground. So his soul is no longer bound. Signed, Malcolm de Moray." She held the note to her chest. "I just love him. Do you think Malcolm is the 'he' referenced here?"

Malcolm de Moray had once been King of the Picts and ruler of the druids and an earth druid, himself. He'd held such a burden on his shoulders, and a thousand years ago, he'd halted the apocalypse in Scotland. He was a grandfather who knew they'd be born one day, and he knew that they'd need his guidance. That they'd need these robes. Stitched with love and words of encouragement.

Tierra looked at Aerin a little sheepishly. "There's only ever been a maximum of three de Moray siblings... until now. You didn't have an air druid ancestor or anything to give you your wand so...your robe might not have a note."

Aerin shrugged it off, having come to terms with the same idea. "That's okay. Let's get it on. We don't have much time."

Moira opened the final trunk and took out the robe, a shimmering confection of every conceivable color of sky, from stormy gray to blue threaded through with shots of silver and white. Aerin shucked it on with her help and gasped as something scraped at her arm in the billowing sleeves.

She closed her eyes for a moment. Just so, so, *so* relieved she hadn't been left out. Disconnecting it from the sleeve she looked down into something like ancient cardstock upon which was scrawled semi-neat lettering. She read, "I was once one with the darkness. A demon born for destruction. I was sent to end Malcolm de Moray, and I fell in love with him instead. I saved his life and he saved my soul, and together we bought the world a thousand years. You can change what is written in the sky. So that he can touch the world. Signed, Vian."

Beneath it a hasty line was scrawled that Aerin read silently. *Forgive me, I have no care for rhymes.*

Aerin didn't realize she was crying until she laughed.

Vian. A demon and a kindred spirit. She'd have to ponder that later.

She turned to her sisters and realized they were standing in a circle, each a point of the direction they'd been assigned by their elements.

"We leave the familiars this time," Claire said sagely. "Someone has to look out for things in case..."

She didn't have to finish her sentence.

Aerin glanced around at them, marveling at how resplendent they were in their robes. How their crowns had transformed them into something regal. Symbolic.

And powerful.

It was Tierra who turned to the portal first, taking a deep breath before she stepped through. Moira followed, then Claire and Aerin gripped her wand tightly as she brought up the rear.

It was time to save the world.

Or end it.

Until this moment, Aerin hadn't known it was possible to be seized by both marvel and terror simultaneously. The sight before her both moved her deeply and caused her heart to plunge into her belly as if to hide from the enormity of what was about to happen.

The cliff known as Siren's Cry loomed skyscraper tall above Discovery Bay, a handful of miles outside of Port Townsend proper. The de Morays had stepped through the portal to several standing stones adorning the pinnacle like a jagged crown, the stones replaced with a flick of Tierra's wand.

Below them, a churning sea barraged the cliffs. And before them, acres of verdant meadow unspooled down the gentle slope that would have been called a moor in a more ancient land. It was besieged by dense forests of both evergreen and deciduous trees.

This meadow made for a perfect battlefield.

The armies had assembled and were, even now, facing each other like players on a chessboard.

Lucifer levitated in a cloud of writhing black mist in front of an army thousands strong of wrathful wraiths and the undead. They stretched back into the trees and disappeared beneath the shadows. Bodies under complete control, whose souls she lusted after.

Souls they would fight to save today.

Aerin had never truly understood what the word *horde* meant before now, but the numbers of hissing, screaming, cackling cadavers were incalculable.

And fucking creepy.

Melody stood at the Devil's side, the apparent general of the dark-clad witches who arced out behind her. Each chanted and taunted in equal measure. Calling their powers to lend to the darkness. It was odd to see several of the witch hunters join their ranks, but times like these often created unlikely bedfellows.

Against the onslaught, creating a protective arc around the stones, the coven of witches stood like infantry behind four magnificent figures mounted on their famously colored horses.

Conquest astride his white horse, draped in a suit of armor that might have done any Roman legionnaire proud, managed to look both civilized and brutal as he held his bow at the ready, an arrow nocked between two strong fingers.

War had painted his red steed with various symbols and adorned it with the same dark armor plating he wore. He gleamed like the edge of his frightening blade, as the horse danced beneath him in anticipation of the coming violence.

Pestilence eschewed ornamentations, donning only a long black hooded robe that draped majestically over Archimedes. He sat tall and proud, cultured but merciless, brandishing his scales like a banner. In his offhand he held an onyx-tipped spear Aerin hadn't been aware he knew how to wield.

Death had stowed his wings in favor of his pale horse, but he wore only simple black leather across his wide chest. His wicked scythe glinted in the dying sun, and Aerin could see the blood moon reflected in the devilish blade.

It wasn't the sight of the Horsemen, awe-inspiring as they were, that pricked Aerin's eyes with tears.

It was who stood with them.

Sir Norman Barriston and his cadre of students, swords drawn, and patchwork armor clad. His elegant wife stood next to him clutching a cleaver from her kitchen.

Tacklebox, er Sunny—obviously not worried about being stabbed if all the piercings in her body were aught to go by— was armed with a chainsaw she'd pilfered from their shed. She revved it often and chortled manically, but Aerin sensed the fear beneath her bravado.

Uncle Sal, Mookey, Red, and Little Earl were armed to the teeth with enough firepower to give John Wick wet dreams.

These brave souls had gathered to buy them the time they needed to work their magic.

The Star of the Morning looked as she should, a woman of astonishing beauty. Tall, blond, and almost skeletally thin, her dark eyes as soulless and unfeeling as her farcical smile. She wore a robe not unlike theirs. Black, of course, just to avoid any confusion as to what anyone's powers were, Aerin guessed.

She held a staff topped with Labradorite, and it swirled with dark power as she opened her arms as if to welcome them to the Apocalypse. "Don't mind me, ladies, you're here to end the world. I'm only here make certain you don't do something stupid. Like save it."

Claire notched up her chin. "We'll end you first."

"How many times must I tell you, you cannot," Lucifer scoffed. "I am eternal. I am fed by the dark and I am—"

"Eat glass, Devil Barbie," Aerin interrupted, all mature and stuff, before she held her wand to the sky, evoking bright forks of lightning. Her robes stirred in the summoning wind. "You are nothing but the archaic evil leftover of some long-forgotten vengeful God who's been twisted through time to be a monotheistic ass weasel. You're sloppy seconds. Old news. Yesterday's bullshit. And you're about to fall. Again."

"Yeah!" Sunny yelled over the loud idle of her weapon's motor.

"*En garde*, Beelzebub," Norman dropped into a fighting stance, his hand in the air behind him as his brave charges did the same.

Drawing her palm over the stone in her staff three times, the devil conjured something like a projection onto the blazing sunset. "Whatever happens here, whatever battle you think you might fight, it won't matter. The world is imploding. You've already lost." Images of global devastation flashed above them. Crumbling pyramids, cities ablaze, people fleeing in fear.

"No," Moira said gently, her voice somehow clear above the din. "We haven't lost." She pointed her wand and summoned a skein of water over part of the image, using it as a magnifying glass. There, in a throng of terrified refugees, people were lifting those who had fallen. They heaved the wounded onto their backs and carried children who did not belong to them. Witches the world over stood against the onslaught of disaster. Calming the fires and holding back walls of flood water so others could escape with their lives.

"Women—witches—know that they shouldn't take power from each other," Tierra addressed the opposing coven. "They should give. They should lift. They should empower. Because this still exists in the world, it means Lucifer has lost already." She lifted her wand and the world began to shake. "We're just here to finish the job."

Lucifer's laugh raised every hair on Aerin's body. "Say your little spells if you must," she cackled unleashing whatever chains held back her minions. "You won't leave those stones alive."

❦ 50 ❦

Nothing Aerin had seen on HBO could have prepared her for the sight of what Lucifer unleashed. The army of the undead advanced, their weapons often rudimentary, but no less terrifying for it. Machetes, axes, pipes, and even pistols—for those few who had tendons and fingers left.

She learned that too late, as one of Norman's students fell to a bullet before someone could hack off the gun arm.

The Horsemen spurred their mounts, launching into the fray, their weapons cutting down entire swaths of undead not unlike those monstrous harvest machines chewed through fields of wheat.

The Coven wove wards against the magic of their lost sisters, slowing Lucifer's advance.

Aerin looked to the left and the right of her as she and her sisters shared a moment of hesitation. They had to cast together to break the final Seal. They had to end this, so they could mend it.

Moira breathed in and reached for her hand, "I am the storm of the sea," she began.

Claire's hand slid into the other side, clenching it tight. "I am the dance of the flame."

Aerin drew from their bravery, glowing with love. "I am the breath of the sky."

Tiera completed their chain, creating an unbreakable bond. "I am the heart of the earth."

They all said, "Through me the prophecy is fulfilled."

Four times, they chanted the words together. *I am the storm of the sea.*

Clouds gathered in the south, rolling and climbing over each other, clashing with lightning and thunder. Ice and hail pelted at the battle sharp and devastating, taking several of the undead out of the fray.

And elsewhere it was shown that storm surges overflowed their banks. Rivers redirected and floods swelled to encompass monuments to past invasions and surrenders, victories and defeats. Piles of trash that had been thrown into the sea were belched back up.

I am the dance of the flame.

A spark ignited the forest, setting the undead waiting in the trees on fire and arcing round them, ensconcing their battle in flames and evening the odds. Many of them ran for the cliff, hurling themselves into the ocean.

Elsewhere, other fires burned. Tempers ignited and passions and evils that had been held back now exploded into chaos and battles. Forests and plains alike were chewed up by flames so powerful their plumes blotted out the sun.

I am the breath of the sky.

Where lightning touched down on the battlefield, scores of undead were blown for yards where they landed, mangled and useless.

Elsewhere, tornadoes and hurricanes churned the skies, feeding the sea storms, fanning the flames.

I am the heart of the earth.

Sinkholes opened up in the earth, swallowing entire sects of Lucifer's host. Vines lashed and pinned them to the ground, immobilizing them so the Horsemen could do more efficient damage.

Elsewhere sinkholes devastated roads and railways. Landslides and earthquakes changed the geological maps of entire nations.

A distressing knowledge opened up a pit in Aerin's chest as she felt the final Seal give way. It vibrated inside of her with that silent, terrible stillness right before an earthquake. The sky turned dark. The moon barely glowed, it was so red with blood, so smothered by volcanic ash.

It was done.

Goddess help them all.

She sought Julian in the battle and found him easily. His features both savage and focused, his movements controlled and choreographed, he devastated dozens at a time with his sharp spear.

Next to him, Dru hacked at limbs and heads and Nick stood on the saddle of his horse, surfing through the horde and taking them out with three arrows at a time. With sweeps of his long scythe, Bane created a constant circle of bodies, and with their concerted efforts, they'd managed to keep the host of Hell at bay.

But it wasn't enough.

Taking advantage of the chaos, Lucifer advanced. She'd broken through the line of witches, and was coming straight for the stones. Her lips murmured dark incantations, and behind the ash and destruction razed everything to the ground.

"It is done," she said, her eyes gleaming with dark intent as she raced for them. "There is no need for you now."

"We need more time!" Tierra shouted over the din. Keeping their hands clasped, she folded them over until she clutched at Moira's other hand, forming a circle. "A protection spell. Quickly!"

Now, their wands were each held by themselves, and another.

Moira touched her wand to Aerin's and motioned the other two to do the same. An orb of light and energy pulsed between their circle, and then, as if fed by the air of a child blowing bubbles, it undulated and grew. Encompassing them first, then expanding to cover the stones.

"Everyone fall back!" Claire screamed into the fray.

Now that the final Seal had broken, power coursed through Aerin, but she wasn't certain what to do with it. Something told her that if she used it to destroy, it would be lost. Diminished.

It was meant for something else.

But what?

The Coven helped Sunny, Barriston, and the uncles safely back into the shield just in time to watch the chomping, straining undead crash against it like a rogue wave.

It held.

The Horsemen battled their way into the stones, pulling their mounts up short and breathing with the exertion of battle.

"We were beating them back!" War raged. "Send us out there, we can protect you!"

"This is only a skirmish," Tierra said. "I can feel the earth in pain. The broken Seal is rending the world in two. We have to do something now. Something bigger than this."

Aerin put a hand to her head, staring up at the moon. "I thought once the prophecy was fulfilled the answers would become clear. I thought our spell would fix things, not make them worse."

Claire turned to Lucifer, who hovered outside the shield, her features gathering with the same darkness threatening to overtake their one last glowing ball of light. "What if this is how we fix it?" she pointed to the projection, which currently showed the black forest in flames.

"What?" Tierra gaped, aghast.

"Destruction is essential to rebirth," Claire explained smoothing the shimmering garment. "If I've learned anything as the fire druid, it's *that*. Think about it, if we want to build a new world, we have to let the old one burn. It's not an ending. It's a beginning. A cataclysm between all of this shit-stained patriarchy, war, and oppression and what we've done to bend to it."

Moira nodded in fervent agreement, her eyes catching with the same spark. "We've been through all of this, together. Zombies, zealots, witch hunters, ex-boyfriends, zombie ex-boyfriends, poltergeists, bitch fights, witch fights, the devil and the prophecy. And through it all, I've always sensed, the only thing that could truly destroy us is ourselves. We are sisters and priestesses and lovers and women. We are rare and pure and somethin' this world has never seen. We were chosen to bring about the Apocalypse. So we get to fuckin' decide what the Apocalypse is. We get to build the world our children will protect and balance."

Tierra put her head on Moira's shoulder for a brief hug. "You're right. So wise. We were born to do this, but we fought it because of fear. Beneath that fear, was a knowing. Something more is out there. Something better. Something beyond what we imagined. We are wild creatures of this earth, and we've silenced the instinct within us. We have a knowing in here." She held her fist to her gut. "Inside of us. We are all born to bring something forth into this world. Perhaps *we* were born to set that free."

"What about all this?" Aerin pointed to the horror film still playing in the sky. "All of this hatred and conquest, war and pestilence and yes. Even death." She turned to the Horsemen. "What if *you* are the enemy? Not as men, not even as Horsemen, but what you stand for? What you've been forced to become. To do to others." That knowing rose within her wild and terrifying. "What if...we are fated not only to love you. But to *stop* you."

For a moment, time stood still.

Julian looked deep into her eyes, and whatever he saw there held him in thrall. His features softened and the trust that glimmered in his liquid gaze filled her with a sky full of grace. "What do you propose we do?"

"We change our skies," Aerin whispered, thinking of Vian's note. "We change our skies, so you can touch the world."

"Come again?" Conquest looked at her as if she'd lost her mind.

Aerin expounded. "What if the Goddess is not a singular being of creation? What if she is not above us in a heaven, or below us in the earth. But...within us? Perhaps she is the warmth, the compassion and the liquid fire inside of us. Perhaps she is unseen because she *is* us. We have known, instinctively, that the way things are is unsustainable because she has been lost. And we all know, when we are silent and alone, that there is a better way. A way where every voice is heard, and every life is equal. I don't want to live in a world where conquest is the only way to victory. Where warlords reign with fear and violence. Where our children suffer from famine, privation, and illness while so many of us have too much. I no longer want to live in a world where people die before their time. Where people *exist*, but do not *live*. It was all meant to be more beautiful than this. We cannot wait for death or the promises of the other world. Nor give ourselves over to it. We have to birth it here and now. Together." She stared up at each one of the mounted Horsemen challenging them to understand. "We must change not *who* you are, but *what* you are."

"What would become of us?" Killian asked, his brow crimped with befuddlement.

Aerin shook her head, a weighty grief weighing her shoulders. "I don't know."

"Oh for the love," Moira konked her head with her palm as if she'd just gotten a puzzling joke. "Hope will be your gift. So, *he* may mend the rift!" she exclaimed. "It makes sense now.

"You will win the day. So he can light the way," Claire murmured.

"You will hold the ground. So his soul is no longer bound." Tierra locked eyes with Killian. "No longer bound to her. To death. To anything but us."

"That's the hope." Aerin said. "I'm sorry, but we have to destroy you Conquest, War, Pestilence, and Death. Together."

Horses stomped and snorted. The men in their saddles sitting straight and proud their weapons aloft. They shared a long look, holding a silent conclave.

Aerin caught her breath and stood against the man she loved, but she didn't waver.

It terrified her that she might lose him.

Julian threw one leg over his raven black horse and slid to the ground. He held the scales in one hand and lance in the other.

"Together," he whispered. Kneeling, he laid both of his weapons at her feet. "Together with the sky above us."

Conquest's boots hit the earth and he marched toward Moira clutching his bow with knuckles turned white with rage. His eyes burned into hers with the force of his disbelief and something dangerous and indefinable. Taking an arrow from his quiver, he stood in front of her, staring down at the mother of his child with a silent, masculine intensity.

Then, he hit a knee, and drove his arrow into the earth. "Together, with the sea around us."

Dru jumped down from his steed and adopted the same posture in front of Claire before plunging his sword into the ground and wrapping his hands around it like a knight of old pledging his fealty. "Together, with the fire within us."

Killian likewise prostrated himself at Tierra's feet, Death ceding to life. "Together, with the earth below us. We are one."

We are one.

It was the truth that had created them and would unmake them. It was the fire that would consume them. The flood that would overtake them. And the storm that would sweep them away.

The de Moray sisters turned toward Lucifer whose power battered against the shield and they chanted,

"Together with the sky above us."

Winds redirected tidal waves while twisters and hurricanes quieted and disappeared.

"Together with the earth beneath us."

Volcanoes receded and the earth ceased its trembling. Chasms mended and landslides rolled to a stop.

"Together with the sea around us."

Rain fell on forest fires snuffing them out, and the sea retreated and calmed draining from streets and overrun civilizations.

"Together with the fire within us."

Gathering camps of marauders and looters and warlords ignited. Missiles were disarmed or detonated harmlessly. The risen undead everywhere were bombarded with fiery wrath turning them to ash.

They lowered the shield against Lucifer, and she surged forward, her darkness settling upon them, threatening to smother all light.

And still they chanted.

"We are one. We are one. We are one."

Suddenly there were more witches chanting. Not only the ones in the Coven but Melody and what was left of her minions, as well.

Beside them, in the stones, Mirelle appeared, and their father, iridescent shimmering specters of light. Malcolm, Morgana, and Kenna. A woman with black hair and eyes smirked as she held onto the druid king, adding her voice to the fray. She smiled at Aerin as she chanted and Aerin knew this was Vian.

We are one.

Dozens more apparitions appeared, then hundreds, then tens of thousands, women in every form and time of dress spreading over their hill, the peninsula. The continent. The world.

We are one.

The spirits of every woman burned in fires for her knowledge, spurned for her body, killed by violence, sex, or villainy.

We are one.

Every woman who had ever loved, lost, hated, railed, cried, and died. Their voices ringing across the earth begging for the return of their Goddess. For the love that was lost and the time that had come.

We are one.

Everyone that had had enough. *Enough*. Enough violence and rage and greed and malice. Enough evil. Enough pain.

The Horsemen's armor fell away, the earth swallowed their weapons of offering. The power flowing through Aerin rushed into her mate. Her man. And then she suddenly knew that now they shared it. They had a balance. Because she had the Goddess inside her, and so did he, and they shared a God, as well. A masculine balance as well as a feminine.

Everything. This was everything.

An inhuman scream rent the chaos, sending shivers through her entire being.

When the darkness receded, Lucifer and her minions were nowhere to be seen. And Aerin knew that she'd been finally vanquished, because she couldn't sense the evil stain on her soul any longer.

Aerin enfolded herself in Julian's arms and then stepped back to watch as he embraced each of her sisters, tears streaming down his regal features.

He could now touch the world.

❧ 52 ❧

The celebration was like nothing Aerin had attended.

Of course, when had there, in the history of the world, been another, "Congratulations on inheriting Satan's dark powers!" party for a one-month-old?

Maybe never?

She certainly couldn't find a banner for it.

It wasn't the first celebration they'd had since the Apocalypse, but it was fast becoming her favorite.

Mostly because she was gathered around the firepit in the de Moray gardens, seven shots into some kick ass apple pie moonshine. And, judging by how green Little Earl was getting around the gills, he was going to lose the no-puke competition, as they were the last two standing.

Well sort of standing.

"Suck it John Deere," she slurred. "Not even Pestilence could make me puke, what makes you think these weak-ass sips of swill are going to do the trick?"

However, if Dr. Lecter was going to insist on being two or three bats at a time as he circled the warmth of the fire, she was going to be mighty ill.

Red, who now sported an eye patch due to the devil's douchebaggary, leveled half of a skeptical glare in her direction. "Who you callin' John Deere, fancy pants? Those *bourgeois* thangs would drown you in the Bayou."

Aerin shrugged. She had really no idea what John Deere (deers?) were, just that guys that looked like these cretins wore the caps and drove big machines with big motors and chopped stuff. "Y'know?" she said, downing her eighth shot and waiting for the liquid fire to strip her esophagus. "Y'aren't so bad when you're not eating vermin and copulating with livestock."

"Don't make me weep, woman!" Mookey's voice broke over his yodel. "I done explaint to you already, t'weren't never meant to be, me and y'all. I belong to the crawdads and you to the city. My soul—*belch*—is like a bayou." He held his hand out as if it contained Yorick's skull from Hamlet.

"Full of muck and decay?" Aerin asked, swatting her hand past her nose as the gastronomical stink cloud of garlic and intestine-based sausages reached her across the fire pit.

"Spread over several states, not belonging to a one. Full of dangerous, mysterious things."

"And dangerous critters," Moira snarked fondly, as she came up behind them holding little Seraphine against her chest.

Mookey horked into the fire and Aerin grimaced at the sizzle.

"Can't hogtie this catfish, is what I'm getting at." He waggled wildly bushy eyebrows at her.

Red nodded sagely, scratching at his kidneys beneath his overalls. "Thus, are we all alike. We'll only slip away, don't matter none how many fists you try to shove in our mouths to git us catched."

Alarmed, Aerin looked to Moira for help.

"Still a catfish metaphor," she said helpfully, patting little Seraphine on the back to produce her own little belch.

"Thank God," Aerin breathed, looking on as Moira took the baby from her shoulder and rearranged her on her lap.

The child was happy and squirmy, and damned adorable in the purple onesie Julian had bought her that read, *Pardon me, but I do believe I hath shat my pants* beneath a picture of a waxed mustache.

Reaching out, Aerin booped little Seraphine on the nose. "You're not so bad either," she cooed in that insufferable voice people reserve for babies and dogs. "For a toothless, drooling shit machine. No, you're not. No, you're not."

Seraphine gave her a smile that sent a slimy puddle of drool dripping out of the side of her mouth.

And promptly farted.

Not to be one upped in the noxious gasses department, Cheeto belched a little flame that set Little Earl's one good sock on fire, and he danced away to put it out in the garden fountain.

Sal leaned forward, his wizened face glowing with pride and a little 'shine, though he'd opted out of the current contest. "Hand me the mite, Moira Jo," he crooned. "Then you can eat with both hands."

"Oh, I don't have food, yet," she said, but she passed Seraphine over to her uncle, anyhow, just before a plate appeared in her lap.

Nick, it seemed, never tired of waiting on and worshiping her. The mother of his child. The Goddess who'd gifted him with a life.

Claire drifted to the fire carrying two plates, while Dru hauled two chairs for them, and situated them closest to the flames. They settled in, and Claire passed Dru his food before accepting some moonshine from Mookey.

"See what kinda fire you start after one sippa that!" he crowed, elbowing her one too many times.

"So, you guys are leaving tomorrow, huh?" Dru said

around a bite of potato salad, not exactly able to disguise his anticipation of the event.

Aerin held in a giggle as she watched him bend down to give Kai a little scratch behind his red ears.

"Yup," Little Earl intoned in his slow baritone. "Gotta check on the old place, see what damage were done to it."

"I'll get in contact with the local coven, if you need any help to rebuild," Tierra offered as she and Bane brought their food over and perched on a massive log that had been converted into a bench. Violet bounced on her father's knee, burbling and grabbing at food from his plate, her other hand reaching for the dancing tail of the black cat winding its way around his motorcycle boots.

"Obliged," Red tipped his Hoodoo Shack ball cap as if it were a top hat in a Jane Austen novel.

Aerin couldn't contain her joy, which was such a new feeling for her.

Since the Apocalypse, covens had begun popping up everywhere, many of them having already existed in the shadows. They had no need to protect themselves from judgment and evil anymore. Not because it did not still exist in the hearts of men, but because the truth of the Goddess and her power—their powers—could no longer be denied. So they used whatever powers they had to rebuild and renew.

Entire governmental systems had been dismantled in one cataclysmic night. Monuments to tyranny lost and crumbled. Forests had taken back land, the sea had reclaimed its reefs, and air now sparkled, free of chemicals and toxins.

Mortals drew their energy from the sun now. From the moon. From the magic they'd forgotten existed.

If someone had told Aerin this was possible a year ago, she'd have told them to fuck off and wake up, because they were dreaming.

But she'd have been only half right. People *were* dreaming. People *had always been* dreaming of this. Of paradise. A world without war, without oppression and autocracy. A world where the feminine divine was worshiped in equal measure. A world where all voices were heard and none of them marginalized. These dreamers were finally being listened to.

It wasn't perfect. Because people weren't perfect. But it was better. And improving with each step they made toward mercy. With each dream and imagining that became a reality.

There was no more need for Conquest, War, Pestilence and untimely Deaths. With the power of the Goddess restored to the earth, the Horsemen became protectors of the elements and rebuilders of a global utopia, right alongside them.

Each of the witches had their own time, their own season to reign and their own season to wane. And the balance was beautiful and right.

Their immortal mission seemed to be to protect the world from such an imbalance occurring again, and to raise children who would keep it strong from any forces who would endanger this new paradise.

It was as much a joy as it was a burden, one Aerin treasured every day.

Silent footsteps drew next to her, and the glow in her heart told her who had joined them before she even turned to look.

With a squeal of happiness, Violet launched herself from her daddy's knee and hurled her little cherubic body into Julian's arms.

He caught her and pulled her in for a sticky hug. "My darling," he murmured. "What substance is draped all over your face?"

Violet couldn't answer, of course, as whatever magic had sped up their gestation and growing process seemed to have waned since the defeat of the devil. Perhaps, because they were no longer needed in great haste, they would be blessed with a childhood.

Julian pulled a silk handkerchief from his pocket, licked it, and wiped at the squirming angel's sticky mouth while she tried to gnaw on him.

Aerin told herself her vision blurred because of the booze, not real emotion, as Pestilence, the man who could know the touch of no other without deathly consequences, gave Violet a very ungentlemanly raspberry on her round belly.

It had all been worth it. For this moment. For this family. For this love.

Who knew what eternity meant or how long this place could last?

But for now, they had the chance to live in a reality that had once only been a dream.

And *that* was nothing short of magical.

ABOUT TIFFINIE

USA Today Bestselling Author Tiffinie Helmer is always up for a gripping adventure. Raised in Alaska, she was dragged "Outside" by her husband, but escapes the lower forty-eight and returns to her beloved Alaska every chance she gets.

A mother of four, Tiffinie divides her time between enjoying her family, throwing her acclaimed pottery, and writing of flawed characters in unique and severe situations.

Tiffinie loves to hear from readers.
Visit her: http://tiffiniehelmer.com/
Email her: Tiffinie@TiffinieHelmer.com

ABOUT CYNTHIA

Cynthia St. Aubin wrote her first play at age eight and made her brothers perform it for the admission price of gum wrappers. A steal, considering she provided the wrappers in advance. Though her early work debuted to mixed reviews, she never quite gave up on the writing thing, even while earning a mostly useless master's degree in art history and taking her turn as a cube monkey in the corporate warren.

Because the voices in her head kept talking to her, and they discourage drinking at work, she started writing instead. When she's not standing in front of the fridge eating cheese, she's hard at work figuring out which mythological, art historical, or paranormal friends to play with next. She lives in Colorado with the love of her life and three surly cats.

Cynthia loves to hear from readers.

Visit her: http://www.cynthiastaubin.com/
Email her: cynthiastaubin@gmail.com

ABOUT CINDY

Amazon bestselling author Cindy Stark lives in a small town shadowed by the Rocky Mountains with a kindle of kitties, working her way toward official Cat Lady status. She writes fun, witch cozy mysteries, emotional romantic suspense, and sexy contemporary romance. She loves to hear from readers!

Cindy loves to hear from readers.
Visit her: www.CindyStark.com
Email her: CindyStark19@gmail.com

ABOUT KERRIGAN

Kerrigan Byrne is the USA Today Bestselling and award winning author of several novels in both the romance and mystery genre.

She lives on the Olympic Peninsula in Washington with her wonderful husband and Willow the Writer Dog. When she's not writing and researching, you'll find her on the beach, kayaking, or on land eating, drinking, shopping, and attending live comedy, ballet, or too many movies.

Kerrigan loves to hear from her readers! To contact her or learn more about her books, please visit her sites:

Kerrigan loves to hear from readers.
Visit her: www.kerriganbyrne.com

www.ingramcontent.com/pod-product-compliance
Lightning Source LLC
Chambersburg PA
CBHW011114100726
47898CB00011B/3082